Wildflower Wedding

"Sweet romance with small-town Southern charm. . . . McLane weaves together walks in the moonlight, stolen glances, and kisses under the stars with seduction and sizzling sex, populating the carefully crafted story with a cast of affable characters." —*Publishers Weekly*

"In this modern Southern romance, charming bad boy Reese and sassy Gabby's chemistry sizzles. McLane gives readers characters they'll care about, as she expertly weaves a tale of love and past regrets. Her writing is heartfelt, her characters sympathetic, and her pacing steady." —*RT Book Reviews*

"A lovely, sweetly sexy, terrifically enjoyable read. . . . McLane's Cricket [Creek] series is similar in style to Susan Wiggs's bestselling Lakeshore Chronicles." —*Booklist*

Moonlight Kiss

"Alluring love scenes begin with the simplicity of a kiss in this romantic Southern charmer." —*Publishers Weekly*

"A sweet love story set in the quaint Southern town of Cricket Creek. Reid makes for a sexy hero who could melt any heart." —*Romantic Times*

continued . . .

"A very charming story, and I would be more than happy to read the entire series."　—The Bookish Babes

"McLane nails the charm, quirks, nosiness, friendliness, and sense of community you'd experience in a small Southern town as you walk the streets of Cricket Creek. . . . Engaging and sweet characters whose chemistry you feel right from the start."

　—That's What I'm Talking About

Whisper's Edge

"This latest foray to McLane's rural enclave has all the flavor and charm of a small town where everyone knows everyone else and doesn't mind butting in when the need arises. With a secondary romance between members of the slightly older generation, *Whisper's Edge* offers a comforting read where love does 'trump' insecurities, grief, and best-laid plans."　—*Library Journal*

"Visiting Cricket Creek, Kentucky, feels like coming home once again."　—*Romantic Times*

"Cute, funny, and full of romance."

　—Love to Read for Fun

"LuAnn McLane has a rich and unique voice that kept me laughing out loud as I read."　—Romance Junkies

Pitch Perfect

"McLane packs secrets, sex, and sparks of gentle humor in an inviting picnic basket of Southern charm."

　—*Ft. Myers & Southwest Florida*

Sweet Harmony

A CRICKET CREEK NOVEL

LuAnn McLane

A SIGNET ECLIPSE BOOK

SIGNET ECLIPSE
Published by the Penguin Group
Penguin Group (USA) LLC, 375 Hudson Street,
New York, New York 10014

USA | Canada | UK | Ireland | Australia | New Zealand | India | South Africa | China
penguin.com
A Penguin Random House Company

First published by Signet Eclipse, an imprint of New American Library,
a division of Penguin Group (USA) LLC

First Printing, October 2014

ISBN 978-0-451-47048-5

Printed in the United States of America
10 9 8 7 6 5 4 3 2 1

Sweet Harmony is dedicated to musicians
and songwriters everywhere.

Acknowledgments

I would like to take the opportunity to thank everyone in the music industry for all of the hard work and dedication it takes to bring music into our lives. From live bands in small venues to huge shows in large arenas to simply turning on the radio, I can't imagine going even one day without listening to music.

Thank you to the amazing staff at New American Library. From the beauty of the covers to the attention to detail in copyediting, I couldn't ask for a better team. I also want to thank Jessica Brock for her marketing expertise and for all of the help with social media. And a very special thank-you goes to my wonderful editor, Danielle Perez. From small details to big scenes, you've made my writing better on every level.

As always, a heartfelt thank-you goes to my wonderful agent, Jenny Bent. From the moment we met, you gave me the confidence to believe in my writing and to fulfill my dreams. I couldn't have done this without you!

Thank you so much to my loyal readers. Your continued support over the years has kept the joy in writing my stories. My goal is to bring you love, laughter, and, of course, a happy ending.

1

Here Comes the Sun

"RIGHT TURN IN FIVE-POINT-TWO MILES," THE FEMALE voice of Cat's GPS said with staccato precision. Although she was tired to the bone, Cat had to grin. "Is it my imagination or do you sound as road-weary as me?" Cat glanced at the screen on her dashboard, half expecting Rita, the name she'd given the voice, to answer. Earlier Cat had accused Rita of being a bit tipsy when she sounded as if she were slurring her words.

Cat glanced at the map showing her SUV driving down the two-lane road and sighed with relief. "Yes! I'm almost there." After driving all day from her parents' home in Chicago, she was anxious to reach her destination near the city limits of Cricket Creek, Kentucky. Because Cat wanted solitude for songwriting, her friend Mia had hand-picked the location of the log cabin nestled in the woods and with a river view from the back deck. Cat knew the cabin was nicely decorated with rustic yet stylish furnishings because Mia had sent dozens of pictures. Cat was also aware that the fridge was fully stocked, including a chilled bottle of Cupcake Chardonnay, because Mia sent even more pictures of the contents of the fridge. To say that Mia was excited about Cat's move to Cricket Creek was a vast understatement.

"It sure is pretty here, Rita." The sun was dipping lower in the sky, casting a soft golden glow over cornfields in the early-spring stages of growth. In the distance, tender green leaves made the woods appear fresh, and redbud trees added a splash of bright reddish purple to the landscape. When she passed cows lazily grazing in the grass, Cat waved and offered a tired "Moo."

Although Cat knew she would miss living in Nashville, her switch to small-town life already felt like the right choice. So did leaving Sweetside, her big corporate record label, for independent My Way Records in Cricket Creek. But changes, even ones for the better, still held an element of fear that Cat couldn't completely shake.

"In one mile turn right on Riverview Lane," Rita reminded her.

"It's not soon enough." When the sign appeared, Cat smiled, having been worried that the road out here in the countryside wouldn't be marked. She turned down the dusty gravel lane and, even as weary as she felt, her pulse kicked up a notch. This was going to be her home.

Cat had sold her sprawling home in Brentwood, Tennessee, completely furnished except for the music industry awards and personal items she'd taken with her. She'd donated most of her designer clothes to charity and sent dozens of shoes to Mia's Cricket Creek–based foundation, called Heels for Meals. Cat wanted a fresh start, a new beginning, to go back to performing and writing songs for the love of music and not worry as much about record sales and concert attendance.

A sudden stiff breeze caused dust to kick up, and the field of wildflowers on either side of her started dancing in the wind. *I'm going to like living here,* Cat thought, and she felt a sense of peace chase away her lingering fear. During the past year of legal entanglements with her record label, selling her home, and ending a toxic relationship, Cat had vowed to keep negativity out of her life. She longed for less chaos and more simplicity. Through it all, her charity work had kept Cat grounded, bringing her some joy along with the constant reminder that there were those in dire need which made her own problems seem somehow trivial.

Luckily, Mia had done the legwork with the local real estate agent and found the location on Riverview Lane. Not only did Cat trust her best friend's judgment, but the never-ending pictures already had her in love with the quaint cabin.

The fields of flowers gave way to woods with only fingers of lingering sunlight able to reach down through the trees. Cat knew that there were a few other cabins nestled in the woods, but they were mostly for weekend use by tourists or fishermen putting their boats in Cricket Creek, which led to the Ohio River. So for the most part Cat should have the solitude she'd been craving for the past year.

"Five Riverview Lane is located on the left. You have arrived."

"Thank goodness," Cat nearly shouted as she pulled up in front of the cabin. After killing the engine she inhaled a deep breath and then blew out a sigh. Staying up late with her mother and father the night before was catching up with her, but her parents were heading out of the country to do some charity work, so she knew it would be a few weeks before she'd see them again, making her fatigue worth it.

"Oh . . . wow," Cat said when she spotted a doe walking up from the edge of the trees on the opposite side of the lane. Knowing she would frighten it away, Cat sat there for a moment and drank in the deer's quiet, gentle beauty. As she'd suspected, as soon as she opened her door the deer bolted, doing a graceful jump back over the gulley and then disappearing into the woods.

Cat walked around and opened the tailgate of her white SUV, now covered with a light sheen of golden brown dust. She leaned in to drag out her overstuffed suitcase, but the doggone thing barely budged. Thinking of the hearty snacks and chilled wine waiting inside, Cat tugged harder, grunting with the effort. "Apparently I need to do some lifting at the gym," she grumbled, but then remembered it had taken both Cat and her father to heft the suitcase up into the SUV. With a quick intake of pine-scented air, she braced the heels of her boots into the gravel, grabbed the handle with both hands, and gave the suitcase her best tug.

It worked.

The suitcase slid across the slick tailgate much quicker than Cat had anticipated, making her backpedal, but not nearly fast enough. The painful impact of the heavy luggage smacking into Cat's legs sent her stumbling backward. Cat's butt hit the gravel with a bone-jarring thud. After a stunned grunt she uttered a string of words that didn't even fit together, but she was so spitting mad that she continued saying them, adding a random curse word here and there. "Stupid, ye-*ouch*, oversized damn piece of luggage. Dear God, that hurt. Oh, my shins . . . Sent from holy hell." She sat there breathing as if she'd just run a marathon and then glared at the suitcase as if it were somehow to blame. "Wow, ohhh, that hurt like . . . ohhh. I hope your blasted wheels are broken, you lousy piece of ugly . . ." she whimpered and then added weakly, "leather . . . *crap*."

Cat desperately wanted to dislodge the luggage from her legs, but all her brain could deal with was the pain shooting up her shins. Rocks bit into her denim-clad butt and both elbows stung. "Don't you know I bruise easily?" She intensified her glare but then sudden tears welled up in her eyes and with a little groan she shoved hair that had escaped from her ponytail off her forehead. Cat considered herself a tough cookie, but this past year had tested her mettle in more ways than one, and in that moment she threatened to fall to pieces. "This is your new beginning! No negativity," she reminded herself and swallowed hard. "Get a damned grip!"

Cat gritted her teeth, determined to shove the suitcase aside. "Get off me." But just as she leaned forward she heard the crunch of gravel and her heart rate increased. Could it be another wild animal from the woods? But this time, instead of a doe, could it be the kind with claws and big teeth?

Before she could turn around to face her fear, the suitcase was suddenly lifted from her legs as if it didn't contain piles of clothing that had the lid bulging like a muffin top. From her sitting position Cat looked at scuffed brown cowboy boots and jean-clad legs.

"Hey, are you okay?" His deep Southern drawl oozed with charm and a hint of concern.

Cat leaned back on her palms and tilted her head up. Wow, he was tall. And even through the pain throbbing in several places she noted that he filled out his flannel shirt quite nicely. "Define *okay*." She meant it as a joke but her voice had a slight hitch in it.

"*Okay* as in, are you hurt?" The tall cowboy flashed Cat a slight grin that caused two very cute dimples in his cheeks, which were covered in dark stubble that matched the dark hair clipped close to his head. He had a strong jaw and straight nose but a full mouth that suddenly captured her attention. "No, really—are you okay?"

"Sorry, but I was distracted by . . . ah, your sudden appearance." She blinked at him, thinking he looked familiar. She wondered whether he'd recognize her, but with her hair pulled back and not a trace of makeup hopefully he wouldn't. Cat wanted to remain on the down low while she got her life together. "To answer your question, um, yes."

"*Yes* as in *okay*?"

"*Yes* as in *hurt*. Everywhere. In fact, I think I'm one giant bruise. Where did you come from, anyway?"

He jammed his thumb over his head. "I heard your . . . um, rather colorful shouts of distress and decided I needed to jog up here and investigate. So just bruises?"

"And maybe broken bones." She frowned at her legs.

His grin disappeared, and his green eyes suddenly appeared concerned. "Are you serious?"

"Yes . . . well, kinda. Oddly enough, I've never had a broken bone, so I don't know, but it sure feels like my legs are crushed." Okay, she might be a teensy bit overly dramatic, but she was a singer, an entertainer, and an only child diagnosed with ADD. Drama was in her blood.

"Well, I've had a few broken bones, and, believe me, you'd have a pretty good inkling."

"Come on, it was the attack of the killer suitcase. That thing is a monster on wheels. Do you really think I'm overreacting?" she asked with an arch of one eyebrow.

"A little." He gave her a slight grin. "Although that overstuffed monster does weigh a ton." He tilted his head in the direction of the suitcase. When he knelt down beside her she got a subtle whiff of spicy aftershave that made her want to lean closer. "So do you think you can move?"

She made a show of wiggling her toes. "That's a good sign, right?"

He nodded. "Think you can stand up?"

"I'm sort of afraid to try," Cat admitted with a wince. "I think I'll just chill here for a few minutes. Or maybe overnight."

"Out here with coyotes and raccoons?"

Cat glanced toward the woods. "Okay, scratch that idea."

"Do you want me to carry you inside?"

His question made her eyes widen. "No!" Cat replied, but in truth his offer held more than a little bit of appeal.

He held up both hands in surrender. "Gotcha."

Although Cat could be a bit dramatic, she also thrived

on being independent, so her unexpected, rather needy reaction to this perfect stranger felt confusing. She blamed it on fatigue. Or maybe low blood sugar. Or maybe she was damned tired of being strong and wanted a shoulder to lean on other than her parents, who didn't fully understand what was going on in her life and career. No, it wasn't that last one! Fatigue and hunger were the culprits. She glanced at those wide shoulders. Maybe.

"Well, then at least let me help you up."

Cat gave him a quick nod conveying more conviction that she felt and then accepted his outstretched hands. His grip was warm and strong as he effortlessly tugged her to her feet. Cat was tall and had a solid build, but he suddenly made her feel feminine. He held on after Cat stood up, presumably to make sure she remained steady on her feet, which she wasn't. To her dismay her legs hurt and her knees felt wobbly.

"The offer remains," he said with a hint of concern.

Cat inhaled a deep breath. "I'll be okay, really." She stiffened her spine. "I've just had a long day of driving and I pushed too hard to get here. Low blood sugar," she added. She swayed slightly as she pulled her hands from his, and he immediately put an arm lightly about her waist.

"Are you sure about that?" His question still held concern but a slight hint of amusement.

"I'm fine," Cat insisted. In the cool air, his body felt warm, and she fought the urge to snuggle closer.

"Hey, just let me help you inside. Look, I know we're strangers, but not for long. I live in the cabin just around the bend in the road. My family owns this property and it butts up to our farm. The local real estate company handles the rentals for us. I didn't realize you'd be moving in or I would have come over to help earlier. That's the way we do things around here."

"Oh." Cat wondered why Mia hadn't mentioned that she would have a cute country-boy neighbor, but then maybe she didn't know.

"I'm just being a neighbor and a gentleman. I'll bring your suitcase to you once you're inside."

"Okay, thanks. But now that I'm standing, I'm feeling better," she lied. "It was just the initial shock of pain that threw me for a loop. I can make it on my own."

"My mother always told me to err on the side of caution."

"And do you?" She tilted her head up to get a better look at his face. Again, Cat felt as if she somehow knew this guy, but she met so many people, and it was embarrassing when she failed to remember names. Having ADD certainly didn't help matters. "Well?" she prompted, still racking her brain for his name.

"No." Oh, there were those dimples again. "Dare me and I'll do it. It's kind of a country boy thing."

He helped her up the three steps to the front porch that Cat knew wrapped around to the back to overlook the river in the distance. She knew there was a grill, a swing, and a hot tub, all visible in Mia's pictures. Unfortunately, her friend had had to head out of town to watch her husband play baseball, or she would have been there to greet Cat. "Oh, I forgot. There is supposed to be a packet with keys and instructions in the mailbox."

"Sit down here in the chair and I'll go get it for you."

"Thank you." Cat eased into the big wooden rocking chair and watched her neighbor walk across the lawn. While she wanted the cabin in the woods for solitude, it was comforting to know she'd have what seemed to be a nice guy nearby to rely upon if an emergency occurred. He certainly oozed small-town charm, and she suddenly wondered whether he had a girlfriend, but then quickly squashed that thought. She was on a mission to switch gears in her music career and didn't need any complications to get in the way.

And yet Cat looked at the flannel stretching across his shoulders and suppressed a sigh. Because she stood at five foot nine, Cat was always attracted to big, tall men.

Throw a sexy Southern drawl into the mix, add arresting blue eyes, and he was quite a pleasant package. The dimples and crooked smile were just an added bonus.

Mia must have known that Cat would find this guy attractive, and she wondered whether the location of her cabin near his was more than a coincidence. Cat nibbled the inside of her lip. Surely her friend wasn't trying to do any matchmaking. Well, if so, Mia's efforts weren't going to work. Although Cat did have an unfortunate knack for ending up with jerks for boyfriends. Maybe a matchmaker wasn't such a bad idea after all.

Cat watched his long, lazy stride and realized she was staring. She cleared her throat and squared her shoulders, trying to act nonchalant as he approached.

"Here you go." He handed her the packet. "By the way, in all the commotion I forgot to introduce myself. I'm Jeff Greenfield."

"Really?" Cat raised her eyebrows. So *that's* why he seemed so familiar. "'Outta My Mind with Lovin' You'? I was singing along just a little while ago when it came on the radio. I love the lyrics. Did you write it?"

"I did." Jeff smiled. "Thanks."

"You're with My Way Records."

"Yes . . ." Jeff said, then tilted his head sideways. "Oh boy—wait. You're Cat Carson." He shoved his fingers through his hair. "You sang at my brother's wedding."

"Right. A couple of years ago! Gosh, that slipped my mind."

"Wow, I'm sorry. I can't believe I didn't recognize you. I guess I was so concerned with you being hurt . . ."

Cat waved him off. "If you don't mind, I'd like my residence here to be kept under wraps. I'm planning on doing some songwriting and I'd like some peace and quiet."

"Aren't you with Sweetside Records?"

"Not anymore," Cat answered darkly.

"Wait. Did *you* sign with My Way Records?"

Cat paused. "Yes, but keep it quiet, please? It was a year from hell with legal issues. Plus, Rick wants to make an official announcement after I get some songs written and a single ready to release. He's going to team me up with Maria Sully!" She looked at Jeff to get his reaction.

"She's one of the best songwriters in the business," Jeff agreed. "I've always been so proud that Maria's from Cricket Creek."

"You should be, but I have to admit that I was surprised. I thought she lived in Nashville."

Jeff nodded. "Maria moved to Nashville years ago when she and Pete Sully split up. He owns Sully's Tavern, not far from here."

"So when did Maria come back to Cricket Creek?"

"Maria returned last Christmas when Clint came home from California because Pete was having health problems."

"Clint?"

"He's their son. Clint let Maria know what was up when he came here to check up on his dad. Of course, everybody's hoping they get back together."

Cat raised her eyebrows. "You know all of this?"

"Of course." Jeff chuckled. "Oh, the story gets better than that. When Clint came home to look after his dad, he reunited with his high school sweetheart, Ava Whimsy." Jeff's grin remained. "To be fair, Ava's family farm butts up to the Greenfield farm, so we know her family well."

"But still . . ."

"It's a small town, Cat. That's how we roll. You'd best get used to it."

Nibbling on her lip, Cat mulled his statement over for a moment.

"Hey, it's not idle gossip. We care about each other," Jeff said with a hint of defensiveness.

Jeff looked so sincere that Cat couldn't help but smile. She had the odd urge to put her hand over his, but refrained. "I believe you, and—trust me—I am so thrilled. I can't wait to meet Maria and get started at My Way Records."

"But you just came off a big year. I don't get why you'd want to switch to a small label when you were with the big dogs."

Cat shrugged. "It's simple. Rick Ruleman will let me take my music in the direction I want it to go."

"Which would be?"

"Less pop-sounding and more traditional," Cat answered, and watched for his reaction. He tried to hide it, but she could feel Jeff's slight but sudden withdrawal. She understood. Jeff's music was traditional country, much like legendary George Strait, and she bet he wasn't a fan of her songs. Old-school country artists often felt as if singers like her were simply jumping on the country bandwagon. Although popular with fans, they weren't taken seriously by the icons in the industry.

"That's . . . um, good," Jeff said, but shoved his hands in his pockets and his gaze flicked away. "I mean, I do get it. I wanted complete control over my career too."

Cat arched an eyebrow. "So, I have to ask, do you switch the station when one of my songs comes on?"

"No," he answered a bit too quickly. "Why would I do that?"

"Oh, if I might be so bold to ask, do you have a favorite song of mine? Just curious." She gave him an innocent look and waited.

His mouth worked but nothing came out. "Um, 'Sail' . . . um . . . 'Moonlight,' um . . ."

"'It's a Sail-Away Summer'?" Just because she wanted to go in another direction now didn't mean she wasn't proud of her beach-themed songs, many of which she had written. Cat just didn't want to do them exclusively.

Jeff rocked back on his heels and nodded a bit too hard. "Yes, uh, that one."

"Or did you mean 'Moonlight Dance'?"

"Oh, I like them both."

Cat suspected he liked neither. "Thank you."

Jeff nodded but appeared a bit uncomfortable.

Cat gave him a smile that felt rather stiff. She'd certainly felt the backlash of having her star rise swiftly, making some artists feel as if she hadn't paid her dues. And because her music bridged the gap between pop and country, she had a wide following, much like Sheryl Crow, Kelly Clarkson, Taylor Swift, and Carrie Underwood. When she'd won female vocalist of the year at the Country Music Awards two years earlier, Cat had felt the heat in more ways than one. That's when she'd started to reexamine where her life and her career were headed and found the need to make changes.

"You have a huge fan base," Jeff added, as if that would make up for his obvious lack of interest or knowledge of her music.

"I'm lucky to have such loyal listeners." Cat adored her fans and loved her songs, but she was tired of doing the same themes, which were starting to blend together and feel stale. "I don't want to disappoint them, but I'm going to explore more traditional country with a splash of bluegrass," she explained, thinking that admission might change the expression that he was politely trying to hide. Although she'd moved to Nashville three years before, most people thought she was a city girl from Chicago, where her parents still lived. In fact, she'd spent her early childhood in South Carolina. "And get back to my Southern roots," she finished.

He only nodded.

"Let me guess—" Cat gripped the arms of the chair. "You don't take me seriously."

"I didn't say that."

"You didn't have to."

"Wow." Jeff tilted his head to the side. "So you can read minds?"

"No, I read faces and it's written all over yours."

"Really?" Jeff leaned back against the railing. "And maybe you are making assumptions that you shouldn't."

And maybe she was suddenly tired and sore and grumpy. "Right. Listen, I can get my things from here."

"Don't be stu—silly. I'll get your suitcase. You'll have a tough time getting it up the steps."

"Watch me," Cat boasted, knowing she sounded stubborn and childish. "Thanks for your help," she added, but didn't sound all that thankful. What was wrong with her?

"No way. I won't allow it," Jeff insisted and turned on his heel.

"*Won't allow it?* Are you kidding me? Did you really just say that?" Cat stood up, but when the blood rushed down her legs she sucked in a sharp breath. She was going to be so sore tomorrow. She knew she was overreacting, but she'd been pushed around enough for the past year and she wasn't about to be told what she couldn't do any longer.

Jeff turned around and gave her a concerned frown. Well, she was standing now, so she was invested. Gritting her teeth, she took a tentative step forward. Not too bad. Apparently she was just going to have massive bruising—not that bruises were anything new. Cat had a knack for getting distracted and running into things. With a bracing intake of breath, she moved forward, brushing past Jeff, but had to grab on to the handrail for dear life.

"What exactly are you trying to prove?"

More things than she could begin to count. "That I don't need your help." Petulance wasn't in her nature, but she just couldn't stop.

"This sudden burst of anger is all because I don't know your songs?"

Are you that vain? remained unspoken, but Cat felt it when Jeff glanced over at her. She was used to having people make assumptions, but in reality her daily life was nothing remotely close to the rumors or gossip that showed up in the tabloids. Cat also tended to be outspo-

ken about issues that she believed in and that also sometimes landed her in hot water. She usually had a fairly
thick skin, but for some reason Jeff's apparent judgment
put her on the defensive.

When he folded his arms across his chest and looked
at her expectantly, she refused to dignify his question
with an answer.

"Thanks again for your help, but you can leave now.
I've got this." Cat felt his eyes on her as she walked stiffly
across the lawn to the suitcase. Her legs did hurt in an
achy kind of way, but she did her best to ignore the dis-
comfort. Carly Simon's song "Haven't Got Time for the
Pain" filtered into her head, and Cat had to smile. Her
mind continuously revolved around lyrics, sometimes
making her feel as if she were living in her own personal
musical. Her brain was a Wikipedia of songs and she
could give anybody a run for their money with music
trivia. There was so much more to her than catchy beach
tunes, and she longed to prove that she had more depth
and talent than people were giving her credit for.

Grabbing the handle, she raised it upward and rolled
the heavy thing awkwardly across the lawn, hoping Jeff
would get bored with the embarrassing situation and decide to leave her to her own devices.

Of course she was wrong. With his arms still folded
across his chest, he leaned against the railing looking all
smug. And hot. *No!* Scratch the hot part. Cat paused at
the first step, gathering her waning strength. This was
silly. She should allow him to help and yet she couldn't
bring herself to give in and ask for it.

Cat took a deep breath and muttered a silent prayer,
but before she could even begin to try to lift the suitcase
Jeff swiftly descended the steps and grabbed the handle
from her.

"Hey!" Cat protested, but secretly she was very glad
for his help. "I could have managed," she added, trying
not to admire his nice butt in his Wrangler jeans.

"I have no doubt." Jeff positioned the suitcase close to the front door and then turned around to face her. "But my mother taught me to be a gentleman. Put some ice on those bruises." He waited until she nodded. "My number is listed on the contacts in the packet. If you need ice packs or anything, please don't hesitate to call. Okay?"

"Sure." Cat nodded, but she wasn't about to call him.

Jeff hesitated and then said, "It wasn't my intention to insult you. I'm really not like that."

"And it isn't in my nature to be so stubborn."

"Really?"

"Maybe a teensy bit . . ." She held up her finger and thumb to demonstrate.

His slight grin and the appearance of the damned dimples got to her in ways she couldn't begin to understand. Cat pressed her lips together, suddenly feeling oddly vulnerable, needing a hug so badly that she took a quick step backward and knocked the suitcase over. When it landed with a loud thud, she yelped and then felt super silly yet again. Cat closed her eyes and sighed. "Look, it's all good," she assured him, but when she attempted a smile, to her horror it wobbled a bit. She hoped he didn't notice. "It's just been a long day." She faked a yawn. And a long year.

Jeff's expression softened even more and when he stepped forward Cat thought for a heart-pounding second that he was going to give her the hug she so sorely needed. But he moved past her and righted the suitcase.

Cat swallowed hard and tamped down her disappointment. "Can I help you get the suitcase or anything else inside?"

"No, I can manage. Well, from here, anyway. My clumsiness knows no bounds."

"You don't look clumsy."

"Trust me—I can trip over my own shadow. Walking forward while looking sideways often ends in disaster. But I've got this from here."

He looked as if he were about to protest but then nodded. "Welcome to Cricket Creek, Cat."

"Thank you, Jeff," Cat said, and watched him walk away. She inhaled a deep breath. "Well, that was an interesting little Welcome Wagon," she whispered. Then she reached inside the packet to retrieve her keys and open the door to her new life.

2

Hello Good-bye

ON THE WAY BACK TO HIS CABIN JEFF RELIVED HIS CON-
versation with Cat Carson and then scrubbed his
hand down his face. As first impressions go, he knew that
one pretty much sucked. But seriously, why in the hell
hadn't someone given him a heads-up that she was moving to his little neck of the woods? Granted, over the
past few years some pretty extraordinary people had
landed in Cricket Creek, but it was still big news that Cat
Carson was moving here. Jeff understood why she would
want to keep her residence quiet. Maybe it wasn't per-
manent. He certainly couldn't imagine someone of her
stature living in the little cabin for very long.

"Damn." Jeff hadn't meant to be rude, and, even
though he'd tried to smooth things over he still felt as if
he somehow owed her an apology. Could he help that he
didn't listen to her pop music, which in his opinion
shouldn't get airplay on country music stations? It wasn't
as if he hated Cat's trendy beach-themed songs. And she
did have an amazing voice. When she sang "From This
Moment" at Reid and Addison's unexpected wedding,

he'd been blown away just like the rest of the audience. He remembered feeling disappointed when he found out she wasn't staying for the reception. He also recalled now that when she'd signed with My Way Records, Sweetside had fought her tooth and nail, so it really must have been a tough year for her.

Plenty of big-name country stars had similar-styled hits. They were fluffy and fun, he supposed, but were songs to be played at parties and not to be performed at the Grand Ole Opry. Jeff just didn't want that kind of music to be considered classic country, because it wasn't.

Like many traditional country artists, Jeff worried that country music was becoming a vanilla genre, casting too wide a net, causing his beloved genre to lose its identity. But unfortunately, record labels were in it to make money, which was the reason Jeff had signed with My Way Records. Owner Rick Ruleman had assured him that his career would go in the direction he wanted and that it would be all about the love of the music. Rick had told him that he wanted to create legends, not the flavor of the moment.

Jeff had to wonder what Rick had in mind for Cat Carson. While he applauded her decision to embrace a more traditional sound and write her own songs, what did she know about the hardships of everyday life, the backbone of great country lyrics?

Jeff entered his A-frame cabin, headed to the galley kitchen, and opened the fridge. He suddenly had the need for a cold beer. After popping the top he glanced at his guitar, but felt too restless to try to work on the song lyrics that had been giving him trouble. Instead, he slid open the door to his back deck and walked outside.

Sunset brought with it a chill, but Jeff inhaled a deep breath of earth-scented air before sitting down on a lounge chair. He took a long drink of his beer and then looked above to where Cat's cabin sat up on the ridge, just to the right of his cabin. When he saw the soft glow of lights, Jeff suddenly wondered what she was doing. But then his curiosity shifted to concern. That heavy-ass suitcase must have left some serious bruising, and Jeff considered taking her ice, just to make sure she had enough. Maybe she needed dinner. Or perhaps a shot of bourbon to dull the pain? No, she was probably a wine kind of girl. He had several bottles in his wine rack. Would she prefer red or white?

Just what the hell was he thinking? He inhaled a deep breath and tried to get Cat Carson off his mind.

Jeff leaned back in the chaise longue and gazed up at the darkening sky. There were a few streaks of deep pink and red lingering from the sunset and in just a little while the stars would pop out, glittering against the inky blue backdrop. The lack of city light out here in the woods made for amazing night skies, so much so that Jeff had downloaded an app on his smartphone that showed the constellations.

"I need music," Jeff murmured, but just when he was about to head inside to turn on his outdoor speakers, his cell phone rang. Jeff looked at the screen and grinned when he read the caller ID. "Hey, Snake. What's up, man?"

"Nothin' much. Just thought I'd give ya a holler." Snake's real name was Wes Tucker, but his snake armband tattoo earned him the nickname. Snake's mother was about the only person who still called him Wes. "We still jammin' at Big Red tomorrow night?"

"Far as I know," Jeff answered. Big Red was the former barn down by the river that they'd converted into a practice studio way back in high school when they'd first formed the band South Street Riot.

"Sweet. Man, it feels good to have the band back together again. It still seems a little bit surreal . . ."

"I feel ya." They'd broken up not long after graduation, when they'd gone separate ways. Guitarists Jackson Pike and Sammy Slader went off to college. Snake, the drummer, left Cricket Creek to backpack across the country. Keyboardist Colin Walker had remained in Cricket Creek to work on his family farm but played solo gigs at places around town. But here they were, all of them nearly thirty years old and finally closing in on a dream none of them thought would happen. "But you gotta admit it's pretty damned cool."

"Dude, no doubt."

"Jammin' at Big Red brings back old times." Rather than have strangers assembled for his road band, Jeff knew he wanted South Street Riot with him if he could get his friends on board. Colin was already doing some sessions work over at My Way Records. Most people didn't realize that road bands weren't always the same musicians who recorded in the studio. In this case Jeff had lobbied for South Street Riot to do both. "There's nobody I'd rather go on the road with."

Snake chuckled. "You sure about that? Remember that trip to Panama City Beach after graduation?"

"Um . . . some of it," Jeff answered with a laugh. "We've matured, though, Snake."

"Speak for yourself."

Jeff laughed harder. "Yeah, well, I don't think you'll ever grow the hell up."

"Part of my charm," Snake answered. In truth, Jeff had been envious when Snake took off for parts unknown. Guilt had kept Jeff working on the struggling Greenfield farm before finally heading to Nashville, much to the sorrow of his parents and especially his older brother, Reid, who thought he was being irresponsible. All of them were convinced he was chasing a pie-in-the-sky impossible dream.

When Jeff found some success and then signed as a solo artist with My Way Records, he convinced South Street Riot to join him as his backing band in the quest for stardom. Although Jeff recorded his first single with hired session musicians at My Way Records, his friends really were the guys he wanted with him both on tour and in the studio.

"So everybody's down with jammin' tomorrow?"

"Colin's got a singing gig at Wine and Diner for the happy hour crowd but he said he can make it by eight o'clock."

"Cool, well, I was just checkin' in. Anything else goin' on?"

Jeff glanced up at Cat's cabin. "Can you keep something under your hat?" While Jeff knew that Cat's presence in Cricket Creek wouldn't stay under wraps for long, he wanted to respect her wish to remain on the down low. But he knew he could trust Snake.

"Yeah," Snake replied. When Jeff hesitated, Snake urged him on. "Damn, do you need a drumroll? I can provide one but only on my legs at the moment."

"Cat Carson just moved into the cabin on the ridge."

"Seriously?" he asked with a low whistle.

"I kid you not."

"Aren't you the lucky one."

"Why do you say that?"

"Have you seen Cat in the music video for 'Sail-Away Summer'?" Snake asked.

"No," Jeff answered in what he hoped was a bored voice. But he just might have to look the video up.

"Well, Cat is smokin' hot in it. She's in a bikini on this sailboat . . . Dude, she has a bangin' body. Forever legs and a real nice—"

"That's enough, Snake. I get it."

"Whoa, now. That sounded pretty damned protective. You got a thing for her?"

"No!" Jeff scoffed, but then glanced up at Cat's cabin again. "First of all, I don't even know her. And secondly, she's not my type."

"Type?" Snake gave Jeff a short laugh. "I never did get that whole type thing."

"Not everybody loves all women like you, my friend."

"Why limit yourself to a certain . . . type? To me that's kinda like sayin' you like candy but only peanut butter cups. Sorry, but I just don't get it."

"We all have preferences," Jeff insisted.

"Really? Then what's yours?"

Jeff was momentarily startled when a vision of Cat slid into his brain. "I don't know," he sputtered. "How'd we get on this sorry-ass subject anyway?"

"Um, I think we were talking about your hot new neighbor. The one you have no interest in. You didn't say what it was like meeting her."

"I think I kind of insulted her."

"What? But you're always the picture of perfect politeness. I didn't think you knew how to be rude."

Jeff blew out a sigh. "Well, I kinda insulted her music."

"Well, damn, it's like one and the same, bro. I mean, what the hell?"

Jeff looked up at the night sky. "Yeah, I know. She asked what song of hers was my favorite and I was stuck for an answer."

"Awk-ward. Hey, but you gotta hand it to her. Cat does have an amazing voice. Pure, but with a little bit of a sultry edge here and there. Remember when she sang 'The Star-Spangled Banner' for the Cougars on opening day?"

"Oh, wow. I'd forgotten about that."

"Dude, she killed it."

"Yeah . . ." Jeff felt himself nodding in agreement.

"And didn't she sing at Reid and Addison's wedding?"

"Yeah, I think Cat and Mia Monroe go way back and Addison is Mia's cousin. So there you have it."

"Cat wasn't nearly as well known back then, but, man oh man, she shot to the top of the charts fast not long after that. In just a couple of years Cat Carson went from opening concerts to headlining."

"Too fast, in my opinion."

"You're not the only one with that opinion. When she

won vocalist of the year two years ago, some people were royally pissed. You gotta admit that it must be tough to win an honor like that and then have to take some serious heat from your peers."

Jeff stood up and leaned against the railing. "Blame the record companies who create artists rather than artists creating themselves," Jeff responded tightly.

"And you're throwing Cat into that category?" Snake asked. "Part of the criteria for the honor is sheer numbers and she has them."

"Well, yeah, I get that." Jeff gave Cat's cabin a guilty glance. "I don't know, Snake. I guess she just seems one-dimensional. I mean, yeah, she has a great voice with some serious range, but no depth or emotion to her music."

"I don't know if that's a fair statement."

"Come on . . . 'Sail-Away Summer'? Are you kidding me? Snake, there was, like, a dance remix. And now she claims she wants to do more traditional country? Give me a break."

"But sounds like she's trying to take control of her career mold. You gotta give her credit for that."

"Why? Because she's tired of singing about her toes in the sand? And suddenly she's a serious country artist?"

"Rick Ruleman must see something more in her than just a great voice. I mean, I read where she had a pretty big disagreement with Sweetside, so I guess that's why she ended up here. So she's not just about fame or the money."

"Maybe she just likes getting her way," Jeff answered, knowing he was being unfair. "It's no secret that she *comes* from money, so she doesn't need it."

Snake laughed. "Sounds to me like you're trying really hard to talk yourself out of liking her."

"I don't even know her."

"Well, you might try not to like her, but she's your

neighbor and will be at the studio on a regular basis. So odds are that you're going to get to know Cat Carson a lot better in no time. If not, I'll be glad to do the honors. She is my type."

"Stay the hell away from her, Snake," Jeff growled, and then felt a little bit stupid.

"Okay . . . so, what are you trying to tell me?"

"I'm not trying to do anything more than drink a damned beer. As a matter of fact, I think I need another one," Jeff added, even though he hadn't finished half of the one he held in his hand. Meeting Cat still had him feeling a little bit off-kilter and he didn't even know why. And seriously, why the hell did he just jump all over his best friend? "See ya at practice tomorrow."

"I might get there early."

"I'll meet you there. Just give me a call when you're on your way." After Jeff ended the call, he took another swallow of beer and then set the can down on the railing. Usually an even-keel kind of guy, Jeff didn't understand why his reaction to Cat Carson was so strong in more ways than one. Despite butting heads, his instant attraction to her caught him off guard. Maybe it was because he'd been concentrating on his career for so long that he'd put even the thought of a relationship on the back burner and Cat had suddenly lit that fire. Or maybe it was because his brother Reid and sister, Sara, were both happily married with a baby. His other brother, Braden, had a girl in his life, which made his mother concentrate on *his* lack of a love life during their Sunday dinners at the farmhouse. She was always trying to fix him up with someone, and now that she had grandchildren she wanted to fill the farmhouse with them.

"Whatever," Jeff mumbled. He did need to concentrate on his music. Although he'd signed with My Way Records and had a top-twenty hit single, his career continued to move more slowly than he'd hoped. Everyone thought that once you had a hit single you became an instant millionaire, but that was so far from the truth it wasn't even funny. Opening for a big name was an honor, but mostly on the artist's own dime. Jeff knew he still had a lot of dues to pay before making the big time.

Jeff sighed. He could take the easy route and put out something with a catchy hook that was part of the popular new country sound but that felt like a sellout, and he refused to go in that direction. But now that Jeff had brought his band on board, he felt the pressure for continued success at a faster pace. They'd all taken a leap of faith and put their regular lives on hold to try to make this happen. Still, Jeff wanted to give this his best shot, but in his own way and on his own terms. If not, he'd just as soon go back to farming. But if things didn't take off, he just might have to do that pretty damned soon.

Jeff drained the rest of his beer and crushed the can. In order to keep the momentum going, he needed another hit single fast, or would risk being on the long list of one-hit wonders.

Pushing away from the railing, Jeff thought about grabbing his guitar and starting work on the song that had been giving him fits. Songwriting usually came to him pretty effortlessly, but Jeff guessed the pressure to write something fantastic was getting to him and screwing around with his creativity. He just needed a spark of inspiration and knew the melody would slide into his brain like magic. The question was . . . where could he find the elusive spark?

3
Let It Be

CAT INHALED THE RICH AROMA OF COFFEE BREWING AND smiled. "Bless you, Mia, for hooking me up with all of the essentials," Cat said and then reached past wimpy cups, searching for the largest mug in the cabinet. "Aha," Cat announced when she found a giant thermal mug decorated with the Cricket Creek Cougars logo on it. "I designate you as my official coffee container." Cat poured the steaming brew into the mug, leaving enough room for vanilla-flavored creamer.

Sunshine streamed through the floor-to-ceiling windows at the back of the great room, drawing Cat over to take in the lovely view of the river. She cradled the mug in her hands and smiled at the sunshine sparkling off the water. She moved a bit gingerly on her sore legs, but ice and ibuprofen helped dull the ache a little bit. Although the cabin wasn't huge, the layout made the space seem bigger; in truth, she liked the cozy feeling much better than her big house in Brentwood. Later, Cat had a lunch meeting with songwriter Maria Sully at Wine and Diner up in town, but right now all she wanted to do was sip her coffee and lounge in sweatpants and a hoodie.

After a year of turmoil Cat finally felt as if her life was back on the right path. She inhaled a deep coffee-scented breath and blew it out. Okay, well, at least she was heading in the right direction. Switching gears and taking time off from touring to get back to the basics of music put a smile on her face and joy in her heart. She hadn't felt this sense of freedom in a long time.

Cat's smile faltered a little bit when she thought of the staff who no longer worked for her. While Cat hadn't fired any of them, her move to small-town Cricket Creek, coupled with taking her career in a new direction, had her crew staying in Nashville. And honestly, Cat thought there likely was some pressure from her former record company for her staff not to follow her. This meant that her manager, personal assistant, and road manager were no longer working with her. Cat took a sip of coffee while feeling a little stab of guilt. She wasn't just Cat Carson, country singer, but a franchise. A lot of people's livelihoods had depended upon her success—probably the reason that Cat had taken one album too many to seriously consider making some life and career changes. She cared about all of them, which had made her final decision a difficult one.

Cat stared down at her coffee and swallowed some emotion. She missed them, especially Amy Peterson, her personal assistant. Not only was Amy a sweet person, but she helped Cat keep her scatterbrained ways under control. Cat took solace in that she'd given them all glowing referrals, and the last she'd heard they had all found employment. In the meantime, the front desk secretary at My Way Records, Teresa Bennett, had taken on the task of keeping track of Cat's mail, appointments, and personal appearances. She would have to eventually hire a new staff, but for now all she wanted to do was concentrate on her songs and get the opportunity to do more charity work, perhaps with Mia and her Heels for Meals in Cricket Creek. She also felt huge satisfaction from visiting fans going through a tough time. Just the month before she'd been a prom date for Colby Hughes, a high school football star diagnosed with leukemia. Putting a smile on Colby's face made her legal troubles seem trivial.

Cat knew that she was being portrayed as a stubborn star by Matt Stanford, president of Sweetside Records. He claimed she was difficult to work with and the tabloids were having a field day. His unfounded words hurt. Cat trusted in Matt as a father figure with her best interest at heart, but in the end all he cared about was money, not her as a person or artist.

Although his unfair portrayal of her still stung, it only reiterated that she was doing the right thing by stepping back and reevaluating where her career was going. Being in the limelight came with the territory, but losing control of her creativity had made her feel as if the life was being sucked right out of her. Rick Ruleman of My Way Records understood. After a hit record, he'd been pigeonholed into hard-core rock and roll when his real love was ballads and bluegrass. Rick had lived a life pretending to be something he wasn't, and Cat didn't want the same scenario to happen to her. All she wanted was control of her destiny, and Rick had promised he'd hand the creative reins over to her.

Just when Cat had decided to go out onto the deck to drink her coffee, she heard a knock at her front door. Her stomach did a funny little lurch when she wondered whether her visitor might be Jeff, since there weren't too many other people it could be this early in the day. She glanced down at her attire and winced, but then squared her shoulders and headed toward the door. What did she care how she looked? She wasn't about to let her judgmental neighbor get to her the way he did last night.

Lifting her chin, Cat swung open the door so hard that she sloshed hot coffee onto her bare feet. "Oh . . . damn!" she blurted, and then felt heat in her cheeks when she glanced up at . . . Jeff. Of course he had the nerve to appear calm, cool, collected and oh so sexy in worn jeans and another faded flannel shirt.

"Not the reception I was hoping for, but I guess I sort of deserve it," Jeff admitted with a slight grin. He held up a tinfoil-covered plate. "I brought a peace offering in the form of homemade coffee cake."

"You baked a cake for me?"

"Of course!"

"Seriously?" She suddenly pictured him in a *Kiss the Cook* apron, stirring batter with a wooden spoon. Kinda sexy . . .

"No." He laughed, and Cat found herself liking the rich sound of his deep chuckle. "No, actually, my mother brought it over very early this morning. Warm from the oven, I might add."

"Earlier?"

"We're farmers. We get up when the rooster crows."

"Does that really happen?"

"Getting up early or the rooster crowing?"

"The rooster crowing."

"Yes." Jeff inched the cake forward. "And there's no snooze button. The best you can do is put the pillow over your head and groan."

"So you're giving your mom's cake to me?"

"Yes, and it's a cinnamon cake. My favorite." Jeff held the plate up higher. "I'm not as big a jerk as you think."

"Let's hope not," Cat mumbled, and he laughed. She caught a whiff of cinnamon and then stood back for him to enter. "It smells divine. I accept."

"The apology?" He put the plate onto the breakfast bar and turned to face her.

"The cake." Cat lifted the tinfoil and took a pinch of cinnamon crumble and popped it into her mouth. "Oh, now that's delicious. Okay, I guess I will have to accept your apology too," she tried to joke, but he frowned. "What?"

"How are your legs? Not bruised too badly, I hope?"

Cat shrugged. "Like I said, I bruise easily and run into random things. Not a good combination, but let's just say I'm used to it by now. Most of the pictures of me as a kid growing up show bruises on my shins. It didn't help that I liked climbing trees," Cat added, and then wondered why she'd felt the need to share this information with him. "But the attack-of-the-suitcase thing was over the top even for me." She'd blame her runaway chatter on nervousness, but Jeff didn't make her feel nervous exactly . . . just *aware* in a way she hadn't felt in a long time.

Jeff nodded. "Hey, I get it. I told you I was a daredevil, remember? I've suffered many a broken bone."

Cat grinned. "Right. If I dare you to do something, you will do it."

"And I'll tell you to watch me. Typical country boy behavior, I'm afraid." His grin was a little shy, and yet had a hint of something in it that made her pulse flutter. He cleared his throat. "Well, I hope you enjoy the cinnamon cake."

"Would you like a cup of coffee?" Cat found herself asking. "And I'll be happy to share the cake with you. You should at least have a slice."

"I would, but I'm running late. My sister, Sara, runs an educational program for grade schoolkids on the Greenfield farm. It's a hands-on thing teaching them about farming, called Old MacDonald's."

"*E-I-E-I-O.*"

Jeff groaned. "And the kids sing it nonstop. My dad usually drives them around the farm on a hayride, but he's fishing with his buddies so I'm Farmer Jeff for the day."

"So, Farmer Jeff, shouldn't you be wearing overalls or something?"

"My dad does, but I have to draw the line somewhere."

"Well, you're no fun."

"You might be surprised."

"Well, now . . ." Cat arched an eyebrow. "I dare you."

"To do what?"

"Wear the overalls."

Jeff laughed. "You're not playing fair."

Cat shrugged. "I want a picture."

"Okay." He reached in his pocket for his cell phone. "Then I need your number."

"That was smooth."

He grinned. "I have my moments." Jeff extended the phone toward her. "Type it in, please."

"Sure." When Cat reached for the phone, his fingers grazed hers and she felt a nice little tingle. This exchange suddenly felt like flirting, which was a luxury that Cat hadn't allowed herself in a long time. "I fully expect a picture, and you need to have a piece of straw hanging out of your mouth or something," she added as she handed his phone back to him.

"You're pushing it."

"I usually do," she admitted lightly.

Jeff grinned and slipped his phone in his pocket. He paused, and she wondered whether he was reluctant to go or maybe wanted to ask her something. Maybe dinner later? "Well, I should get going. My schoolteacher sister doesn't like tardiness. If there's anything you need, let me know."

"Just the picture," Cat said, trying not to feel a little bit disappointed.

"I have a feeling I shouldn't have divulged the whole dare thing to you."

"You would be one hundred percent correct."

He grinned and there was that slight pause again. "Hope you have a good day," he said.

"You too, Farmer Jeff. And thanks again for the coffee cake. Tell your mom I said thanks too."

"You're welcome." He walked over to the door and then turned around. "Am I going to be Farmer Jeff from here on in?"

Cat grinned. "Count on it."

"Thought so." Jeff nodded and then headed out the door.

Cat watched him walk away and then realized she was standing there in the kitchen still smiling. The light-hearted teasing or flirting made Cat feel a little bit giddy. But then she shook her head. The banter was most likely part of the country boy charm and meant nothing more. Not that she wanted her relationship with Jeff Green-field to be anything more than friendly.

But then Cat remembered the warm tingle she'd experienced from a mere brush of his fingers and had to wonder whether he'd felt the connection too. She shrugged, trying to dismiss the feeling. As a songwriter Cat tried to remain in tune with her senses and emotions. "Stay focused," she whispered, but then walked over to the window in time to see Jeff drive down the road in his red pickup truck. She wondered whether he would send a selfie of himself wearing overalls; then she smiled at the thought.

After locating a small plate, Cat cut a generous slice of the cake and then refilled her coffee mug. She moaned as the cinnamon crumble melted in her mouth. Even though Cat refused to obsess over her weight, she didn't often eat something as decadent as cake, and the indulgence was a party in her mouth. She worked out and tried to eat a healthy diet, but she had lots of younger fans and didn't want to portray the too thin image that girls thought they had to live up to. Although her lyrics were flirty and fun, she was well aware of the influence she had on her audience and made a pact with herself to always remain a positive role model. When she was asked to do increasingly sexy music videos, Cat protested, causing even more friction with her label. Wearing a bikini on a boat was as far as she wanted to go, and for Cat that was even pushing it. When the last video was supposed to be her rolling around in bed wearing little more than a sheet, she'd flatly refused. If Matt Stanford wanted to label her refusal as being difficult to work with, well, then so be it.

"So be it . . ." Cat whispered and was hit with sudden inspiration. "Kinda like 'Let It Be' but with an edge." She scooted back from the table and went in search of paper and pen. For the first time in a long while, words started flowing from her brain onto the page.

4

While My Guitar Gently Weeps

$\mathcal{A}$S SOON AS SHE ENTERED WINE AND DINER, MARIA'S empty stomach reacted to the tantalizing aroma of food being served. She hadn't meant to skip breakfast, but she'd been so engrossed with listening to demo tapes with Rick Ruleman that she'd nearly been late for her meeting with Cat Carson.

The clinking of glasses and silverware, along with chatter and laughter, brought a smile to Maria's face. Originally called Myra's Diner, the renovated restaurant still served classic favorites, but the expanded menu included several gourmet offerings, which drew in both locals and tourists. And while the décor remained true to an old-school diner, with the servers wearing retro uniforms, the atmosphere felt fresh and full of fun. Fifties and sixties music pulsed in the background and when songs like "The Twist" came on it wasn't unusual for servers to encourage dancing. Wine and Diner put a smile on Maria's face, even as she walked in the door.

The line for the hostess station was five people deep so Maria decided to look around to see whether Cat had already arrived. Out of the corner of her eye she saw her friend Myra hurrying her way.

"Maria Sully!" Myra said before giving her a huge hug. "It's so good to have you back in Cricket Creek, where you belong."

"Myra Robinson!" Maria answered with a laugh. "Are you going to tell me that every time I eat here?"

"I want to remind you so you don't ever move away again. And remember, it's Myra Lawson now."

"I keep forgetting that you got married to Owen Lawson!"

"Yeah, I finally found some fool crazy enough to have me." Myra shook her head slowly and chuckled.

"I'd say Owen's a lucky man," Maria said with a lift of her chin.

"I happen to agree with you but I also think that might be open for lively debate," Myra admitted with a wince. "But never a dull moment, that's for sure."

"I thought you'd retired when your niece came back and took over the diner. And yet you seem to be here every time I come in."

"That was the plan," Myra said. "But then Jessica had to go and get married and have a baby. I don't think I'll ever be able to retire," she said with a roll of her eyes.

"I have a feeling you love every single minute."

Myra tossed her long braid over her shoulder and laughed. "I do. And little Ben is such a pistol, but I love him to pieces."

"I imagine you do. I can't wait for Clint and Ava to make me a grandmother. And it's so wonderful to see your restaurant doing so well."

"Ah . . . Wine and Diner might be all fancy-pants now, but I still get requests for my apple pie and chicken-fried steak."

"And how's your sweet niece Madison?"

"Happily married to Jason Craig and writing her plays."

"Right, Jason built the outdoor concert stage for Pete, didn't he?"

"Yes, and he did the initial remodeling of the diner and builds the sets for her plays. That's how Maddie and Jason met." She shook her head and chuckled. "Those two sure did butt heads at first."

Maria grinned. "If I remember, Madison is a sassy little thing. Big blue eyes and bouncing curls."

"You remember correctly and it still holds true." Myra pulled Maria to the side and then leaned closer. "Gets it from me, not her easygoing mama." Myra stepped back and angled her head. "You know, the two of you should get together and write a musical someday. It could be . . . What do the kids say?"

"Epic?"

Myra snapped her fingers. "Yeah, epic!"

Maria nodded slowly. "Funny you should say that because I've always wanted to write the score for a play. We should discuss it sometime soon."

"Maddie would be so thrilled. Maria, we are so proud of your songwriting success, but it's so damned good to have you back, my friend." Myra reached over and squeezed Maria's hand. "And I know Pete's happy you're back too. I haven't seen him smile so much since . . . well, since before you two split. And having your son move back from California last Christmas and reunite with Ava? You must be over the moon."

"Oh, I am." Maria pressed her lips together, suppressing sudden emotion. "Look, I know the whole town hopes Pete and I will patch things up." She closed her eyes and swallowed hard. To this day Maria found it painful to think that her husband had cared more about saving his business than saving their marriage. "It's just not that simple."

Myra nodded. "Life never is." She put a hand on Maria's shoulder. "Love sure never is."

Maria felt a little jolt at hearing the word *love*. "I'm just taking it a day at a time."

Myra gave Maria's shoulder another squeeze. "That's a good plan. So do you need a table or do you want to sit at the counter?"

"Actually, I'm here to meet Cat Carson. Do you know if she's here?"

Myra leaned and whispered, "At the last booth in the back on the left. Cat's wearing a baseball cap pulled low. She made it clear that she wanted to keep her presence quiet if at all possible. I don't think she's comfortable with all that hoopla. Sweet girl."

Maria frowned. "I probably should have just met her at the studio. I wasn't thinking. In Nashville having famous artists walking around town is normal."

"Her back is to the restaurant and so far no one has recognized her, or if they did they're leaving her alone. Around here people tend to be respectful."

"I'm not surprised. Thanks, Myra. I'll find her. And tell Madison that I'd love to get together. Oh, and hey, I'm planning on starting a songwriters' roundtable at Sully's sometime soon. Madison should come."

"I'm sure she'd love that. I'll tell her."

"Good. And you're right—I loved Nashville but it feels right to be back in Cricket Creek. You and I really do need to get out together too. Do some two-steppin' at Sully's."

"Deal," Myra said. "It was great talking to you. Enjoy your lunch with Cat."

Maria nodded and then headed to the back of the dining room. She slid quietly into the booth and smiled across the table at Cat. "Sorry I'm a little bit late. I was talking to an old friend." She extended her hand. "I'm Maria Sully."

Cat grasped her hand and gave her a bright smile. "You've written some of my favorite songs. It's an honor to meet you."

"Thank you, Cat. I'm a fan of yours too."

"Really?"

Maria tipped her head sideways. "Why on earth would you think otherwise?"

Cat toyed with the straw poking out of her iced tea and shrugged. "I'm sure you know that I'm not always viewed very seriously. I've taken some heat for my pop-sounding songs."

Maria arched an eyebrow. "You want to know what I think about that?"

"I would." Cat nodded and leaned forward.

"Pardon me for being so frank, but that's . . . well, bullshit."

Cat's eyes widened and then she sat back and chuckled. "Really?"

"Absolutely. Listen, you're an artist and you don't have to fit into any mold except for the one you create." Maria pointed at her. "You. Not your label. Not what the fans want. And not what anybody says you can or can't do. If you love singing about the beach and sailing off into the sunset, then do it. And if country calls it too pop and Top 40 radio calls you too country, then who cares? Just be true to yourself. Sing from your heart." Maria patted her chest. "And whoever doesn't like it can shut their mouths and listen to something else."

Cat grinned. "In other words, kiss my Southern sass?"

"I couldn't have said it better." Maria wanted Cat to be completely at ease with her and not pull any punches.

"May I take your drink order?"

Maria paused to order a sweet tea from the server and then picked up the menu. "You're never going to please everyone, so don't even try. At My Way Records, Rick and I want to develop talent and create something that lasts, not—as he calls it—the flavor of the moment. Don't get me wrong. We want hit records. We want to make money, but not at the expense of the integrity of the label or the artist. Quite simply, we want to develop talent with the hope of creating legends, which means music that transcends time. All of the great artists had their critics. Look at Elvis or the Beatles or Johnny Cash. But they thumbed their noses and did as they pleased. I know it sounds cliché, but you have to think outside the box."

"Wow. I don't know if I can live up to all of that," Cat admitted.

"That's the beauty of it. You don't have to live up to *anything*. Just dig deep into your heart and soul and the rest will come naturally." She smiled her thanks for her drink to the server and then looked at Cat.

"You make it sound easy."

Maria took a drink of her tea and then nodded. "Oh, it's not one bit easy to tap into your deepest, sometimes darkest, feelings and pour them into a song." Expressing this to Cat, Maria felt a tug of emotion and then looked down at the menu without really seeing it.

"And that's what you've done?" Cat asked in a quiet tone.

Maria looked up. "Yes. Pretty much, anyway."

"Then why don't you consider my songs pure fluff?"

"Well, Cat, not every song can be about heartbreak. Tell me, why did you write about the sand and the sun?"

Cat shrugged. "I love it there. It's my happy place. Many of the songs were actually written while at the beach, or at the very least I'd had the thought or wish to be sitting in the warm sunshine while enduring the blustery winters in Chicago."

Maria tapped a fingertip on the speckled table. "Exactly. And your fans feel the same way, I'm sure. Listening to your music brings a smile and the desire to sing along with joy. And joy is a wonderful emotion to express and bring to listeners. Who doesn't want to fantasize about being at the beach or on a sailboat? Don't you agree?" Maria smiled when she saw the emotion play on Cat's face.

"I've never thought of it that way." Her frown suddenly turned into a bright smile and she put a hand to her chest. "Oh my gosh. Thank you for validating me, Maria."

"I'm just pointing out the obvious," Maria said, then paused when the young server approached them.

"Are you ready to order?" the server cheerfully asked Maria.

"Oh, I'm not sure," Maria replied and looked at the menu.

"What's the soup of the day, Courtney?" Cat asked, and Maria thought it was sweet that Cat called her by name. She could tell that Courtney recognized Cat.

"Jessica's stone soup."

"Stone soup?" Cat repeated.

Courtney pointed to the menu. "It's basically beef vegetable soup but named for the folktale about feeding the hungry. The menu explains it; Jessica recently started a charity with the same name. For every bowl of stone soup ordered today, one dollar will be given to the local soup kitchen. Jess does it every Monday, but you can make a donation as well."

"That's so cool," Cat said. "Remind me to leave a donation, so I don't forget."

"Yes, that's wonderful," Maria agreed. "I'll have the stone soup and a garden salad with ranch on the side."

"I'll have the stone soup as well, but I'd like an order of the hot slaw."

"Oh, good choice! Gotcha. I'll bring out yeast rolls in a minute."

"Courtney recognized you, Cat."

"I know. I'm going to leave her a note on a napkin."

"How nice of you."

Cat shrugged. "It's not always fun to get hounded for autographs or pictures, but it's part of the drill and I'm so grateful for my following. I'm just not always comfortable with the recognition."

"You're very genuine. I admire your attitude. Not everyone is as gracious as you."

Cat shrugged. "Doing something like leaving a note is the least I can do." She smiled at Courtney when she dropped off the basket of rolls. "Those smell amazing. I don't think there's anything better than homemade rolls."

Maria groaned. "I'm going to have to start jogging instead of walking. I can't pass Grammar's Bakery down the street without stopping in. By the way, Mabel Grammar has always donated day-old bread and cookies to the soup kitchen. I thought you might like to know."

Cat reached for a roll. "I believe it's important to give back." She slathered on some butter. "I'm starting to like this little town even more. No wonder Mia loves living here."

"Good thing they're closed today, or I'd have to get a dozen butter cookies and maybe a cinnamon cake."

"Yes, who knew cinnamon coffee cake was so delicious?" Cat asked.

"Oh, so you've been to Grammar's Bakery already?" Maria liked that Cat wasn't reed thin and afraid of carbs. Too many artists worried way too much about weight and gave the wrong message to adoring fans.

Cat paused while Courtney delivered the slaw and salad. "Anything else I can get you?"

"I think we're good to go," Maria answered, and Cat nodded.

"Um, well, actually Jeff Greenfield brought one over to me this morning freshly baked by his mother."

"So you know Jeff?" Maria stabbed a cherry tomato and lightly dipped it into the ranch dressing.

"We met last night when I was attacked by my very own suitcase," Cat said with a nod. "I remember him being the best man in Addison and Reid's wedding, but I'd never been formally introduced." She then took a bite of her hot slaw as if her statement about being attacked by her suitcase was perfectly normal. "Oh, bits of bacon makes everything better, doesn't it?" She held up a forkful of hot slaw and smiled.

"Wait . . . Attacked by a suitcase? Okay, seriously, you've got to elaborate," Maria probed.

"You promise not to laugh?"

"Of course." Maria nodded her agreement, but then starting giggling uncontrollably while Cat weaved the crazy tale. "Oh my . . ." She sniffed and then dabbed at the corners of her eyes with her napkin. "Do things like suitcase attacks happen to you often?"

"Pretty much. I have ADD and get easily distracted. For example, looking sideways and walking forward isn't a good idea, but I can't seem to help myself. I always have bruises in odd places."

Maria pointed the fork tongs at Cat. "Ah, but being rescued by cutie pie Jeff might be worth a few bumps and bruises, right?"

"No!" Cat scoffed. "He's one of those traditional country singers who look down their nose at my music. He couldn't even name one of my songs." She lifted one shoulder. "Not that I give a fig what Jeff Greenfield thinks," Cat added, but judging by the sudden pink in Cat's cheeks, Maria thought otherwise.

Maria reached over and patted Cat's hand. "But the coffee cake was a nice gesture."

Cat shrugged again. "I suppose."

"And he is really cute."

"If you like the Wrangler-jeans-and-cowboy-boots kind of thing. Or get sucked in by those dimples of his." Cat gave a dismissive wave of her hand.

"And you don't and won't," Maria said firmly.

"Not on your life," Cat insisted, but then rolled her eyes. "Okay, I do and I have. Not that he will ever know it and let's keep this our little secret."

Maria laughed and made a show of locking her mouth and throwing away the key. "You're going to be such fun to work with, Cat."

"Ah . . . you say that now."

Maria leaned back when Courtney brought their

stone soup. "You know, you've got some sass. I think you could pull off some kick-ass lyrics, kind of like Miranda Lambert or Kimberly Perry from the Band Perry."

"You think so?"

Maria dipped her spoon into the steaming soup. "I do. But you've got this sense of humor that I think we can tap into as well."

"I think most of the time my humor is accidental. I'm like, why are they laughing . . . ?"

"Oh, Cat." Maria laughed. "Something tells me you're much savvier than you're admitting, but that's part of your charm. Listen, stage presence is essential to the total package. Today you have to do more than simply stand behind your guitar and sing. Garth Brooks broke that country music mold years ago."

"I understand what you're getting at." Cat nodded. "Taylor Swift has her wardrobe changes. Miranda Lambert has her attitude. Keith Urban has his intense emotion. Luke Bryan has his baseball cap and hip thrusts . . . but what would be my thing? Please don't say twerking."

Maria laughed. "No, definitely not twerking."

Cat tilted her head to the side. "Do I have a thing?"

"Absolutely. Look, I know that Sweetside Records was trying to make you this sexy beach babe, but it just didn't seem genuine to me. Am I right?"

"I love the beach," Cat said. "I wrote the songs so the lyrics are a part of me but in more of a whimsical way . . . not just the sexy stuff. And it was heading in a direction that made me uncomfortable."

Maria dabbed at the corner of her mouth with her napkin. "Rick sees so much potential that you haven't even begun to tap because you've been viewed as only one thing. You have so much to offer."

"I do want to explore so much more," Cat admitted while she crumbled crackers into her soup. "And I do love songwriting."

"We will, Cat. But like I explained, there will always be critics."

"Oh, believe me, I know."

"Country music, like anything else, has to grow, change, and evolve. Anything that doesn't, simply withers and dies. I love the classics as much as anybody else and many of them were groundbreakers who were criticized at first. Not everybody took Dolly Parton seriously, and she's an amazing singer and extremely talented songwriter. Not many people realize she wrote songs like 'I Will Always Love You.'" Maria tapped her head. "And she's smart. Look at Willie Nelson. He didn't really break in until he let his hair grow into that long ponytail." She scooped up some soup.

"So what do you think my thing is?"

"Your brand?"

Cat nodded.

"We will have to peel away the layers, Cat, and discover who you are and where you want to go with this. You have to connect with the audience. If you truly want to become a legend, your fans will not only love your music but love *you* as well. But I want your brand, your connection, to be authentic, not something contrived. Do you agree?"

"Totally."

"Well, then, we'll start bouncing ideas off each other and then showcase some of our favorites at a songwriting venue. I'm going to talk to Pete about hosting a songwriters' showcase at Sully's, much like the Bluebird Cafe in Nashville."

"Oh, I love the Bluebird Cafe. So many great artists were discovered there. Like Garth Brooks."

Maria nodded. "Eventually, Rick and I would like to team up with Pete and open Sully's South up in Restaurant Row, the lovely mall overlooking the river. We will showcase songwriters and new talent. I hope to discover new artists and test songs there. Of course, that's in the future but it's on my list of possibilities. I'm even hoping to snag the legendary Bob DiPiero for a session."

"I adore the idea," Cat said and then glanced down when her phone beeped. She chuckled.

"What?" Maria asked.

Cat tapped the screen and then handed the phone to Maria. "It's Jeff Greenfield wearing overalls and sitting on a big green tractor. He's playing Farmer Jeff for his sister's educational hayrides for schoolkids. I dared him to wear them and he took me up on it."

"That boy manages to make bib overalls look good, doesn't he?" she said and looked at Cat's reaction.

"I suppose."

Maria rolled her eyes.

"Okay . . . he does."

Maria looked at Cat for a moment and then inspiration hit her like a smack to the back of the head. "Cat . . . I have, well, an idea."

"Okay." As if sensing this was going to be something big, Cat put her spoon down. "Shoot."

"I could see you and Jeff Greenfield singing a duet."

Cat leaned back against the booth and nibbled on the inside of her cheek. "Seriously?"

"You've got the fan base he needs to boost his career and he has the classic sound you're looking to break into. I think it's brilliant."

"Mark my words, he'll never agree to it."

"Why would you say that? It would certainly help his career, and artists teaming up for a song has been popular for a few years now. I loved the Miranda Lambert and Keith Urban duet. Oh, and Taylor Swift and Tim McGraw? Perfect."

Cat inhaled a deep breath and nodded. "I'm not disagreeing with you, but I had a conversation with Jeff about how we're both taking control of our careers. I just don't see him agreeing to do something with me."

"Well, would *you* do it?"

Cat swallowed hard. "You mean one song, right?"

Maria nodded. "Yes," she said, but in reality she could already hear their voices blending in her head. They were both such talented artists but Maria thought they could be amazing together. And country music was hungry for duos. And judging from the reaction Cat had from meeting Jeff, Maria had a pretty good vibe that there was some chemistry there. She smiled. "So let me get this straight. You're willing, right?"

"Sure, why not?" Cat said with a slight lift of her chin. "Bring it on."

5

We Can Work It Out

$\mathcal{F}$EELING A BIT OF APPREHENSION AT BEING SUMMONED
to Rick Ruleman's office at My Way Records, Jeff
rolled his shoulders to get the kinks out. His new single,
"Second Chances," refused to budge on the *Billboard*
charts, and after the success of "Outta My Mind with
Lovin' You," the sluggish sales felt like a huge letdown.
He suspected that Rick and Maria felt the same way.
After inhaling deeply, Jeff raised his fist and rapped on
the door.

"Come on in," Rick called out in his raspy voice.

Jeff opened the door and stepped inside the spacious
office, which smelled pleasantly of leather and furniture
polish.

"Hey, Jeff, have a seat." Rick pointed to the chair
from his red leather chair behind a huge mahogany desk.

"Hello, Mr. Ruleman." Jeff nodded at Maria Sully,
who sat in a smaller chair bedside the desk. "Ms. Sully."

"I keep telling you not to be so formal. I think we
both feel old enough as it is," Rick protested with a grin.
"Right, Maria?"

"Rick, it's part of his Southern upbringing. My son, Clint, is the same way. But that being said, I do prefer Maria—and whatever you do, don't call me ma'am. Now *that* does make me feel ancient."

"'Nuf said. Just don't tell my mama." Jeff raised both hands in surrender. They were both smiling so he felt his tense muscles relax. "Let me start again. Hey, Rick and Maria."

"Ah, now that's more like it." Once a hard-core rocker with long spiked hair and a beard, Rick Ruleman now sported a short haircut and clean-shaven face. The only thing giving away his past were the tattoos peeking out from his rolled-up sleeves.

Jeff sat down, crossed his ankle over his knee, and waited.

"You're probably wondering what this is all about." Rick looked across his desk at him.

Jeff nodded.

"Well, we have an idea," Rick announced and then glanced over at Maria. "Why don't you elaborate?"

Jeff felt another twinge of nerves and had trouble not fidgeting in his chair.

"Sure." Maria shot Jeff a friendly but businesslike smile that reminded him of when his mother would *ask* him to do something but really meant he *had* to do it. "We think that it would be an excellent idea for you and Cat Carson to sing a duet. With your slow Southern style and Cat's sultry voice, your voices will blend well together."

Jeff glanced at Rick, who added, "And from a business standpoint her popularity will boost record sales."

"But Cat's fan base and mine aren't the same," Jeff pointed out.

"Exactly." Rick nodded. "This would benefit you both. Kind of like Taylor Swift and Tim McGraw, but you two have the added benefit of being around the same age so you could include some chemistry onstage and maybe in a music video."

A music video? Jeff felt unease wash over him and this time he did shift in his chair. "Look, I get where you're going with this and I really appreciate the effort you're putting into marketing my music, but I just don't feel like this is right for me . . . or my band. Cat just won't fit in." He swallowed and added, "And I have to tell you that we've already sort of butted heads."

"Jeff," Maria said, "you know that we love your music. But this could be a game changer and benefit you both, not to mention the label."

Jeff hated feeling guilty. He'd felt that way when he left his family farm and headed to Nashville. "With all due respect, I signed with My Way Records to do things . . . well, my way. I don't want . . . *didn't expect* to team up with anyone." He looked from Rick to Maria while trying to gauge their reaction to his resistance. "Um, what does Cat think about all this, or have you asked her yet?" He couldn't imagine she would agree.

"I ran it past her," Maria said. "I'll admit that she was a tad reluctant. Cat's got a mind of her own—otherwise she'd still be with Sweetside—but she is willing to do one song with you." Maria held up her index finger.

For some reason Jeff felt a little bit miffed by Cat's apparent reluctance, even though he didn't want to do this either. But still . . . "One song, huh?" So he wasn't a big enough star for her? "Do you have a song in mind?" Or was Cat calling the shots?

Maria and Rick exchanged a glance. "'Second Chances.'"

Jeff sat up straighter. "But we've already released it. I don't get it."

"It's not really going anywhere," Rick pointed out. "We feel strongly enough about Maria's song to give it another chance, if you'll pardon the pun."

"There's just a spark missing and we think that you and Cat singing together will change all that. After you rehearse we plan on having you sing it together at Sully's

first to get the reaction and if it's positive we'll cut another single and re-release it," Maria explained further.
"Kenny Rogers did something similar with 'Islands in
the Stream' when he teamed up with Dolly Parton. The
song was going nowhere until they added Dolly, who was
actually right down the street when she got the call to
record it with Kenny. So what do you say?"

Jeff felt a flash of irritation at being railroaded. Did he
really have a choice? But then he remembered that he
was sitting across from a former rock legend and one of
the best songwriters in the business. He should be over-
joyed at being in a position most new artists would give
their eyeteeth for.

"Sure, I'll give it a shot." Jeff hoped his smile didn't
appear as forced as it felt. "And thanks for the opportunity. So when do we get started?"

"Right now, if that's okay?" Maria raised her eyebrows.

Right now? "Sure, but is Cat here?"

"She's due to arrive in ten minutes," Maria replied.

"You were that sure I would agree?"

Maria angled her head. "I was hopeful, but I don't
want you to feel strong-armed. If you don't want to dive
in this quickly, I can do a songwriting session with Cat
instead. She was coming in regardless, so don't feel pres-
sured."

Jeff took a deep breath. He had agreed, so there
wasn't a valid reason to put this off. "No, I'm free, so let's
give this a shot."

"Super! You can head into the studio and warm up.
I'll send her in when she arrives. Need anything? Coffee
or water?"

"Water would be great," Jeff answered and forced one
more smile. If they thought he was going to make "Second Chances" into some pop-sounding bullshit, they
were dead wrong. He'd do this, but on his terms, not Cat
Carson's. He wasn't about to get talked into teaming up

with her and then having her run the show. Jeff had waited far too long for this opportunity to have it ruined by compromising what he believed in.

"Thanks." Jeff accepted the bottle of water and headed into the state-of-the-art studio. Wondering how his band would react to this new development, he inhaled deeply. So Cat Carson would agree to one song, would she? Jeff took a swig of water and squeezed the thin plastic too hard, splashing water down his shirt and onto his jeans, which made it look like . . . well, that . . . "Dammit!" He was trying to remember whether he had a change of pants in his truck when the door swung open.

Cat walked in. No, she didn't walk. She breezed in looking confident while he stood there looking as if he'd just wet himself. He wondered whether he could grab a guitar to hide it, but judging by her grin it was already too late. "Nervous, Farmer Jeff?"

"I spilled water."

"Sure you did."

"Evidence." Jeff held up the crushed water bottle, and she laughed.

"So you don't know your own strength?"

"Apparently not."

"Okay, I believe you now."

Jeff took a step closer and said in a low voice, "Look, I don't want to do this any more than you do."

She raised her eyebrows. "Oh, so you're taking one for the team by singing with the likes of me?"

Jeff opened his mouth for an instant comeback, but Cat flipped her hair over her shoulder and when he caught a subtle whiff of her floral perfume his brain short-circuited. "I, uh . . ." He tried again but his traitorous eyes had to notice that Cat was dressed in a plain white V-neck T-shirt tucked into faded jeans that hugged her curves in all the right places. She tapped her dusty pink cowboy boot and folded her arms across her chest.

Come on, who wore pink boots? And why the hell did he find them cute? He didn't . . . *dammit*. He forced himself to look away.

"So are you?"

"Am I what?"

"Taking one for the team?" she persisted.

"There you go, putting words into my mouth again. Oh, right, what I'm thinking is written all over my face." Jeff felt the need to point straight at his nose and do a circle.

"Let's just say I'd kick your butt in poker. And it was *you* who put words into *my* mouth. I didn't say I didn't want to do this."

"Right, but you will only grace me with your voice for one song."

"What? So you want to be a duo? Cut an album?" She raised her arms akimbo and eyed him as if they were about to start a boxing match instead of sing a song.

"Ha," was all Jeff could manage because he was distracted by her mouth, sheer pink and glossy. "You wish," he added. He raised his chin but then felt ridiculous and rocked back on his heels.

"In your dreams," Cat shot back.

"More like a nightmare," Jeff told her. Since Cat was tall, her boots made them stand almost eye to eye. The thought that they would, in fact, look good onstage together slipped into his mind, but he shook it off. When she opened her mouth to retort, Jeff heard the loud clearing of a throat.

"Um, shall we get started?" Maria asked lightly.

"Oh . . ." When had Maria entered the room? Jeff backed away quickly, oddly feeling as if caught in an embrace instead of bickering. "Sure." He nodded and then glanced at Cat, who appeared just as guilty-looking.

Maria handed them sheets of music. "I've created this arrangement. Look it over while we wait for Rick to join us. Remember that this song is about embracing a second chance at love," Maria added with a soft smile. "It doesn't happen often," she said, and there was an odd twist to her lips that gave Jeff pause. He had to wonder whether the song was a reflection of Maria's own life. The entire town of Cricket Creek was pulling for Maria and Pete Sully to reconcile. Jeff thought it would be pretty darned cool if they did.

Jeff sat down on the tall stool and looked over the arrangement. The song weaved a story about love lost but never forgotten and the hope of someday getting that elusive second chance to begin again. Jeff loved the lyrics about eternal hope and never giving up.

"This song is so sad," Cat said to Maria. "I didn't realize when I first heard it." She glanced at Jeff.

"That's because it's not," Jeff protested, defending his interpretation of the song. "It's about hope."

"That never comes!" Cat sputtered.

"Until tomorrow," he argued.

"Always tomorrow," Cat countered. "That's what the lyrics say. The tomorrow that never comes."

"The tomorrow that is always there for the taking," Jeff argued. "Are you that cynical?"

"Are you that naive?"

Jeff started to reply, but Rick entered the studio. "Okay, let's get started." Rick rubbed his hands together and gave them a smile. If he sensed the tension between Jeff and Cat he chose to ignore it.

"I don't know the song the way Jeff does, so bear with me," Cat said with a slight frown.

"No, you sure as hell don't," Jeff mumbled and was rewarded with a glare from Cat. Jeff shrugged at her and when the music began the result was like a singing sparring match. Jeff sang of hope and Cat countered with despair. The result became angry, edgy, and chock-full of emotion. Jeff turned and moved toward her pleading, but Cat countered with resistance. But when he finally gave up Cat lured him back with the lyrics, and at the conclusion of the song Jeff leaned closer . . . close enough for a kiss—and for a crazy moment he thought Cat was going to give him one. Then she abruptly turned away, leaving him feeling lost and needing her.

Jeff wanted to turn her around, but the sound of silence in the room made his heart thud and he remembered that Maria and Rick were watching. Jeff removed his headphones and shoved his fingers through his hair. Damn, he'd been that emotionally into the song!

Oh boy . . .

Jeff looked at Cat's back. Her shoulders raised and lowered as if she was breathing hard. Upset? Angry? He told himself he didn't care and yet he had an odd urge to draw her into his arms. He told himself his reaction was to the powerful lyrics, but he found himself frowning. What the hell was going on here?

This time both Rick and Maria cleared their throats, bringing Jeff back to reality. Well, that performance most likely killed the whole duet idea. Good. Problem solved.

Right?

"That blew my mind," Rick said, drawing Jeff's attention. "I mean, wow, man. Sorry to be so blunt, but . . . *holy shit.*"

Cat whirled around as well. She glanced at Jeff with a total I-blame-this-on-you slight narrowing of her eyes.

Rick turned to Maria, who was dabbing at the corners of her eyes. Good God, they'd reduced her to tears? Did this really just happen? "Thoughts, Maria?"

"I totally agree." Maria swallowed hard and then gave them a shaky smile. "Pardon me for saying so, but I think holy shit says it all."

"We could run through it again," Cat offered and then gave Jeff another glare. "Can't we, Jeff?"

"S-sure." Jeff nodded but returned her glare with a this-totally-wasn't-my-fault stare down.

"You think you can top that performance?" Rick asked. "I'm already blown away."

"Top it?" Jeff asked hesitantly and then it hit him. They'd liked it. He heard Cat suck in a breath and he glanced her way. She was frowning as if confused.

"That edgy, hard-hitting version was super unexpected," Maria admitted. "But the emotion was raw and powerful and quite frankly took my lyrics to a new level. But that's what music is all about. Touching you with fierce emotion and you two have it in spades. Chemistry. Explosive." She raised her hands skyward. "Boom!"

Jeff looked at Cat, who seemed a bit stunned.

"The question is, can you capture that same emotion again?" Rick wanted to know.

Jeff turned his attention to Cat. She lifted her chin and then narrowed her eyes ever so slightly at him once more. She didn't have to say it, but Jeff knew it was a silent dare.

"Yes," they answered in unison.

"Excellent," Rick said. "Based on what I just heard, you two have the potential to be an amazing duo."

"We agreed to one song," Cat reminded him with a touch of firmness.

"I know," Rick said in a light tone and raised both hands. "But you both need to hear that. Trust me, I'm not trying to force you into anything you don't want to do, but you should be aware of the fact so you can make decisions down the road. Fair enough?"

Jeff looked at Cat and they both nodded.

"Good. Well, the studio is open for the rest of the afternoon if you want to rehearse. If possible, I'd like for you to perform at Sully's on Friday and get the reaction from a live audience. Is that okay with you?"

"Sure," Jeff said. Cat nodded again but she didn't look all that pleased. Jeff understood. He didn't want to be a damned duo. One song! And that was going to be it.

6

Got to Get You into My Life

WHEN PETE LOOKED UP TO SEE MARIA ENTER THE FRONT door of the tavern, his heart started to thud. Taking a deep breath, he grabbed a towel and started wiping down the already clean bar top. Ever since Maria's return to Cricket Creek last Christmas, Pete had been hoping to find a way to get his ex-wife back into his life. When subtle hints failed to work, Pete decided it was high time to step up his game. He reached up to stroke his beard—a nervous habit he'd formed over the years since Maria had left him—but encountered smooth skin and then he remembered.

That morning he'd shaved.

During the week after Maria had left Cricket Creek for Nashville and Clint had left for college, Pete had let himself go and the result was a beard that he'd ended up keeping for the following seventeen years. After the divorce, beer and bar food became other habits, resulting in weight gain and ultimately health issues.

While Maria visited Cricket Creek for family events, they would only see each other in passing, resulting in a polite hug and forced smile that would haunt Pete afterward. When Clint didn't come home from California after he'd failed to get drafted into major-league baseball, Pete had been sure his son would return to Cricket Creek. Instead, Clint chose to stay and coach college baseball. Pete had missed his son like a physical ache. So much anger and words left unspoken had resulted in years of unhappiness and regret. Clint chose to visit his mother occasionally in Nashville, and Pete had heard that Maria had made several trips to California. Visits to Cricket Creek, however, had been few and far between. And when Clint confessed that he'd stayed away because he thought Pete was disappointed that he hadn't made the major leagues, it had torn Pete apart.

Why hadn't he reached out to them?

Pete gripped the edge of the bar and closed his eyes.

Foolish pride. It had taken heart problems to knock some sense into Pete. Years of not caring about himself finally reared its ugly head.

The return of Clint last Christmas changed all of that, and Pete now worked out on a regular basis over at the Cricket Creek Cougars baseball stadium, where Clint worked as a coach. Clint had also insisted on adding healthy choices to Sully's menu and the result was Pete being in the best shape he'd been in for a long-ass time, and it felt damned good.

While Pete wiped the same spot over and over he watched Maria's progress out of the corner of his eye. She wore dark blue boot-cut jeans and a fitted tan leather jacket that she removed and hung on a row of hooks lining the wall. A crisp white collared shirt was tucked into her jeans, revealing an intricate silver belt buckle studded with turquoise. Maria always did love Western and Native American jewelry, and she looked amazing. Pete reached up and tried to stroke his beard once more and then wondered what Maria would think of his clean-shaven face.

Would she even give a flying fig whether he had a beard or not?

Pete quickly looked down so Maria wouldn't catch him watching her, but when he heard the heels of her boots clicking across the hardwood floor, he couldn't resist glancing up. *Damn.* John Jameson, newly elected state representative and oh so full of himself, slinked over and extended his hand toward Maria. She smiled politely and accepted the handshake, but when John clung to her hand and leaned in to say something in Maria's ear, it was all Pete could do not to hop over the bar and plant his fist in Jameson's face.

Maria smiled, but when Jameson gestured toward the high-top table he'd been sitting at, she shook her head and pulled her hand away. Pete let out a sigh of relief. Had Maria joined that smarmy-ass politician, Pete didn't know what he would do but it would most likely not end well. Maria had that look about her that said she wanted no part of his bullshit, but John Jameson's mouth kept moving. And, although Maria's smile remained, it looked a bit strained. Pete really wished he could hear what was being said, but the music along with the clanking of pool balls and the dinging of the pinball machine interfered with his ability to listen in on their conversation. Dammit!

Still nodding, Maria glanced around as if looking for someone she knew to help her escape, but happy hour was still a good thirty minutes away, so only a few other patrons were scattered around the room.

Soon people would start pouring in and Pete would crank up the music, but right now all he wanted to do was tug Maria away from Jameson.

Pete sighed again when Maria finally turned on her heel to go but the damned man reached out and put his hand on her shoulder, impeding her progress. Pete felt hot anger wash over him. He tossed his towel down and wondered whether he could still hop over the bar without doing himself bodily injury—it would be a pretty impressive move. Pete placed one palm on the smooth wood and was wondering how much heft it would take when Maria reached up and deftly removed Jameson's hand.

"Oh, come on. Just one drink?" Jameson said loudly enough for Pete to hear. "You know you want to, sugar."

Pete wondered whether the doofus realized that Maria was his wife? Okay, ex-wife, he reminded himself. But seriously, couldn't the man feel Pete's gaze boring into his back like a red-hot laser?

"The name is Maria and I said no thank you." Pete watched Maria raise her eyebrows. When she tilted her head just slightly, Pete wondered what she was about to do. Pete had witnessed similar behavior from Jameson on numerous occasions but Pete thought he might be messing with the wrong woman this time. Was John Jameson about to finally get the slap across the face he so richly deserved?

Pete sure as hell hoped so. He just might have to applaud.

Instead, Maria abruptly turned away. . . .

And Pete's gaze locked with hers.

Maria's eyes widened and her mouth parted, making Pete wonder whether she was pissed that he hadn't intervened, and then he remembered his clean-shaven face. She walked toward him with a slightly bemused expression that he wished he could read. After sliding up onto a barstool, she finally asked, "So what made you shave your beard?"

"You never did like to beat around the bush," Pete replied, glad that his voice didn't sound as nervous as he felt.

"There's no reason to." Maria pointed to his face. "So?"

"Ah, just felt like a change."

"And how does it feel?"

"Cold."

Maria tilted her head to the side and laughed. God, how he loved the sound. . . . How he missed the sound.

With a move bolder than he felt, Pete leaned across the bar. "Wanna feel how smooth?"

Her eyes widened again and Pete's heart dropped when it appeared as if she was going to refuse but then she reached up with both palms and cupped his cheeks. She rubbed her thumbs back and forth and nodded. "Somebody replaced your face with a baby's butt," she agreed, and Pete wondered whether he imagined a slight breathless tone in her voice. As if reading his thoughts, she abruptly dropped her hands and cleared her throat.

"Can I get you something? An Arnold Palmer?" he asked, making sure she knew he still remembered her favorite mix of lemonade and iced tea.

Maria nodded and then lifted her chin. "I know it's not five o'clock yet, but add a shot of vodka. The good stuff."

Pete pointed to a sign hanging on the wall that read: "IT'S FIVE O'CLOCK SOMEWHERE."

"Good point."

Pete nibbled on the inside of his lip. "I just thought of something you might like even better. Are you willing to try?"

"Sure." She gave a smile that appeared a bit shy, reminding him of the first time he asked her out on a date, and it went straight to his heart.

Pete went in search of some tea-flavored vodka, and after adding a splash of lemonade proceeded to make an Arnold Palmer–flavored martini. He shook the ingredients until it was ice cold and then strained it into a chilled glass that he'd rimmed with sugar. Pete added a curl of lemon zest and placed the fancy concoction in front of her with a flourish.

"Wow, now that's very pretty," Maria said, and he was mesmerized as she moved her fingers up and down the stem of the glass. She lifted the glass to her lips and took a sip.

"Well?"

"Oh, now this is some good stuff. Could be dangerous," Maria added and then licked a few grains of sugar clinging to her bottom lip. "You do make an excellent martini, Pete."

"Thanks. I'm always trying out new recipes. I'll add this one to the drink list. I'll call it the Maria Sully Special," he said, and then wondered how she'd take that comment. He was trying his best to flirt. "Is that okay with you?"

"I think it's really cool to have a drink named after me." She lifted her glass. "Maria Sully it is."

"You forgot the *Special* part."

Maria flicked a glance at him and smiled. She took another taste. "Ah, it gets better with each sip."

"Even better with the next glass. There's more in the shaker. You know what they say about a martini. One martini is all right. Two is too many and three are not enough. James Thurber."

Maria laughed and then raised her glass. "I'll drink to that."

"I never go jogging. It makes me spill my martini," Pete said in his best George Burns imitation.

Maria arched an eyebrow. "I like to have a martini, two at the very most. After three I'm under the table; after four I'm under my host. Dorothy Parker," Maria said with a chuckle.

Pete had another martini quote on the tip of his tongue, but the image of her under the host slammed into his brain and slid south. Judging by the sudden pink in her cheeks, Maria might be thinking something similar. Or perhaps it was just the alcohol, he reasoned. "So what brings you over?" Pete asked, hoping she might say to see him.

Maria reached for the small bowl of peanut mix and,

just as he thought, picked out the sesame sticks. "I wanted to talk to you about starting the songwriters' showcase here at the tavern that we talked about. An open mic night kind of thing, but not cover songs, only self-written music. Are you interested in getting it off the ground?"

Oh, so this was business. Pete shoved his disappointment to the side and nodded. "I like the idea. We could eventually open up Sully's South in Restaurant Row."

"This could get the ball rolling and if we publicize it I think we can get some pretty big names from Nashville."

"We already have a big name," Pete said with a smile. He was so damned proud of her accomplishments and wished he'd stood behind her years earlier and not let his pride or fear get in the way. The knowledge that he'd hurt the only woman he'd ever loved plagued him every single day after she left. How many hundreds of times had he picked up the phone to call? Grabbed his truck keys to go after her and bring her back to Cricket Creek, where she belonged? But after Maria became an acclaimed songwriter Pete worried that she would think he wanted her back because of her success.

And so the years passed . . .

Maria smiled, but he saw a haunting sadness in her blue eyes. She dropped her gaze to her drink. "I'd also love to have Cat Carson and Jeff Greenfield here on Friday to debut a duet they're working on. It it garners good audience appeal then we plan on releasing it as a single."

"But I thought Jeff had a band."

"He does. But Jeff is the star and he needs to remember that little detail. Besides, this is just a little experiment." She picked up another sesame stick.

"So what's your opinion of them?"

"They're amazing together. The chemistry is downright explosive. But neither of them is really all that keen on collaborating, especially Jeff. I hope that a strong audience reaction will change their minds. So is it okay?"

"Sure. And, hey, would you like to get together and talk about open mic night over dinner?" Pete's heart beat rapidly while he waited for her answer. "We could put together some publicity ideas. I'm sure that the *Cricket Creek Courier* will want to do an article. I know Trish Daniels, who writes about local cuisine and entertainment. I can give her a call."

"Oh, is she a friend of yours?" Maria lowered her eyes and picked up a peanut.

Was Maria jealous? Pete felt a flash of pleasure at the possibility. "Trish did a nice write-up about Sully's a while back. She raved about my martinis and she was duly impressed that we offer more than traditional bar food and have healthy choices on the menu. Of course, as you know, I can thank Clint for that."

"Oh, how nice." She popped another peanut into her mouth and washed it down with a sip of her drink.

Pete hid his grin. "Yeah, but listen to this. Trish wrote a rather bad review of River Row Pizza and Pasta."

Maria frowned. "I heard the pizza there was delicious."

"It is. She was there the day they opened and it was a disaster. But get this—I overheard a few days ago that she is engaged to Tony Marino, the owner."

Maria laughed. "Well, I guess he must have forgiven her."

Pete risked putting his hand over hers. "Yeah, he sure did." He cleared his throat. "So how about that dinner, Maria?"

"Do you mean eat here?"

"No." Pete shook his head. "Maybe we can go to Wine and Diner Saturday night? The Cougars have a day game so Clint can keep an eye on things for me. I'm thinking about hiring more staff. I'd like to get away from here for a night if that's okay with you?"

"Um, yeah, sure," Maria finally agreed.

"I'll even put on a shirt with a collar and wear my

dress boots," Pete said with a grin. He'd wear a damned suit and tie if that's what it took to get Maria to spend an evening with him.

"I'm flattered," Maria said with a crooked smile. "I know how you detest dressing up."

Pete always dressed up on their wedding anniversary and took her out wherever she wanted to go. He looked at her and his heart constricted. So many lost years. Would she ever even consider taking him back? "Not for you," he said, and saw her startled expression.

"Pete . . ." She gave him a wary look that hit him in the gut.

"Some things do change, Maria," he interrupted quietly. He wondered when he would have the nerve, the courage to tell her that he'd never stopped loving her and never would. He wanted to say more but the crowd started pouring in and he was going to have to tend to his customers. This wasn't the place or time to go there and he told himself to be patient and to earn her trust. He would not, could not *ever* cause her hurt or pain again.

"I need to get going," Maria said.

"Can't you stay for a while?" Pete asked, but reluctantly removed his hand. There was a time when his pride would allow him to plead and it had cost him bigtime. "You still have the rest of your martini in the shaker."

"I'm meeting up with Rick Ruleman a little later. I know we've already bounced around some ideas about doing this but needed to run this by you first to make sure you're still on board."

"I understand," Pete said, but then, needing to touch her, reached over and covered her small hand with his. "I'll pick you up at six Saturday, or do you prefer later?"

"Six is fine," she said with a small smile and then stood up. "Oh, how much do I owe you for the martini?"

"You know better than to ask me that," Pete said gruffly.

Maria nodded and the smile she gave him this time was bigger. She started to turn around but then said, "Oh, and Pete?"

His heart thudded. "Yeah?"

Maria pointed to his face. "I like the clean-shaven face. It takes years off you."

"Then I'm keeping it shaved," Pete promised.

I did it hoping to please you, Pete wanted to say, but the words stuck in his throat. "Like I said, I needed a change," he replied with a slight shrug.

"Ah . . ." Something flickered in her eyes, making him wonder whether she'd guessed the truth. When he opened his mouth to confess, someone called her name and she turned to greet them.

When the customers started coming up to the bar, his lack of beard was going to cause quite a stir. Good. It would take his mind off wishing Maria would come behind the bar and help him serve and then get up and sing just like the old days before he'd told her she needed to give up her pie-in-the-sky songwriting dream and raise Clint. He'd been so damned wrong. "Maria, wait a minute."

"Okay."

Pete hurried from behind the bar and pulled her in for a quick hug. Her floral scent washed over him and it was all he could do not to drag her into the back hallway and kiss her, but he knew he needed to go slowly, tread softly. "It was good seeing you," he said in her ear and then stepped away.

"Same here." Maria nodded, but when he would have said more she quickly turned away. He stood there and watched her walk out the door and felt an immediate sense of loss. But she was having dinner with him Saturday night. It might be about business, but it was at a restaurant and not here. It was a start and Pete planned on taking full advantage, pulling out all the stops to get her back. If he didn't win her love again, his heart would be forever broken, but this time he wasn't going down without a fight.

"Hey, baby face, could you quit yer daydreamin' and get me a Kentucky Ale?" Jack Kemper shouted to Pete. "By the way, you're lookin' kinda girly without the beard," Jack added. He pointed to his own bushy growth of several inches. "Now this is the face of a real man."

"Here ya go." Pete slid a cold longneck down the bar with an expert flick of his wrist and Jack deftly caught it. "And if ya care to arm wrestle I think I'll prove who's the real man, beard or no beard," Pete challenged.

"Maybe later," Jack replied with a wave of his hand. "I wouldn't want to embarrass ya."

Pete chuckled. Other than his son, Clint, or some of the Cougar baseball team players, there were few men in Cricket Creek who could best him in arm wrestling. He listened to more jokes about his clean-shaven face. Some patrons didn't even recognize him and when he went to the bathroom in his office and looked in the mirror he was momentarily startled. He did look much younger without the beard—and physically fit too, thanks to Clint. Pete reached up and rubbed his hand over his chin. Did Maria find him attractive? Damn, she worked with countless famous singers. How could he begin to stack up next to the men in the circles she ran in?

Pete shrugged his wide shoulders and then leaned his hands against the cool edge of the sink. "All I can do is give it my best shot."

Pete sighed. Seeing her in passing when she popped into town had been tough as hell. But now that Maria lived in Cricket Creek and he'd been seeing her on a regular basis—if only for business—he had to wonder how in the world he'd managed to live without her for all these years without going completely crazy. If she'd dated, he didn't know about it and never asked Clint anything more than about her well-being. Imagining her in the arms of another man was just too much to bear, so he never let his brain go there. Pete shook his head. Damn, just seeing smarmy John Jameson touch her was enough to make his blood boil.

Pete gripped the sink harder and then pushed back. Although they'd been divorced for years, he'd never really stopped thinking of Maria as his wife. And he'd never even considered dating, because he knew no one would ever be able to take her place in his heart. So why even bother?

Pete felt a zing of excitement at the thought of the romantic setting on the patio at Wine and Diner. Maria might think this was all business, but to him it was so much more. He wondered whether he should show up with flowers, or would that seem like a date? Would the prospect of a date scare Maria away or was it what she'd been waiting for all along?

And then another thought hit him. Just what in the hell was he going to wear? His wardrobe had never been much to write home about in the first place, and the recent weight loss made the selection even smaller. He ran a hand over his smooth cheeks. If he wanted to put his best foot forward, he was going to have to enlist some help or end up on Maria's doorstep looking like a big-ass dork. No, he wanted to have her look at him with admiration and perhaps desire.

Pete closed his eyes and swallowed hard. He'd gotten a hug out of her here and there but he wanted more. How would Maria react to a kiss?

God, Pete's heart thudded at the mere thought of having her mouth pressed to his. But the big question was, would she fall into his arms or shove him away?

"Ah, boy." Pete inhaled a deep breath and looked at himself in the mirror once more. "I guess there's only one way to find out."

7

I Wanna Hold Your Hand

CAT LET THE SERENE BEAUTY WASH OVER WHILE SHE FOL-
lowed the worn path through the woods. Spongy
moss cushioned her feet and the clean, earthy scent of
nature filled her head. She didn't plan to hike very far,
and Jeff had advised her that she'd be fine if she stuck
close to the path. If she did happen to lose her way, all
she had to do was follow the gurgling creek that fed into
the river and it would lead back to her cabin. Her sense
of direction was sketchy at best but this was simple
enough . . . right?

As Cat hiked, snippets of lyrics slid into her brain, and
if she'd had a pen and paper, she would have sat down
on a rock or fallen log and started writing. The quiet, the
solitude, felt so peaceful and helped ease the stress of
knowing she and Jeff were going to perform "Second
Chances" at Sully's on Friday evening.

Cat knew that Jeff's band wanted nothing to do with
her. She'd overheard a phone conversation about jam-
ming at some place called Big Red and she wasn't in-
vited. While she understood that South Street Riot didn't

want Cat and Jeff to become a duo—they thought it would change the dynamics of where they wanted to take their music—Cat knew they were talented musicians and she wouldn't be opposed to going on the road with them. Because, like it or not, after a couple of days of rehearsal it was completely clear that her and Jeff's voices blended together and complemented each other perfectly. Cat had been in the business long enough to know they had that elusive special *something* that would set them apart from others. Maria certainly knew it, and she wasn't shy about reminding Cat whenever she got the chance.

Cat stopped to catch her breath. A light breeze cooled her skin and brushed her hair across her cheek. She gazed up at the tall pines reaching toward the blue sky. The treetops seemed to be poking toward puffy cotton ball clouds snagging at them as they lazily drifted by without a care in the world.

Although she'd never admit it to Jeff since he remained so stubbornly opposed, the idea of becoming a duo was kind of growing on Cat. She nibbled on the inside of her bottom lip and thought about it for a moment.

Or maybe Jeff Greenfield was growing on her.

Cat closed her eyes for a moment, trying to chase away the vision of Jeff, but it failed to work.

Okay . . . there was no *maybe*.

Cat was totally attracted to him. She kicked at a jagged rock with the toe of her hiking boot and sighed. Jeff represented everything she ever wanted in a man. He came from a solid background and made no bones about how much he cared about his farm and his family all the way down to his dogs, especially Little John, who was evidently as big as a horse. Cat tilted her head to the side. What would it have been like to be raised in a big, sprawling farmhouse filled with laughter and chaos? Cat knew they still shared a big family Sunday dinner; Jeff had spoken of it, and Cat secretly wished he'd invite her.

And during a break when Cat had heard Jeff chatting on the phone with his mother, begging her to bake an apple pie, she'd all but melted. His gentle, teasing tone had been laced with love. Jeff might not have realized he'd been grinning the entire time he'd spoken with his mom, which Cat found endearing and oh so very sexy.

Cat took a sip from her water bottle and then started walking again, this time at a slower pace. She loved her parents dearly, and while she was so very proud of the charity work they did, Cat missed them so much. A little ache settled in her chest, and she sighed. Sometimes she just felt so alone.

While people might envy Cat's wealthy family, all money had done was make her childhood lonely and then isolated after a kidnapping incident left her parents shaken to the core. Eventually, Cat's parents sold their sprawling estate in South Carolina and moved to Chicago, where they'd poured most of their time and money into doing good works. Cat smiled softly and then shook her head at the memory of what her mother had disclosed on the evening before Cat had left for Cricket Creek.

"Mom, whatever made you and Dad decide to devote your lives to charity work?"

A shadow had passed over her mother's face.

"I'm sorry. Did I ask something wrong? I'm totally proud, but I've never really completely understood."

Her mother had stared down at her wineglass as if the rich red liquid held all the answers, and then glanced at her father, who nodded as if to say, *Tell her.* "I . . . We made a promise." When she swallowed hard, Cat's father reached over and took her mother's hand.

"Jules . . ." he'd said in a gruff voice. "You don't have to speak of it," he added.

"It's okay, Daniel," she'd assured him with a shaky smile. "Cat, when . . . when there was the . . . the kidnapping. I promised God that I'd devote my life to good

works if he'd . . . if we got you back safely." She sniffed
and then smiled at her father with such love in her eyes
that Cat had felt her own throat constrict. Her parents
were completely devoted to each other and it showed.
"Nothing mattered to us but your safety."

"We wouldn't relive that horror for absolutely *anything*," her father explained. "But the result was living a
rich and rewarding life helping others. We were forever
changed, but for the better."

"Why didn't you ever tell me this?" Cat had asked
gently.

"I never speak of it," her mother had said, "because it
brings back that horrific fear." She'd put a hand to her
chest and shuddered.

"Well, I don't remember anything," Cat assured them.
But that wasn't entirely true, even though she'd been
only two years old when the incident occurred. Every so
often she had nightmares about a small dark space and
she suffered from claustrophobia. To this day she slept
with a night-light. The smell of car exhaust sometimes
made her break out into a cold sweat, making Cat guess
that she'd been locked inside of a trunk. Although she
wanted to know whether that was the case, the stark
look of fear on her mother's pale face always made her
refrain from asking more and she'd turned the subject to
something else.

Deep in thought, Cat climbed a rather steep incline,
grabbing on to branches for support. She wondered
whether the kidnapping had been the reason her parents
had never had more children. Although she had friends,
she'd never been allowed to spend the night at anyone's
house, and her parents had been understandably overprotective. And while her childhood hadn't been un-
happy, there were times when she'd felt isolated. In her
loneliness Cat had often turned to reading, losing herself
in stories as if she were the main character. But after
learning to play the guitar, she discovered that music

soothed her restless spirit in a way nothing else could, and that remained true to this day. With her guitar in her hands, melodies filled her head and the rest of the world drifted away, leaving her in peace.

When she reached the top of the hill, the first thing Cat noticed was the sheer beauty of the view. "Oh, wow." She could see the creek in the distance, and judging by the color of the sky, the sunset was going to be spectacular.

Wait . . . sunset?

How long had she been walking? And the creek was way down . . . *there*. When her ADD kicked in, she often got into a zone, a daydream kind of state that made her lose track of time. She wasn't hyperactive, just scatterbrained and often had difficulty staying focused. She was forever losing things but tried to overcome her ADD by making lists and trying to keep organized. Smartphones with alarms and calendars certainly helped, but now, without a personal assistant, she had to be particularly careful.

Cat pulled her cell phone from her jeans pocket. "Oh, damn, it's going on seven." A little flutter of panic hit her in the stomach when she realized she'd been hiking for over an hour instead of the thirty minutes she had allotted to clear her head. An hour back meant it would be dark before she arrived back at the cabin.

Wait. Where was the cabin? She turned in a complete circle thinking it would somehow help, but all it did was make her feel slightly dizzy.

"Okay, calm down." She lowered her palms downward and inhaled a deep breath. "I've got this. Just follow the creek. Damn!" When her mouth went dry, she took a few gulps of water and then had a wild thought that she'd better conserve the rest. She told herself she was being silly and then turned to make quick work of the huge hill she'd climbed. Quick, however, wasn't the smartest move. She slid and then with a yelp grabbed for an overhanging branch that stopped her precarious progress. Cat dangled from the branch trying to regain her composure. The toes of her boots grazed the ground, so she was only inches from safety, except she might start a downward plunge if she let go. Maybe if she just eased her grip oh so slowly. "Yes," Cat whispered.

And the branch broke with a loud snap that sounded like a gunshot. Or was it a gunshot? She'd seen *Justified*. Shit got real in the Kentucky woods.

The snapping sound collided with her scream, and she did a rapid shuffling of her feet in an effort to slow her forward momentum, which resulted in her immediately falling and sliding on her butt. When she ducked to avoid a low-hanging branch, she started a sideways roll, picking up leaves and sticks along the way. Cat grabbed for something, anything, but only ended up with a fistful of weeds. A rather steep patch had her rapidly rolling at an odd angle that thankfully slowed her descent, and when she saw another branch, she grabbed for it and almost had to laugh when it also broke. She came to an abrupt halt, her heart pounding as she wondered whether she was on a ledge and one slight movement would cause her demise. She slowly turned her head and realized she'd landed at the bottom of a hill that seemed like a mountain.

Cat rolled onto her back, breathing hard and not knowing whether to laugh or burst into tears. She remained undecided while humor warred with frustration. "Maybe I should laugh until I cry and let it all out," she mumbled and then sat up. The world started to spin and for a wild moment she thought she might be sick to her stomach. With a hand to her stomach she took a deep breath and willed the dizziness to pass. "Damned motion sickness," she muttered. Everyone thought she was a scaredy-cat (which she was) for not riding on a roller coaster, and she would have sucked it up except that she knew she would throw up afterward.

Cat let out a miserable moan. Remembering one of her near fainting incidents of stage fright, she recalled that she was supposed to raise her knees and dip her head between her legs. Or was it breathe into a paper bag? Wait—or pinch the bridge of her nose? Whatever. She leaned forward and rested her forehead on her knees. After taking deep gulps of earthy air her tilted world started to slowly right itself.

"Holy shit . . . Cat, are you okay?"

"What? Jeff? How did you get here?"

"I took the metro."

"Ha ha, aren't you the funny one?" she grumbled.

"I try."

"*Humph.*" Humiliation rolled over her in droves. How in the world had he found her? Perhaps he wasn't looking but wanted to see the sunset from on top of that . . . *that mountain.* Mortified, without raising her head, Cat muttered, "I'm perfectly fine."

"What in the world are you doing?"

"Meditating." Cat felt something tug at her scalp. "Ouch! Why are you pulling my hair?"

"You've got sticks and leaves poking out everywhere. How did that happen?"

"I like the look. Very bohemian," she mumbled. "You can go away now," she said rather testily and then remembered she was lost. She would sneakily follow him. "I'm not Zen yet."

To her dismay, or rather relief, Jeff sat down.

"Did you trip?" he asked so gently that Cat's eyes smarted with tears. "No. I kind of . . . rolled."

"Rolled?"

"Well, maybe it was tumbling with a bit of sliding involved."

"Down the hill?"

"All the way down the *mountain.* On purpose, of course. It makes the meditation afterward seem much more calming."

"What?" His tone was incredulous, as if he'd never fallen down a hill before. Okay, he probably hadn't. "Are you serious?"

"Almost never."

"Are you hurt?"

"Define *hurt*." She refused to look up.

"I feel as if we've had this conversation before."

"I'm certain it won't be the last time. I told you I'm, well, accident prone." She felt him gently tugging foreign objects from her hair.

"Wow, there's a feather," he observed with a sense of wonder.

"Part of the whole Zen thing. Very spiritual. Go ahead and roll down the mountain."

"Please don't dare me."

"It's like being so close to nature. Oh God, wait—do you think I took out a bird on the way down?" She searched her memory. "Surely I would know that, right?"

"Know what?"

"If I murdered a bird."

"I'm sure you didn't. Oh, damn—you're bleeding."

"I am?" Cat's heart started to thud and she raised her head. "Like from a gash or something?" The dizziness must have masked the pain. Or maybe she was just getting tough from always getting hurt and her body refused to register pain any longer.

Jeff reached over and examined a rather nasty scratch on her arm. "Damn, Cat, how'd you do this?" He started to examine her in other places. She wanted to give him a few suggestions.

"I think it's kind of obvious. I fell down an entire mountain. Look, if this is where you play doctor and ask me to disrobe, it won't happen," she said, but then thought it could be fun. She sucked in a breath as she flexed her hand. Her pinkie finger looked a bit odd. She held it up. "Do you think it's broken?"

Jeff failed to laugh and gently examined her finger.

"Maybe," he said, looking at her with concern. "We need to get you back to your cabin. Do you have a first aid kit?"

"I . . . I don't think so." She looked at the scratch and winced. Why was it that it didn't hurt until he'd pointed it out?

Jeff shook his head. "You of all people should have one, preferably on you, at all times, maybe hanging around your neck."

Cat didn't argue. "Ha. Aren't you just so very funny today."

"I'm not really kidding." When Cat noticed the concern remaining in his eyes, her stomach did a weird little thing that had nothing to do with being dizzy. "Can you walk?"

"Why are you always asking me that?" she tried to joke, but just as he leaned in to pull a twig from her hair she bent forward and they bumped faces. His mouth caught the edge of hers . . .

And suddenly they were kissing.

This was when she should shove him away with a sputter of indignant protest, but Cat clung to his shoulders and kissed him back with the pent-up passion of having wanted this for the past week. His tongue touched hers and Cat moaned. Sliding her fingertips down, she fisted her hands in his shirt, pulling him closer. He threaded his fingers through her hair, tilted her head back, and kissed her deeply, hotly, on and on until the kiss turned gentle, sweet . . . and blew her away.

Jeff pulled back and rubbed the pad of his thumb over her bottom lip. She was about to suck his thumb into her mouth but wondered whether that would be sexy or weird. Before she could decide, he said, "I'm kind of surprised that you kissed me instead of punching me."

"Kissed you?" Cat squeaked.

"Isn't that what it's called when you press your lips to someone else's lips? Kissing?"

She shook her hands, still fisted in his shirt, making him bob back and forth. "You, kind sir, kissed *me*." Hadn't he?

"Um, I don't think so. Seriously . . . you called me *kind sir*?"

Cat felt heat in her cheeks. Her odd vocabulary was a direct result of her love of romance novels. "How's this: Dude, you totally kissed me." She gave his shirt one last little shake and then let go.

"I like *kind sir* better."

"I can think of a few other things . . . *rake* for starters."

"Better than a hoe."

Cat tried hard not to laugh.

"You wanted to kiss me." He gave her a confident grin, and she was momentarily blinded by the dimples as he leaned closer. "Just like you want to do right now."

"I do not!" Fuming, Cat wanted to scramble to her feet, but she knew that in her current condition doing anything quickly wasn't in the cards, so she said, "You need to . . . to get over yourself."

"You talking to yourself there, Cat?"

Inhaling a sharp breath, Cat willed every molecule in her body to gather together for a massive scramble. Not quite confident she could pull it off, Cat bought more time. "Why are you even up here, anyway?" She raised her eyebrows. "Were you following me?"

"I was simply looking for you. I was worried when you didn't come back."

A little wind went out of her angry sails as she thought about him being concerned for her safety. "So you were spying on me?" she asked with less heat.

"I was taking out my trash when I saw you cross your yard and head over to the path into the woods. I don't spy, by the way. I'm not a creeper."

"No, but you do like to blindside someone with an unexpected kiss," she sputtered. "And don't even try to—" she began, but then heard a scurrying noise that sounded very close. "What was that?" she whispered.

"I don't know. It's getting dark soon. Nocturnal animals are coming out to feed."

"Feed?" Cat swallowed hard and looked around for beady little eyes. "Oh."

"You shouldn't have decided to take a hike this far this late in the day. It's really not safe, Cat."

Cat squared her shoulders. "You're just trying to scare me."

Jeff nodded. "Yes, I am."

She heard the sound again and wished she hadn't let go of his shirt. "It's working."

"And when it gets dark up here, it's pitch-black and becomes colder."

"How long do we have?" she asked, sounding like total doom and gloom. They didn't even have anything to ration and she'd lost her water bottle in the tumble down the hill.

"We're not going to make it back before dark—that much I can tell you."

Cat felt a shiver slide down her spine. Had he not come after her, she would be all alone *in the dark*. With hungry nocturnal animals coming out to feed.

The dark.

Her stark fear must have shown on her face because his grin faded. "Don't take this the wrong way, but I want you to hold my hand." She nodded; then he stood up and assisted her to her feet. "You okay?" He tilted his head and looked at her without the dimples, just concern.

"Must you keep asking me that?" she asked in a tone meant to be flippant, but she clung to his big warm hand. Cat was aware that she often masked her fear with humor. Part of her stage fright was due to the darkness just before she went on a stage, but when the lights came up she was fine. Mostly. She clung to his hand like a lifeline.

"We don't have to go fast," Jeff assured her. "I know these woods like the back of my hand."

"I've never understood that saying. How well does anyone really know the back of one's hand, anyway?"

He gazed down at his hand as if considering. "My cell phone has a flashlight." He stopped walking and looked at her. "But seriously—don't go hiking after dark unless I go with you."

"It wasn't my intention."

"To walk without me?"

Cat let out a huff. "No, to be out this long. I was just thinking about a song and kept walking without paying attention to where I was going and ended up on top of that . . . that giant mountain."

"It's just a hill, my little city girl," Jeff said with a grin, and then started walking. "Let me know if you get tired and we can rest."

"My childhood was spent in South Carolina," Cat told him. "So I do have roots in the South, for your information. I'm not entirely a city girl."

"Why did you move?"

Cat shrugged. "My parents thought we needed a change," she briefly explained, not wanting to disclose the real reason.

"Do you have siblings?"

"Nope. I guess I was all my parents could handle," she said breezily.

"Makes sense," he said, and she shot him a look. "Hey, you said it."

"And both of my parents' extended families are scattered all over the United States, so I didn't have cousins around either."

"Ah, so that's why you don't play well with others. It's all making sense to me now."

"I always wanted brothers and sisters. I asked Santa every year."

"Maybe you were always on the naughty list."

"Most likely," she said with a small smile. "I was forever getting into trouble, even on my own."

"Again, I'm not surprised," he said and gave her hand a little squeeze. "Your sassy attitude reminds me a lot of my sister, Sara."

"Well, then Sara must be awesome."

Jeff chuckled. "She is."

Surprised by his admission, she fell silent. Cat tried to remember the last time anyone had held her hand. It felt nice. "I finally gave up asking for siblings," she added, expecting a teasing comment in return, but instead he squeezed her hand again.

"Sara was always getting into trouble in school, mostly for not being able to pay attention." He paused and looked at Cat. "She has ADD."

"Like me," Cat confessed.

"Yes, so I do understand. My parents were totally frustrated with her until she was diagnosed with attention deficit disorder. She decided to become a teacher, knowing that not all children learn the same way."

"So is that why she started Old MacDonald's?"

"Partly. She says that kids learn well when the lessons are hands-on. She also was trying to save our family farm from financial ruin and the school brings in extra money." Jeff sighed. "Most farms are run by corporations nowadays. Family farms are quickly becoming a way of the past."

"That's so sad."

"Yeah, but it's reality. Farms that have been in families for generations are failing right and left. You have to really love farming to consider staying in business, and my family does." He shook his head. "Most farmers actually have other jobs to put food on the table and to keep the farm running. It's a crying shame."

"I had no idea. So I'm guessing that the barn weddings generate a lot of revenue. I remember that it was a gorgeous setting, both rustic and elegant at the same time. I wish I could have stayed for the reception. I'd love to get married there," she said and then wanted to smack herself. "Not that I think about it much," she added hastily. "So the barn weddings are doing well?"

"Yes, they're booming. Sara actually has to turn people away because the dates are snatched up well in advance."

"Wow, now that's great."

"Yes, it's taken the pressure off my parents. Plus, the school program is always booked and in addition to weddings my father does pig roasts for things like family reunions. Between all that and farming, we do all right. Braden still works the farm and Reid does all the financial stuff. I'm the only one who's no longer hands-on."

"But I'm guessing before all of this you put your music career on hold to help out?"

"Yeah. Reid came home to help get things straightened out. It was a family effort." Jeff chuckled. "Reid was so against the barn wedding thing at first. He and Sara sure butted heads over it big-time. Addison was supposed to be on Reid's side and discourage Sara, but she loved the notion."

Cat arched an eyebrow. "That had to cause some commotion between the two of them."

"Yeah, and now Reid and Addison are married with a baby girl on the way. Go figure."

"Back when Mia asked me to sing, I remember her telling me all about how the wedding was a surprise event. Reid thought he was pretending to be a groom at a mock wedding to showcase the renovated barn, but it was the real deal. Amazing. Addison sure was taking a chance. I don't know if I could be brave enough to do something like that in front of the entire town, not knowing the result."

"Oh, she and Sara put their heads together for that one." Jeff laughed. "To this day I don't know how they pulled it off, but the little town has a history of banding together and making impossible things happen. It still blows me away."

"I think I'm going to like it here."

When the sun totally disappeared, Jeff slowed down and Cat found herself edging closer to him. "It won't be much longer," he said. "But do you need to rest?"

"I'm fine," Cat told him, but then of course she had to trip over a root and stumble as if she'd had too much Chardonnay.

"Whoa, there." He held tightly to her hand or she might have done a face-plant.

"Unless of course you're offering a piggyback ride," she joked to hide her embarrassment.

"If you want one," Jeff offered and halted their progress.

"No!" she said quickly. While Cat kept in pretty good shape, she was a big girl and she'd die of embarrassment if he couldn't carry her. But the thought of having her legs wrapped around him left her feeling breathless.

"Don't say I didn't offer." He tugged on her hand and started walking.

In a few minutes they came to the road, but instead of heading to her cabin Jeff led her up to his place. "What are you doing?"

"You said you didn't have a first aid kit. I want to make sure you clean that cut and put antibiotic ointment on it."

Cat nodded. She had to admit it felt rather nice to have someone looking out for her well-being—someone who wasn't being paid to do it.

"Just watch out for that black bear over there," he added, making Cat shriek.

When he laughed, she pulled up and stomped her foot. "That wasn't one bit funny."

"Yes, it was."

"Are there really black bears around here?"

"No." Jeff shook his head. "We're close to Tennessee, where they do have black bears, so it isn't out of the question. But no, it's a rare occurrence."

"Just when I was starting to like you," she said, and then wanted to bite her tongue. She knew she wasn't Jeff Greenfield's type of girl. He probably went for cute little blondes with a sultry Southern accent and a sweet disposition. Cat had none of those things. It sucked that she got that nervous fluttery feeling when he walked in to rehearsal each day. Her fingers tingled when they brushed his, and holding his hand made her feel secure.

And the kiss?

She wasn't even going there.

No, unrequited love was a big-ass bummer and Cat was going to do everything it took to mask her growing feelings for Jeff. It just wasn't going to be easy. Now that she knew the bone-melting feeling of kissing him, she wanted to kiss him again. And again.

8

Help

JEFF OPENED HIS DOOR AND MOVED ASIDE FOR CAT TO enter. After flicking on the recessed lighting he gestured toward the kitchen to the left of the great room. "Have a seat there and I'll go get my first aid kit."

"Okay." She nodded but appeared a bit pale. "May I have a bottle of water?"

"Oh, I'm sorry. I should have asked if you wanted something to drink. I also have beer, wine, soft drinks?"

"A bottle of water—" She pulled a twig from her hair and frowned at it as if wondering how it got there. "Oh, and a glass of wine. I'm a two-fisted drinker," she said with a chuckle.

"Coming right up." Jeff handed her a bottle of water. "White or red?"

"Do you have a bottle open? Don't uncork one just for me."

"I always have a bottle of wine open."

"Really?" She tilted her head. "You seem like a beer kind of guy."

He retrieved a wineglass from a cabinet. "Maybe you shouldn't make assumptions."

"I'm sorry. I shouldn't. I mean, guys who wear Wranglers and flannel surely drink wine all the time. What was I thinking?"

Jeff laughed. "I'm usually a beer and bourbon kind of guy. But I find wine to be soothing when I write songs. Don't tell anyone about that little secret. I want to maintain my badass reputation."

"Never." Cat gave him a wide-eyed innocent look that said she would surely tell at the first opportunity. "Whatever you have open is fine." She unscrewed the cap of her water bottle and took a swig. "You don't seem like the badass type, though. I mean, those dimples of yours defuse any badassness. I think I just coined a new word."

"Yeah, I'm not the bad boy in the band. Merlot?"

"That will do nicely."

Jeff poured the wine and then paused to pick up her forearm and examine it. The ugly scratch on her soft skin bothered him more than he thought it would, and he had this odd urge to plant a soft kiss on her hand. "Not as bad as I thought." His attempt at a brisk tone came out gruff. Jeff cleared his throat. "I'll patch you up in no time," he added, and then realized he still had her elbow firmly cupped in the palm of his hand.

Cat leaned forward and peered down at the jagged scratch. "I've had worse." Her hair slipped over her shoulder and brushed across his arm. Totally innocent, but it sent a warm rush of longing pulsing through his blood. He wanted to touch her hair, tuck the silky strands behind her ear, pull her into his arms and kiss her. When she looked at him, the desire he felt must have shown on his face because her eyes widened just slightly but she didn't pull away. She swallowed and said, "I really think I broke my pinkie. It's still throbbing, so I might have joined the broken-bone club."

"What?" Jeff looked down and saw a darkening bruise beneath her fingernail. "Oh, I think you're right. Cat, what in the world am I going to do with you?" he asked and then had a sudden vision of what he wanted to do.

"Wind me up in bubble wrap?"

"It's not a bad idea." What he wanted to do was wrap her in his arms, and so he quickly stepped away. He brought her a little baggie filled with ice. "Keep this on your finger. I'll be right back," he said, then headed off to his master bathroom. He quickly located the first aid kit in the cabinet beneath the sink but paused to rein in his feelings. When the sun had started to sink low in the sky he'd started watching for Cat to return, and when she didn't, it had scared the daylights out of him. The woods were no place for her to be wandering around after dark. Jeff tried to tell himself he'd be concerned no matter who it was out there hiking, but deep down he knew better. He was starting to like her way too much, and if he wasn't careful it would complicate his music career. He needed to make choices with a clear head and not have emotion involved. With that in mind, he decided he needed to bandage her arm and send her on her way.

Jeff popped the lid off the kit to make sure it had everything he needed. He hated to think of her in pain and if she'd been lost in the dark he would have searched tirelessly to find her. Although he acted as if she annoyed him at every turn, if he was honest with himself he'd admit that he enjoyed her company—especially her quirky sense of humor. And if he was *really* honest, he would admit that he hadn't been this attracted to someone in a long-ass time.

And the girl could sing her face off.

Jeff felt a bit guilty about not taking her talent seriously. Sara had recently called him a music snob and was dying to meet Cat, who happened to be one of Sara's favorite artists. His mother wanted Cat to come over for

Sunday dinner soon! Jeff had told his mother no way. But the problem was that he really wanted to ask her. He wanted to show her the farm, and after dinner sit on the front porch with their guitars and sing together in the moonlight. But that would be delving into dangerous territory, so he wouldn't ask.

Jeff knew what he needed to do. He needed to patch Cat up, walk her to her door, and then head over to Sully's and find a pretty girl to dance with. Maybe his attraction to Cat was because he'd been neglecting his social life. Yes, he'd call Snake and head to Sully's. A few beers in, a pretty girl in his arms and all would be right with his mixed-up world. Good, he had a plan.

Jeff ignored that slight pang in his stomach when Cat looked over and smiled. It was stupid that thoughts of dancing with another girl made him feel guilty. Cat wasn't his girlfriend, dammit. And she wasn't going to be. End of story.

"You doin' okay?" he asked briskly.

Cat held up the wineglass. "This is helping. Maybe you should pour some bourbon over the wound like in an old Western movie."

"Has anyone ever told you that you're a bit on the crazy side?"

"Yes. Normal is overrated, don't you think?"

"I don't know. I consider myself pretty normal."

She put a hand on his arm. "Oh, that's too bad."

Jeff chuckled. "You need to wash the scratch under the sink. The soap is antibiotic." He frowned. "I'm going to have to get you out of that shirt."

"What?" She actually blushed. "What did you say?"

"Your shirt. You have the sleeves rolled up but you need something loose so you don't mess up the bandage afterward."

Cat glanced down. "Oh, I see what you mean."

"I'll get you one of my T-shirts."

Cat nodded. "Okay."

"I'll be right back." Jeff went to his bedroom and lifted a clean shirt from his dresser drawer, not really paying attention to which shirt it was. Putting a bandage on her arm had turned into wine and her wearing his clothes. How in the hell did that happen? The sooner he got Cat back to her place the better. Jeff hurried to the kitchen and thrust the shirt at Cat. "You can change in the bathroom off the hallway. There's soap in there too and then we can get you bandaged up," he said with a quick smile.

Cat nodded, but Jeff caught the flash of uncertainty in her eyes and he felt like an ass. When she stood up he had the urge to pull her into his arms, but he refrained. He needed to put some distance between them. Anything more than a friendly but business relationship was going to muddy the waters. The kiss had been an absolute bonehead move that wasn't going to be repeated. Blaming her had been nothing short of genius when he knew all too well that he had been the culprit. Jeff scrubbed a hand down his face. All it had taken was his mouth brushing against her soft lips and he'd been a total goner. Not gonna happen again.

"Okay, Doc, here I am," Cat announced and walked toward him. The Keith Urban song "You Look Good in My Shirt" started playing in his head. The blue University of Kentucky shirt was at least two sizes too big, but she somehow managed to make it look entirely sexy. She sat down and put her arm in front of him. "Make me all better," she said with a small smile. "And then I'll get out of your hair."

"Get out of my hair?"

"It's a figure of speech." She waved her hand, wincing as her pinkie throbbed.

"I know that, but why do you think I want you to go so fast?"

"Um, maybe because you're scowling at me?"

"No, I'm not."

She blew out a sigh. "I get it. First you had to trudge up the hill after me and now this. I'm . . . sorry." She lifted one shoulder.

"Sorry for what?" When her gaze flicked away he wanted to gently turn her back to face him, but he refrained. "Cat?"

"For being a pain in the ass."

Jeff couldn't help it. He laughed.

"Why are you laughing?" she sputtered.

"You can't be serious."

"I am completely serious. Why do people laugh at me when I'm being totally sincere? It's very off-putting, I'll have you know."

"Are you really arguing with me over whether you're a pain in the ass or not?"

"I think that says it all. I win." She smiled. "Wait. . . . I think."

This admission only made Jeff laugh harder. "It's kind of hard to take you seriously with twigs and leaves littering your hair."

"Still?" She reached up and extracted a small leaf. "I thought I got them all."

Jeff gently started applying salve to her scratch, hating it when she winced. "I don't mean to hurt you. This has to be done."

"I am a complete wimp when it comes to pain. I think it goes back to being an only child and getting attention. I made scratches and bruises into a huge deal."

Jeff chuckled while he found a sterile pad. He gently wrapped her arm with gauze and then taped it securely over the scratch. "There. Take two aspirin and call me in the morning." He started putting the items back in the kit.

Cat took the last sip of her wine. "Thanks for coming to my rescue or I might still be up there on the mountain. I should get going."

"I'll walk you."

"I've taken too much of your evening already. I can find my way up the road and around the bend. I even left lights on, I think."

"I'm walking you," Jeff said firmly. "I don't mind."

"You're kind of bossy, you know."

"I've been told I'm actually very laid-back."

Cat inhaled a deep breath. "Okay, walk me up if it makes you happy." She started to stand up, but as she pushed up with her hand, she winced again.

Jeff reached over and gently picked up her hand. "You need to put some ice on that."

"Oh, if I had a dime for each time I was told to do that . . ."

Jeff laughed again. "You'd be worth millions?"

"Billions. My mother still jokes that they knew me by name in the emergency room."

Jeff realized he was still holding her hand and quickly released it. "Well, I grew up on a farm, remember? Somebody was always getting hurt." When he stood up, she followed. He wondered what she would do if he asked her to stay. They could order a pizza and maybe watch a movie or ball game, he thought, but then shook his head internally. *No!* As soon as he'd walked her home he was calling Snake. It was ladies' night at Sully's and the tavern should be hopping.

"It sure is dark out here," Cat commented as they walked up the road. "I would have been totally terrified. Thank you again for finding me in my hour of need."

"If you need help with anything, just call," Jeff said, and at her immediate smile he added, "That's how we do things here in Cricket Creek." He wanted to make it clear he was just being neighborly. Of course, kissing her had gone above the call of duty. He wasn't going to bring it up. But when he reached her door, it felt oddly like the end of a date where he had to decide whether to go for the good night kiss. He leaned in and gave her a brief, awkward hug. "Put some ice on that hand."

"Will do."

"Well, I'll see you at the studio tomorrow."

"Sounds good. And thanks again, Jeff. I'll try to keep out of trouble from now on."

"And do you think that's going to work out for you?"

She laughed. "Of course not. But I will give it the old college try. Come to think of it, I did give college a brief try with not so good results."

"What happened?"

"I liked to sing at local bars but forgot to go to class in the morning."

"Ah, let me guess—your parents pulled the plug."

"And to their dismay I moved to Nashville to pursue my singing."

"Well, it worked out pretty well."

Cat shrugged. "Not the way I wanted, but that's why I'm here." She stood there uncertainly for a second, as if she wanted to say more, but then smiled. "Okay, good night. I'll see you tomorrow."

Jeff nodded. As he walked back to his cabin, he started losing interest in going to Sully's. Maybe he'd go back and soak in his hot tub. The thought occurred to him that Cat's sore body would benefit from a soak in the bubbling water, but then he shook his head. "What the hell is wrong with me?" He stopped in his tracks and looked up at the inky blue sky. With determination he took his cell phone out of his pocket and called Snake. He needed a cold beer and a warm woman . . . in that order.

9

Twist and Shout

CAT STARED AT THE SELECTION OF FROZEN DINNERS IN her freezer and wrinkled up her nose. "Well, yuck." Her stomach rumbled in empty protest, but none of the selections appealed to her. She supposed there was nothing like taking a tumble down a mountain to get your appetite going. She wanted something spicy and maybe a little bit naughty, like a cheeseburger or wings. French fries. "No, onion rings!" Cat tried fairly hard to eat a healthy diet, but sometimes a girl just had to splurge.

Nibbling on the inside of her lip, she considered going out to dinner, but the thought of eating alone made her groan. One of the bad things about changing cities was leaving all your friends behind, she thought with another drawn-out sigh.

Cat picked up the lemon chicken with angel hair pasta and tried to get her taste buds interested, but they stubbornly cried out for bar food. She was considering digging into the decadent chocolate chip ice cream when her cell phone rang, making her jump about a foot into the air. When she spotted Mia's name on the screen, she eagerly answered. "Please tell me you're back in town and want to go out and eat some greasy bar food. I need a partner in crime," Cat said in a rush.

"I am back in town, and I want to go out and eat some greasy bar food," Mia repeated with a laugh.

"Oh, Mia, have I told you lately that I love you?"

"No, and I've been wondering about that. What gives?"

Cat laughed. "Well, I love you."

"More than greasy bar food?"

"That might be pushing it." Cat sat down on a tall stool with backs made from bent willow branches. "But you're a close second."

Mia chuckled. "I'll take what I can get. By the way, I'm so glad you like the cabin."

"Oh, Mia, it's gorgeous. Both rustic and elegant at the same time. The splash of color with the quilts brightens up the entire cabin. It's just so cozy and peaceful here. And I just love the view of the river."

"I thought the setting was just perfect. So do you want to meet me at Sully's? I can get over there pretty soon and snag a table. It's ladies' night, so it will be pretty packed with ladies and of course guys looking for ladies."

"Yeah, I can get there in a little while. I just have to brush the leaves and twigs out of my hair."

Mia laughed. "Should I ask?"

"No, just use your imagination."

"I'll drag it out of you over onion rings."

"Onion rings always make me spill my guts."

Mia laughed. "Gosh, I've missed you, girl."

"Oh, me too! But, Mia, do you think I can go out without causing . . . you know, kind of a stir?" Cat hated asking because she thought it made her sound full of herself, but she wanted to be prepared.

"You don't have to be concerned with too much of that. With the recent influx of celebrities moving here, the locals actually try hard to let you maintain your privacy. You might get asked for an autograph or photo or two, but that should be about it. And other than the local paper, there aren't paparazzi like you might find in Nashville."

"That's so good to know."

"People tend to protect their own here in Cricket Creek. You're part of the family now."

"Oh, that's so sweet. This was such a big decision for me to move here, but I immediately felt it was the right choice. It might sound silly, but it was like the wildflowers were waving a welcome."

"You're a songwriter. That's how your brain works."

"I didn't think anyone knew how my brain works."

"Well, I'll tell you this much. I'm sure glad that my car decided to conk out in Cricket Creek, Kentucky. My life changed for the better that day." Mia chucked. "Well, maybe not that *very* day. It took a little living and learning little things like, um, what was important in life."

Cat laughed. "Well, and not to mention you met the love of your life here."

"Yeah, after I caused him to be tossed in jail and almost get kicked off the baseball team."

"This might be a small town, but big things seem to happen here."

"Well, yeah, *you're* here. That's big too. Oh, don't get me wrong. Gossip spreads like wildfire, like in any small town. But . . . for the most part it's just being nosy in a fun and caring kind of way, not to exploit or take advantage of you being a celebrity. You won't find anyone selling pictures of you to the tabloids here, Cat."

"That's sweet music to my ears." Cat sighed with relief. "I'm so over that whole being exploited thing."

"It's a polite, small-town thing to be respectful. Oh, but we are also oh so fiercely proud of who lives here. Like I said, you are kind of a big deal, you know."

"My parents started it all when they bought me that

microphone for Christmas when I was five. But fame wasn't part of my goal growing up. Just the love of music, you know?"

"I do know that about you, Cat. You're one of the most giving people around and you do your charity work without anyone knowing. Those designer shoes you sent for Heels for Meals were just amazing. What's left of the shoes you donated are on display at Violet's Vintage Clothing on Main Street. They went pretty fast!"

"Speaking of—when you have time, I need to go shopping. Purging my closets felt so good but now I'm in dire need of some clothes. Vintage sounds fun. I want to develop my own sense of style and not just dress the way I was told to."

"You of all people know you won't have to twist my arm to go shopping," Mia said. "I just do it a bit differently these days. I love a good bargain."

Cat had to smile. "Oh, Mia, I would have given anything to have seen you waiting tables at Wine and Diner when you moved here and pretending to be Mia Money. I mean, I know you were trying to prove yourself without using the Monroe name, but seriously, how did you even call yourself that with a straight face?"

"I have no idea. But you sure saved the day for me when you agreed to sing the national anthem at the Cougars opening-day game. If I had gotten Cam kicked off the team for getting into that darned fight, he might not have married me."

"Oh, the moment I met him when you came to pick me up in Nashville, I knew you were in love. I'm glad I played a part in bringing you and Cameron Patrick together, but I think you two would have made it against all odds."

"Still, I was so glad you answered the phone that day when I was in Noah Falcon's office pretending to know what I was doing."

Cat laughed at the memory. "That's what friends are

for. And I can't wait to hang out with Cam when he's back in town."

"I still can't wrap my brain around the fact that you're actually living in Cricket Creek. Wait—"

Cat heard her friend squeal. "Mia, what on earth are you doing?"

"The Snoopy happy dance. Sorry—I had to get that out of my system. Okay, *enough*—get your tushy over to Sully's. There should be a slew of cute country boys and baseball players since there's no night game. You might get asked to dance if any of them has the nerve to ask Cat Carson."

"Unfortunately, that can be a bit of a problem. Guys tend to forget that I'm just a person like everyone else. I like to hold hands and be kissed as much as anybody." A vision of Jeff slid into her brain.

"Well, you just let your wingman do the job."

"I pretty much suck at flirting. I think I might actually need a wingman."

"Yes! Oh, I forgot to tell you that matchmaking is the favorite pastime in Cricket Creek right after baseball."

Cat rolled her eyes. "Wait. Okay, then I have to ask you this. Did you pick the cabin I'm living in because it's close to Jeff Greenfield?"

"Of course not!" Mia answered so incredulously that Cat didn't believe her even one little bit.

"Well, it's not going to work."

"He's single, super hot, and can sing. You two are made for each other. And seriously, what's not to like?"

"Nothing. I just don't think I'm his type."

"Wait. Did you just say you liked him, though?"

"No!" If she kept telling people, soon the entire town would know she had a crush on Jeff Greenfield. Of course, there was likely a long list of girls gaga over the hometown country crooner. "You heard me incorrectly."

"Oh, I heard you loud and clear. You've got a thing for Jeff Greenfield. You might as well admit it."

"Well, okay, maybe I have a tiny little *thing* for him. It's those stupid dimples. They should be outlawed. I'm going to fill them in with Silly Putty when he's not looking."

"I knew it!"

"Mia, I will never speak to you ever again if you let *him* know it."

"I can keep a secret," Mia promised so seriously that Cat had to grin.

"And no meddling. There will be no mixing business with . . . you know."

"Pleasure?"

Cat felt a blush warm her cheeks at the thought of pleasure and Jeff Greenfield in the same sentence. "Yeah, it would lead to an epic disaster."

"Really? What about Faith Hill and Tim McGraw? Miranda Lambert and Blake Shelton? Trisha Yearwood and Garth Brooks? Sonny and Cher."

"Sonny and Cher?"

"I was running out of examples."

"Mia, I think I kind of . . . annoy him."

"I seriously doubt that. Cat, you're a bit quirky, but that's part of your charm."

"In other words, embrace my weirdness?"

"I prefer to call it uniqueness, but yes. Can I still be your wingman, though?"

"Absolutely. As a matter of fact, that's exactly what I need. And maybe a tutor."

"A tutor at what?"

"Guy 101. Can you help?"

Mia laughed. "You're so silly. I'll see you soon."

After ending the call Cat stood there grinning. It would be so nice to go out and not get hounded for autographs or pictures. Cat always tried to be accommodating and adored her fans, but it would be so relaxing not to have to deal with that now that she lived in Cricket Creek.

Suddenly super excited, Cat hurried into her bedroom in search of something to wear. Jeans, boots, and a fitted floral blouse seemed like a good choice for a honky-tonk bar. In Nashville Cat loved Lower Broadway, where all the legendary bars were located, but she didn't get to go out all that much since she couldn't go to a bar without causing a stir and usually getting a request to sing. Here in Cricket Creek she hoped that Mia was right and the locals would give her privacy.

Cat inhaled a breath. And when was the last time she'd danced with a guy? Did she even remember how to flirt? Cat thought about the banter back and forth with Jeff. That wasn't flirting. That was . . .

What was it exactly?

Cat was still thinking about that question when she entered the bathroom to freshen up and change, but then sucked in a breath when she saw her reflection. With her hair mussed and wearing Jeff's shirt, she looked like she'd just rolled out of bed. His bed. She looked down at the bandage and remembered the gentleness in his touch and the concern in his eyes.

And then she remembered the kiss.

Had she really kissed him first? God, she hoped not. Cat grabbed the edge of the sink. "No!" she whispered. No matter what Mia said, Cat knew all too well that mixing business and romance would more than likely end in heartbreak. She'd tried that several times when she let Matt Stanford set her up on several dates thinking he was actually trying to find a boyfriend for her when all he wanted was the publicity of hooking her up with another country star or sports hero. It took Cat a while to realize that paparazzi didn't always show up by accident. No, getting involved with someone in the business was just asking for trouble. And she didn't need to even ask for trouble . . . it just seemed to find her.

Cat tugged the T-shirt over her head, telling herself to give it back to Jeff as soon as she could. But when she caught a whiff of his aftershave, Cat put the shirt to her nose and inhaled. "What are you doing?" she sputtered and threw the shirt down. "So he smells good . . . so what?" She glared at the shirt thinking she should take it over to his cabin and toss it in his face. It occurred to Cat that Jeff hadn't done anything to deserve her wrath, but staying pissed at him—even if for no good reason— was going to be her best defense.

Cat decided that she would let Mia be her wingman. Tonight, for the first time in such a long while, she was going to let her hair down and have a rocking good time. She was going to dance and flirt and get all thoughts of Jeff Greenfield right out of her system.

With that thought, Cat paid special attention to her makeup. Then she added soft curls to her hair, letting it fall in beachy waves over her shoulders. After giving herself a critical once-over she sprayed on a bit of her favorite perfume and then added a bit more for good measure. With her hands fisted on her hips she stood back and surveyed her reflection in the mirror. "Look out, boys of Cricket Creek. Here I come."

Of course, in typical Cat Carson style, when she walked up the sidewalk to Sully's front door thirty minutes later, her resolve started to falter. After her childhood years of feeling gangly and clumsy, she still found it difficult to believe that she'd ended up on magazine covers. When her manager had called to inform her she'd been selected as one of *People* magazine's sexiest women, Cat had thought it was a huge joke being played on her and she still didn't quite get it.

When she tugged open the heavy door to Sully's and stepped inside, the rest of her confidence dissolved like a spoonful of sugar in hot tea. The place was packed and everybody was talking to someone, making Cat feel as if she were crashing a party. Inhaling a deep breath, she fought back the urge to turn on her heel and scurry out the door.

You can do this, her inner voice demanded. *You've played onstage before thousands. This is nothing.* But up onstage she let the music take over and she tried to tune the crowd out. She couldn't very well start singing in the middle of a local bar, now could she? Cat eyed the small stage in the far corner and sighed. Well, maybe she could—not that she wanted to. But bringing attention to her celebrity status would undermine her desire to fit in and just simply be one of the crowd. All Cat had ever really wanted to do was to fit in, and all of her life she had stood out. She knew she was an odd combination of self-confidence and insecurity. She could make people laugh, sing at the top of her lungs, and entertain a crowd, but when she was stripped down and just trying to be herself Cat still felt uneasy. Sometimes she felt as if she were always *on*, and it was sometimes tiring.

Cat felt eyes upon her and instantly knew that she was recognized. She saw a few people trying to discreetly take pictures with their smartphones, but no one approached, so that was something positive, she supposed. But in reality it also felt odd and sometimes lonely when people were afraid to just sit and have a friendly conversation with her. As she'd explained to Mia, just because she was a celebrity didn't mean that she didn't want to kick back and have fun like everybody else. It was so weird that people either paid too much attention to her or none at all. Cat was totally grateful for her success, but, boy, it would be so nice for once just to be . . . normal.

Well, she would never be normal, exactly, she thought with a small grin.

A moment later Cat heard a little squeal and spotted Mia hurrying her way. "Oh my gosh, it is so good to see you!" Mia gushed. "Wait—did you get taller?" Mia asked and then rose up on tiptoe to give Cat a hug. She pulled back and tilted her head to the side. "And prettier? Seriously, do those legs ever end?"

"These legs trip over everything." Cat laughed and started to feel more at ease.

"Ha. Well, you're gonna stir these boys 'round here into a frenzy."

"Are you getting a Southern accent, Mia?"

"Maybe. You will too after a while."

"I lived in South Carolina as a child and then in Nashville for three years. If it hasn't happened yet I don't think it will. I still sound mostly Midwestern."

"Southern is a state of mind, Cat. It will happen." Then in true form Mia bounced up and down. "I really am so glad to see you! I have a high-topped table over by the bar. Let's get you a girlie drink and put some of our favorites on the jukebox."

Cat laughed. "Backstreet Boys? Ninety-eight Degrees?"

"Yeah!"

Cat looked around at cowboy hats and baseball caps. "Um, I don't think that would be a popular choice. I think we need to get something in a longneck bottle and play some George Strait."

Mia shook her head. "You're no fun."

"I am very fun! Ask . . . anybody."

"How about I ask that sexy cowboy leaning against the wall?"

"I think I need to get my drink on first."

"Now you're talkin'."

Cat was pretty much a lightweight, so that meant maybe two or three beers at the most. She knew from experience that little bitty Mia could drink her under the table. A moment later a good-looking guy came over.

"Clint, what are you doing here?" Mia asked.

"Filling in for Dad. He needs to hire a few bartenders, if you know anybody interested."

"I'll ask around," Mia said.

"Ava is taking him shopping for a much needed new wardrobe."

"And why are you grinning?" Mia wanted to know.

Clint's grin widened. "Apparently he's taking my mother to dinner Saturday night."

"A date?" Mia bounced in her chair.

"Mom says it's business but I really think Dad has other ideas in mind."

"It's obvious how you feel about it," Mia said.

"All I can say is, it's about time. They are both too stubborn for their own good."

"Wait. So you must be Pete's son," Cat said, extending her hand. "Cat Carson. I'm so honored to be working with your mother. She's an amazing songwriter. She may not know what she's getting herself into, but your mother has taken me under her wing."

"Oh my gosh." Mia shook her head. "I'm so sorry. In my excitement about the date I forgot to introduce you two."

"It's nice to meet you, Cat. I'm a fan, and so is Ava."

"Thanks so much."

"You seem surprised." Clint chuckled. "I lived in California for a long time. Your songs always make me think of the beach and never fail to put me in a good mood."

"You're welcome. I love the beach too, but your mom and I are going to expand my horizons. Dig a little deeper creatively."

"I'm sure I'll enjoy whatever direction you go. You have a great voice." He grinned. "Oh, and whatever you do, don't call the thing with my dad a date to my mom's face. She will set you straight."

"Your mother is a straight shooter, for sure," Cat said. "I love that about her. But don't worry. I won't say anything."

"Thanks. So what will it be, ladies?"

"A bucket of Kentucky Ale," Mia answered and then looked at Cat. "What do you want to eat?"

"Do you have an appetizer sampler of bad-for-us stuff?"

Clint laughed. "Well, at my insistence we do actually have some healthy choices on the menu, but yeah, I can get a platter of bad-for-you stuff."

"Load us up and make sure there's onion rings."

"We hand batter our own," Clint informed her. "A bucket and a platter of bad-for-you stuff coming right up. And welcome to Cricket Creek, Cat."

"Thanks!" Cat said and then smiled across the table at Mia. "Ordering that felt so rebellious. But I guess I'll be jogging tomorrow morning. Note to self: stay on the path and keep the creek by the cabin in sight." She rolled up her sleeve to reveal her bandaged arm.

"What? Stitches again? Did you really take a tumble?"

"Are you surprised?" Cat relayed the hiking incident, but left out the kiss. "Apparently staying on the path is important."

Mia narrowed her eyes. "Why do I think there's more to the story? You're leaving something out."

Cat paused when Clint delivered the bucket of beer. Trying to look innocent, she pulled a longneck from the ice. "I have no idea what you're talking about."

"You have that . . . look."

"I don't have a . . . look." Cat put the bottle up to her lips and took a long swig. "Wow, I'm not a huge beer drinker, but this is tasty. Kentucky Ale, huh?"

"Craft beer brewed in Lexington, Kentucky. We have it on tap over at the stadium. You're avoiding the question."

"What was the question?"

"What are you leaving— Wait. Did you . . . Did something happen between you and Jeff?"

"Yes. He rescued me," Cat said firmly but felt a blush warm her cheeks.

"Come on, Cat—that's not the whole story."

Cat sliced a dismissive hand through the air and felt a twinge in her sore pinkie. "We might have had, well, like . . . a moment or something."

Mia sucked in a breath. "Wait. Did you . . . Did you kiss him?"

"No! I mean, well—he kissed me. Or maybe we kissed by accident. I do most things by accident." She took a drink of the beer and waved her hand through the air. "It wasn't a big deal."

"Liar."

"Okay, it wasn't a big deal to him."

Mia grabbed a beer and then shook her head. "For the life of me, I don't know why you don't get that you're gorgeous."

Cat rolled her eyes. "That's a stretch." She played with her napkin.

Mia shook her head. "Granted, there's nothing conventional about you, but that's part of your charm. Celebrity or not, you stand out in a crowd. And I bet Jeff thinks so too. It's just safer to assume otherwise."

"Bad-for-you sampler," Clint said, setting the tray down with a flourish. "Enjoy, and if there's anything else you need just give me a wave. Now, I have a little favor to ask."

"Name it," Mia told him.

"See that cute girl selling shots? Her name is Tricia Riol and I hired her as a shot girl. It's her first night and she's nervous as hell. Would you mind buying one from her?"

"No problem," Mia said. Cat nodded her agreement.

Mia picked up an onion ring but instead of eating it shoved it toward Cat.

"What are you doing?"

"You said it was your truth serum. So take a bite."

"No." Cat reluctantly put the crispy onion ring down and picked up a deep-fried pickle. After swiping it in the little cup of ranch dressing she popped it in her mouth.

"Cat, you're willing to take a chance with your career. Maybe you need to do the same thing with your personal life."

"Why are you pushing Jeff Greenfield so hard?" Cat asked. She looked at the onion rings with longing.

"I'm not. I just don't want you to push something—make that *someone*—with potential away, that's all."

"Mia, I don't think you even get it. Yes, I find everything about Jeff attractive." She leaned forward and whispered, "Downright sexy. And I don't just mean his looks. But I don't think I'm his type."

"You don't fall for a type, Cat. You fall for a person." Mia waved an onion ring at her. "And come on—what's not to like about you?"

"You said it yourself. I'm . . . different. I just bet that Jeff goes for conventional. The all-American girl-next-door type. And as you already know my childhood was anything but conventional. Let's put it this way. If we were in high school he wouldn't have looked my way. I didn't sit with the cool kids, Mia."

"First of all, you don't know that. Secondly, we're not in high school." Mia grinned. "Although those same kids sure would like to be sitting with a country music star now, wouldn't they? Like the Toby Keith song 'How Do You Like Me Now?'" She put her hands on her hips and wiggled so hard that her chair almost tipped over.

Cat tossed her head back and laughed. "Oh, Mia, I've missed you so much."

"I know. I can't believe you're living here!" Mia handed another onion ring to Cat and gave her a raised-eyebrow challenge. "Okay, take a bite."

"Okay." Cat bit into the crunchy batter. "Oh, this is heaven." She squirted some ketchup onto her small plate and dipped it into the deliciousness before taking another bite. "What?"

"If you thought there was a chance with Jeff, would you be willing to see where it goes?"

"Do you know something I don't?"

"Don't look. But he just walked in the door."

Cat's heart thudded as she twisted in her chair.

"I said don't look!"

"You know full well I can't abide by that rule."

Mia sighed. "It's time to find out if he has any interest."

Cat leaned forward. "What in the world are you going to do?" she asked in a stage whisper.

"Find you a hot cowboy or baseball player to dance with. Make Jeff jealous." Mia drummed her fingertips on the table while she looked around.

"Why do you even begin to think Jeff would get jealous of me dancing with another guy?"

"Because he immediately saw you and his gaze lingered until you turned around and he looked away. Totally a tell sign."

"This is silly. We're beneath high school antics. Do you think I should pass him a note and ask him to circle yes or no?"

"That would be kind of fun. Cute. Let's do it."

"Mia!"

"I'm just kidding. Sort of." She snapped her fingers. "We could put George Strait's 'Check Yes or No' on the jukebox. Think Jeff would get the message?"

"No! Mia, he wouldn't get it because there's nothing to get."

Mia pulled a pout. "Okay, then. Let's snag a dance partner for you. Smile at the guy over by the pinball machine. He's been checking you out."

"Do you have eyes in the back of your head or something?"

"I'm just a really awesome wingman. Follow my lead."

"No, I smell like onion rings and beer."

"It's a bar, Cat. Everything smells like onion rings and beer. Quit being a weenie."

"I'm *not* a weenie."

"Prove it. He's walking your way."

"Jeff?"

"No, the cute cowboy."

"Oh." Cat tried not to sound disappointed. Could Mia be right? Would Jeff actually get jealous? Perhaps it was time to find out.

"Hey there, ladies. Y'all having a good time?"

"Yes," Mia answered and gave Cat's leg a sharp tap beneath the table.

"Sure," Cat answered.

"My name is Devin Daniels."

"I'm Mia and this is Cat." Mia shook his hand and gestured toward Cat. "She just moved to Cricket Creek."

"Well, welcome." He gave Cat a look like he should recognize her but didn't quite know why. She got that sometimes. Onstage she wore dramatic makeup and a variety of hairstyles. When she dressed down she wasn't always recognized in public.

Devin tipped his cowboy hat back to get a better look. "You look familiar."

"I've got one of those faces," Cat said. He might put two and two together soon, but she wanted to remain normal for as long as she could.

"Well, it's a very pretty face."

"Thank you." She knew this was where she was supposed to flirt back, but she wasn't very good at it. Humor she knew. Flirting was still a bit of a mystery.

"Would you like to dance?"

Patient choreographers had turned easily distracted Cat into an excellent dancer and she had fun showing off. Still, she was about to decline when Mia tapped her shin harder. "I bruise easily," she said to Mia, and Devin gave her a curious look.

"I'll try not to step on your toes," he promised in a cute Southern drawl and then offered his arm. "Do you know how to two-step?"

"No. Honestly, I'm lucky to one-step," she fibbed, drawing an eye roll from Mia.

Devin laughed and Cat suddenly felt more in her element. "Well, then, we'll just freestyle. If I'm lucky, the next one will be a slow song." He gave her a charming grin and she relaxed even more.

Cat didn't want to draw attention, so she refrained from busting a move. Instead, she did a safe little shoulder bobbing and tapped her feet back and forth to one of her favorite Keith Urban songs. Halfway through Cat couldn't resist the urge to raise her arms and snap her fingers. When Devin smiled, she stepped it up a little and added a spin move that she used onstage.

And then she spotted Jeff looking at her and her feet reacted by getting tangled up. She did a little stagger to the left and then decided to do it to the right in an effort to make it look like a grapevine dance move. Devin, bless his heart, starting doing it with her like it was a line dance. When he added a little spin, Cat did it too, a bit off balance, but she laughed when he grabbed her hands and started to spin her around with him. When she saw Jeff turn away, Cat felt a little surge of disappointment that he didn't seem at all jealous. But then why should he? Cat tilted her head to the side and gave Devin her undivided attention.

When the song ended, George Strait started crooning "If I Know Me." Devin pulled her into his arms and whispered in her ear, "My wish just came true."

Cat smiled. She couldn't remember the last time she'd slow danced, and it felt really good to be in someone's arms. Devin was tall and she fit nicely in his embrace. He smelled woodsy and masculine and when he pulled her a bit closer she didn't protest. Her hand felt small in his big warm grasp while his other hand rested at the small of her back. Cat loved the song. Everything about the experience was pleasant and she smiled, glad that she'd decided to come out for the evening.

And then over Devin's shoulder she saw Jeff again. Her heart started to thud and she swallowed hard. With determination she put her hand on Devin's neck and allowed her fingers to toy with his hair. He responded by rubbing his thumb over the back of her hand. Cat found the sensation nice . . . *pleasant* . . . but it failed to cause a hot tingle of longing. And then it dawned on her. Dancing with Devin was enjoyable but nothing more.

And she wanted so much more. . . .

10

I Saw Her Standing There

JEFF TOLD HIMSELF TO QUIT WATCHING CAT AND DEVIN Daniels slow dancing, but his gaze kept wandering over to the dance floor.

"You gonna drink that beer or just hold on to it all night long," Snake asked and then gave Jeff's shoulder a shove. "Damn, I'm almost done with mine."

"Oh." Jeff looked down at the forgotten brown bottle and then tipped it up to his lips.

"So you gonna do something about it?"

"I'm drinkin' the damned beer, Snake."

"I mean about Cat." He nodded his head toward the dance floor.

"The duet thing? I told you, it's for one song. That's it. I know you're more open-minded, but the rest of the guys made it perfectly clear how they feel. They didn't sign up for Cat Carson joining us. I respect that. Everyone is making personal sacrifices to make this work, and I don't plan on screwing it up."

"Whoa, there!" Snake shook his shaggy head. "No,

man—I mean, about the fact you can't stand watching Cat dance with another dude."

"Oh, come on. Devin is a damned player. I don't want to see Cat get sucked in by his bullshit." He flicked another glance their way. "That's all."

"Right. Keep telling yourself that."

"He's a douche bag. The damned guy is all over her." And he really didn't like to see Cat's fingers in the jackass's hair.

"Dev is actually pretty legit, Jeff."

"You defending him?" Jeff watched Dev slide a hand down to the small of her back. "If he puts his hand on her ass . . ."

"What will you do?" Snake grabbed another beer from the bucket and looked at him expectantly.

Jeff felt a muscle jump in his clenched jaw. "Nothin'. Let's go shoot some pool."

"Why don't you just admit that you've got a thing for Cat? Do something about it."

"I don't have a thing for her like that. I just . . . She's my neighbor and—"

Snake leaned his elbows against the wooden railing behind their table. "That's a crock, so don't even try it. I said one thing about Cat being hot and you jumped my shit. I don't get it." He nodded his head in Cat's direction. "You're both single. And I saw her looking your way."

"You did?" Jeff asked and then felt like a lovesick fool.

"Go for it."

Jeff took a long pull from his beer bottle. "No way. Getting involved with her could interfere with my career decisions."

"Ah, so you've thought about it?"

"In an abstract way."

"What the hell does that even mean?"

Jeff lifted one shoulder and willed himself to keep his eyes on Snake, but it didn't work. "You know, like, in theory."

Snake made shoveling motions. "Man, it's getting deep in here. Are you for real right now?"

"She doesn't even like me that . . . way either. All we do is kinda fight. We'd suck as a couple." He ran his fingers through his hair. "No. No way. I'm not even going there."

Snaked laughed. "Sorry 'bout your luck, but I'm thinking you already did *go there*. In theory, of course."

"Ya know want? I just need somebody to dance with." Jeff tore his gaze away from Cat and damned smooth-talkin' Devin. "It's been too long since I've had a girl in my arms."

Snake shrugged. "If you say so. There's a whole slew of hot girls here tonight and plenty of them looking your way. Or more likely, looking my way and you're the lucky guy standing next to me." Snake pointed a thumb at his own chest and then lifted up his arm and flexed his biceps, making the snake tattoo move. "It's the tattoo. Chicks dig it."

"Right." Jeff put his empty upside down in the bucket and looked around, anywhere but the dance floor. It had been a pretty long time since he'd even approached a girl. "And the Keith Urban haircut. Why didn't I think of that?"

"Why do you have a burr up your ass?"

"It's been a while and I don't have that bad boy bull-shit going on." He circled his face with his finger.

"You've got those fucking dimples. What the hell else do you need?"

Jeff shrugged. It might be fun to be the bad boy for once instead of the nice guy with the damned dimples. "Damned if I know." But he did know. He needed to have Cat in his arms.

"Look, it's pretty damned easy, Jeff. We're in a bar.

You offer to buy a chick a drink or ask her to dance. Or both. Or send over a shot from Tricia, the sweet little shot girl over there."

"You know her name?"

"Of course. Point to a woman in here and I bet I know her name. Remembering names is crucial and I'm good at it. Just one of my many talents. Use word association. Like with Tricia I said, *wisha* rhymes with Tricia. I wisha had a shot. And that helps me remember she is the shot girl. And imagine her name tattooed on her forehead."

"That's crazy."

"It's only crazy if it doesn't work."

"That's one way of looking at it."

"Using a celebrity name or even an object that starts with the same letter works too. Test me—you know you want to."

Jeff pointed to the bartender behind the tub of beer. "What's her name?"

"Jodi. I think of Jodie Foster and Foster is the name of a beer so there you have it. Chicks love it when you remember their name. And she's cute."

"I hate to admit this, but you're on to something."

"I'm smarter than I look," Snake answered with a grin. "Anyway, Jeff, you're like a celebrity. Did you forget that tiny little detail? It's not like you're gonna get turned down, dude." He gave Jeff another shove. "We started South Street Riot back in high school in order to get the chicks, remember?"

"Yeah." Jeff chuckled. "We were like that Keith Urban and Brad Paisley song, 'Start a Band.' It could have been written about us."

"We sucked at first but it still worked. And we don't suck anymore."

Jeff lifted one shoulder. "I'm just rusty, I guess." Or not interested in anybody except for Cat. *No . . . that's not the reason, dammit!*

"You want me to show you how it's done?"

Jeff pushed away from the ledge he was leaning on. "Hell no. I don't need any damned pointers from you."

"Well, now, I take that bold-ass statement as a direct challenge." Snake raised one eyebrow. "Wanna see who can get somebody out there on the dance floor quicker? Loser gets the next round."

Jeff tapped his bottle to Snake's. "You're on."

"If you wanna get really serious, we could throw a kiss into the wager. The first guy to score a kiss gets a Fireball shot."

Jeff was about to refuse the addition to the bet but then thought it might be the perfect incentive to get past the memory of kissing Cat. "You're on."

"Fine, but none of that kissing on the cheek shit. I mean a real kiss, okay?"

"Like I said, you're on." Jeff felt a little surge of excitement at the challenge and started to scope out the bar, but for whatever reason every girl he spotted didn't seem like the right one to ask to dance or to buy a drink.

Or to kiss.

But he wasn't about to let Snake win. When Jeff spotted his friend chatting up a cute girl at the bar, in true competitive spirit Jeff turned and reached for the first girl within stepping distance of the dance floor . . . and the last girl he should have grabbed.

"Hey!" Cat protested as she stumbled forward toward the floor. "What are you doing?"

"I'm about to dance with you."

"I think you're supposed to ask first."

"Do you want to dance?" Jeff asked, but he'd already tugged her with him, so it was a moot point.

"No," Cat said, but to Jeff's relief she did a few stiff little dance moves. "I'm not a very good dancer."

"Yeah, right." Jeff inched a little bit closer. "You seemed to be doing okay with Dev."

"You know him?"

"This is a small town. Yes, I know *Dev*." He said his

name as if it were some kind of disease. "We went to high school together."

"Well, I was supposed to be following Devin to the bar for a martini." Cat craned her head over Jeff's shoulder.

"You don't want to do that," Jeff said.

"I like a good martini now and then."

"He's a player, Cat."

Her chin came up. "I can take care of myself, Farmer Jeff. I don't need your protection. Is that why you grabbed me? To save me from Devin?"

"No, I wanted to win a bet."

She frowned. "What kind of bet?"

"Snake bet me he could get a girl to dance with him before I could. I win."

"Grabbing someone and dragging her onto the dance floor without asking isn't winning. You totally cheated."

"So why are you still up here with me?"

"You took me by surprise. Again." She danced closer until she was close to his ear. "And because people are *watching*." Cat backed away and then gave him a tight smile.

Jeff danced closer and said, "And why do you care?"

"We're performing here tomorrow night, re-mem-*ber*? I'm being professional or else I'd toss a drink in your face."

"You don't have a drink in your hand."

"I would have had a chocolate martini in my hot little hand by now if you hadn't stopped me with your high school nonsense." She did a slightly off-balance spin move that had Jeff reaching for her waist to keep her from bumping into other dancers. She chuckled and he found her ability to laugh at herself cute. There simply wasn't anything practiced or pretentious about Cat and it was so hard not to be amused by everything she said or did. "I mean, who makes bets like that, anyway?"

"Snake. And you already know I can't back down from a dare. Come on, be a good sport and help me."

"And what's in it for me?" Cat asked, seemingly unaware that his arm was still around her waist. But Jeff was aware. He liked that she was tall and would fit perfectly against him.

And just like that a slow song came on.

When their eyes met, Jeff gave her a look of challenge.

"What are you doing?" she hissed in his ear. "I didn't agree—"

"You're right. People are watching." He pulled her closer and took her hand in his. "I'm creating a little preshow buzz."

"I'm about to do a preshow kick to your groin."

"Well, now *that* would create some buzz," Jeff admitted with a slight grin. "But please don't."

"Give me one good reason not to."

"Because you like me."

"You wish," she said near his ear. The moist warmth of her breath had him swallowing hard. It occurred to Jeff that onlookers were getting a much different impression about what was going on and he had to hide a grin. Damn, she smelled good, like flowers but with a hint of something sultry. When she turned, her hair brushed against his cheek and he longed to bury his face in the sweet scent and tug her even closer. "Come up with something better, Farmer Jeff."

"Okay, how about because I've rescued you *twice*. You owe me. Help me win the wager."

"Are you serious? I'm about to stomp on your foot. And you totally messed things up for me with Dev." She nodded toward the bar. "He just gave my martini to another girl."

"I'm not surprised."

"I'm sure he's pissed that I didn't follow him as I promised and instead I'm dancing with . . . *you*."

"You can thank me later."

"Ha. All because you wanted to win a silly bet. What else is involved? A kiss?"

"Yes."

Cat gasped.

"You asked."

"I was joking."

Jeff shrugged.

"That's despicable. And you're calling Dev a player? You'd ask some innocent girl to dance and then snag a kiss all because of a bet? Who does that?"

"All of this was Snake's idea."

"Who is Snake, anyway?"

"The drummer in my band."

"What kind of name is *Snake*?"

"You'll find out. So are you gonna help me out and kiss me?"

"Not on your life," she ground out.

"Chicken."

"Just how old are you?" Cat sputtered. She put her hands on his shoulders and gaped at him. "And do you really think that lame approach will work?"

"No." Jeff laughed. "I just enjoy the hell out of getting you riled up."

She leaned in close. "You need a new hobby. Take up knitting or something."

"But this is so much fun," Jeff whispered in her ear. "And you make it so easy. Admit that you like me. That's why you kissed me."

Cat pulled back and narrowed her eyes at him. "You know full well that I didn't instigate the kiss in the woods."

Jeff hesitated for just a fraction. This bad boy thing was way more fun than being Mr. Nice Guy. Who knew? "Yeah, actually, I do," he admitted in a more serious tone. Her eyes widened and at first she seemed confused.

Snake's words reverberated in his head. Why not just go for it. But was the attraction on her end as well? The kiss in the woods was . . . spontaneous, almost accidental. What would happen if a kiss was deliberate? Longing stirred inside him at the very thought of sliding his mouth against hers.

"But you did kiss me back," he challenged. But when she made a move to turn away, he grabbed her hand and started swaying to the music. "Admit it, Cat."

She sucked in a breath. "I'll admit no such thing," she sputtered, and started to stalk off the dance floor.

11

She Came in Through the Bathroom Window

*I*N HER EFFORT TO ESCAPE FROM THE DANCE FLOOR CAT forgot that she was holding Jeff's hand, so instead of getting away she was all but dragging him with her. She knew that people were watching, so she smiled as if she were having the time of her life. Cat caught Mia's wide-eyed look of question as Cat hurried past her with Jeff in tow. When they were at the back of the room, she tried to let go of his hand, but he stubbornly hung on and followed her out the door and onto the outdoor deck.

Because it wasn't quite summer season and the nights were still cool, the deck area remained deserted. Shaking off his hand, Cat took a deep breath, thinking she smelled rain in the air. Good thing no one was out there, because she was about to give Jeff Greenfield a piece of her mind. Cat wasn't quite sure just what she was going to say, but it was going to be . . . *scathing.*

She could be scathing, right?

The problem was that Cat really wanted to kiss him,

which was going to make the whole scathing thing rather difficult to pull off. She walked over to the corner of the deck beyond the visibility of the bar, turned, and crossed her arms over her chest. "Okay, I'll do it."

"Do what?"

"Kiss you."

"Kiss me?"

"Isn't that what you wanted?" Cat raised her hands skyward. "So you win the stupid bet. That's the deal, right? The dance and now the kiss." Cat held up two fingers. "I'll do those two things for you. Consider it payback from me, and then we're even."

Jeff looked at her for a long moment. "Okay."

"Good." She tried not to feel disappointed that the dance and kiss were just about winning a silly dare. Maybe she should give him a hot kiss that would knock his socks off. That would show him! "And remember— then we're *even*."

Jeff gave her a slow smile that turned her to liquid. "But something tells me you'll need rescuing on a fairly regular basis."

"A regular basis, huh?" She tapped her foot. "Right."

He nodded slowly. "As in, daily."

"We'll cross that kiss—I mean, bridge when we come to it." She really needed to get a grip on her slips of the tongue.

Jeff nodded. "Fair enough, I suppose. So, does that mean that every time I come to your rescue, I get a kiss in return?"

"I . . . uh . . ." This wasn't going as planned. Was he flirting or poking fun at her? Cat wasn't quite sure. She was going to teach him a lesson of some sort, wasn't she? Cat frowned, trying to remember what that lesson might have been.

Jeff took a step closer, making her heart pound.

"Well . . ." Her gaze dropped to his mouth. Just what in the hell was she doing, thinking about kissing him?

Why did her good sense have to take a holiday every time she was near him? She'd blame it on the beer, but she'd had only one. Cat looked up into the night sky— nope, the moon was only a sliver, not full. Maybe it was in her horoscope. "Maybe . . ."

"What?"

"Maybe if I agree to this crazy-sauce notion of yours, I'll be more careful and not get myself in trouble." She lifted her chin. "Yes, I suddenly think it's a wonderful preventative idea. You're on, Farmer Jeff. And thank you in advance."

"Okay, then. I'm ready," Jeff announced and stood very still.

Losing whatever misguided nerve that had gotten her into this mess in the first place, Cat leaned over and kissed him on the cheek. The slightly abrasive stubble made Cat's lips tingle. Oh, and she had the urge to do it again, but lingering and a little to the left.

"Um . . . no, sorry, Cat, but that won't do."

"What do you mean?" Cat backed up but came up against the wooden railing.

"Snake made it clear that the kiss had to be the real deal."

"How will he even know?"

"Scout's honor." He tapped his bottom lip and then stepped even closer. "Plant one right . . . here."

"This is ridiculous." Her attempt at a stern tone was a complete fail. Her heart pounded and her gaze dropped to his mouth.

"I'm just following the rules. This is your payback, remember?"

"Whatever." Cat made a show of rolling her eyes. "If I didn't want to pay you back and get this off my list, I—"

"List? You have a list?"

Cat swallowed hard. "I'm forgetful, remember? I always have lists. Grocery lists, to-do lists . . ."

"What else is on your list? Other than kissing me."

Several steamy ideas popped into her brain all at once. She wanted to see him shirtless, touch her tongue to his earlobe, and grab his ass with both hands. "Nothing," she replied, hoping that her warm face wasn't glowing in the dark.

"We could make one."

"Punching you in the face is ranking way up there," she said, but he only laughed. "Seriously, do you wake up in the morning trying to think of ways to piss me off?"

"Yes, actually."

"I believe you." Leaning in, she brushed her mouth lightly to his but made a smacking sound. "There." She tried to scoff, but her voice came out low and breathless. She got a whiff of his aftershave and almost dipped her mouth for another taste of his mouth. "You won the bet." She made a shooing motion with her fingers. "Now go and collect your winnings. Oh, and remember—we're even."

When Jeff's gaze lingered on her mouth, Cat's heart started to pound so hard that she felt a little bit lightheaded. He put one hand on the railing behind her, but just when she thought—okay, she *hoped* he'd swoop in for a hot, bone-melting kiss, he abruptly pushed back and stepped away. "Until the next rescue. Unless of course you want to pay it forward?"

"Ha," was all she could manage. A cool breeze replaced the warmth of his body, making Cat long to reach up, grab his shirt, and pull him back where he belonged. She'd never understood those scenes in movies where the couples basically rip at each other's clothes, but damned if she didn't have that urge right now. She wanted to tug at those mother-of-pearl snaps, expose his chest, and put her mouth—

"There you are!" called a deep male voice. Cat looked past Jeff's shoulder to a tall, lanky guy with shaggy sandy blond hair. "I wondered where the— Oh," he said, spotting Cat behind Jeff. "Was I . . . interrupting something?"

His voice sounded innocent, but Cat was on to Snake's game. He wanted to interrupt the potential kiss. These guys were serious about winning.

"Yes," Cat said, drawing a curious look from Jeff. She cleared her throat and then gave Jeff what she hoped was a sultry look, but then thought she was getting in way over her head. "But maybe I should just get going."

"What the hell do you want, Snake?" Jeff demanded, but without waiting for an answer turned back to Cat. "Wait. You're going home?"

"I might after I say good-bye to Mia. I have a heartache—I mean *headache*." She rubbed her temples lest there be any mistake. "Headache. My heart is actually pretty healthy. I eat Cheerios."

Snake cleared his throat. "Look, I'll just—"

"You must be Snake," Cat said brightly. "Nice to meet you."

"Same here," Snake said. He gave Jeff a little shrug and stepped forward. "My real name is Wes Tucker but . . ." He lifted his arm and showed her the snake curled around his biceps. "I've been Snake ever since I got this work of art."

"Oh . . . um . . ." Cat frowned at the odd-looking snake with the lopsided forked tongue and eyes that were too big. "Interesting."

Jeff chuckled, drawing a frown from Snake.

"I know it actually sucks, but . . ." He shrugged and gave her a rather charming grin. "It's part of who I am."

"Sometimes you just gotta own it," Cat said and his grin widened. "Oh, and by the way, you lost the bet," she said and then breezed past them.

"Wait, Cat," Jeff said, but she kept on walking. She opened the door with a *whoosh* and ignored the curious stares. Being watched or whispered about was nothing new, and she took it all in stride with a smile on her face. But the effort really did start to make her head pound, although heartache might actually be closer to the mark.

When it came to Jeff Greenfield, her entire body reacted by going full steam ahead when her brain wanted to put on the brakes.

"Well?" Mia demanded when Cat slid back onto her tall stool. "Are you going to tell me what just happened out there?"

Cat sighed. "If I fully understood, I'd tell you." She felt a little tug of emotion. "But I really don't know. For a minute I thought Jeff was flirting, but I think teasing might be more like it."

Mia shook her head. "No way. Jeff is really into you, Cat."

"Why would you think that? Glancing my way doesn't really mean much in my book."

"Well, then it's *written* all over his face. Put that in your pipe and smoke it."

"What does that even mean?" Cat asked with a chuckle.

Mia laughed. "I overheard Myra over at Wine and Diner say it one day while I was eating lunch. It means it's true whether you like it or not. I've been wanting to use it ever since."

"You're totally wrong." Cat placed her palms on the table and leaned forward. "Mia, he only grabbed me to dance so he could win a juvenile bet with . . . with Snake."

"The drummer in his band?"

"You know him?" Cat asked. She took a swig of her lukewarm beer and wrinkled her nose. She put down the bottle and grabbed a cold one from the soupy ice.

Mia nodded. "Even though South Street Riot broke up shortly after high school, I got them to do a reunion concert at the Cougars stadium a couple of years ago. By the way the girls reacted, you would have thought it was the Backstreet Boys."

Cat laughed. "Backstreet Boys? Somehow I don't think they would like the comparison to a boy band."

"You know what I mean, though. Apparently they were super popular in high school."

"Yeah." Cat could envision girls going gaga over Jeff.

"You know, I really think that concert is what started them thinking about getting back together with Jeff. Regardless, you get the picture. Chicks still dig them."

"What are the rest of the guys like?"

"Snake is the bad boy drummer. Colin Walker plays keyboard and does solo gigs at Wine and Diner. Women young and old swoon when he sings. Jackson Pike, or Jax as they started calling him because he looks like Charlie Hunnam from Sons of Anarchy, is one of those scruffy but somehow sexy guys who doesn't even have to try. Sam Slader, bass guitarist, is as smooth as they come."

"And then you have Jeff as the front man. No wonder they don't want me to mess with the formula. Not that I want to," Cat quickly added.

"You just want to mess *around* with the front man."

"Mia!" Cat picked up a celery stick and swiped it through the ranch dressing.

"Wait. So what was the so-called bet anyway?"

Cat explained and waited for Mia to be disgusted, but her face split into a grin. "That's hilarious!" She leaned closer. "So who won?"

"Jeff." Cat felt her cheeks grow warm. "See, the only reason he wanted to dance with me was to win. Can you believe it?"

Mia waved a dismissive hand. "I'm around baseball players all day long. Believe me—boys will be boys. They do dares and practical jokes all day long. And for the most part they're just having a little harmless fun." Her eyes widened. "And the kiss?"

"Ha—just a little peck is all he got. I only wanted to pay Jeff back for, you know . . . helping me out."

"So all you gave him was a little ol' peck when you had the chance to get a full-blown kiss? Are you crazy?"

"Yes, it's a known fact."

"I don't get it."

"Will you just let this go?" Cat looked down at the

platter of bad-for-them food and realized she'd lost her appetite but picked up a saucy wing anyway. She waved the little drumette at Mia. "Seriously, Mia."

"I am serious. You have to know that Jeff was just using the bet as an excuse to get a kiss from you."

"Yeah, right," Cat protested, but wondered whether Mia could be right. "I just happened to be within handy reaching distance. End of story. I just bet Jeff is already out there with someone else as we speak." She wasn't going to look.

Okay . . . yes, she was going to look, but just a tiny passing glance. To her relief Jeff was talking to Clint Sully and suddenly the wings started to taste delicious once more. She licked her thumb and reached for another one. "The man has it in his head that I'm going to be in constant need of rescuing. And I have to pay him back with a kiss each time. The nerve."

Mia wiggled her eyebrows. "Oh, if I were you I'd take him up on that one."

"Are you kidding me?" Cat crunched on a piece of celery harder than necessary. "That's the sexiest—I mean *sexist* thing I've heard in my entire life. Come to my rescue," she sputtered. "For real? Look, if I need rescuing from someone, Jeff Greenfield is the very last person I'm going to call." She flicked a glance in his direction, noticing how the sleeves of his T-shirt hugged his biceps.

"Can you protest any harder? Really, you are not one bit convincing, so just stop."

Cat groaned. "Okay, I admitted my attraction to him, but how transparent am I to, you know, the general public?"

"You really want to know?"

Drumming her fingertips on the table. "No."

"A plate-glass window."

"I said no! Wait a minute—really?"

"Sweetie, simmer down. I'm only teasing." Mia looked

over at Cat and sighed. "I fought my feelings for Cam for a long time too, but it was a losing battle."

Cat had to smile. "I remember seeing you and Cam for the first time together when you picked me up in Nashville to sing at the Cougars game. I just knew you were in love with him."

"And, Cat, we are from two very different walks of life. But love erases all of that. The past doesn't matter, only the future." Mia smiled softly and looked so happy that Cat felt a flash of envy.

"You can have that in your life too, you know. It's out there for the taking."

"You always could read my mind," Cat said with a shake of her head. "No matter how long we've been apart we immediately connect. I can't tell you how many times you called just when I needed you to."

"That's what friends are for. Well, that, and being your wingman." When her phone buzzed, Mia picked it up and smiled down at the screen. "A text from Cam saying he misses me." She bit her bottom lip and blinked as if holding back tears.

"It must be hard that he has to travel so much."

She nodded. "It is. I offered to give up my job with the Cougars so I could go to more games with him, but Cam knows how much I love it and wouldn't hear of me quitting. Of course, if he gets called up to the major leagues, we'll have to move, but for right now we just deal with it. When you love somebody enough, you make sacrifices. And Noah Falcon gives me time off when Cam is playing within driving distance. Do you mind if I go outside and give him a quick call?"

"No, of course not. Go ahead. But be warned I might eat the rest of the wings and the last fried pickle."

Mia laughed as she scooted from her stool. "I'll be back in a few minutes, but don't give up my seat for a cute baseball player or farm boy." She hesitated and then said, "Only for a super cute country singer who keeps looking your way."

Cat made a point of rolling her eyes but then stared down at her beer bottle for a moment after Mia walked away. Maybe it was the small-town atmosphere or the cozy cabin or seeing Mia so happy, but Cat was suddenly longing for someone special in her life. She looked around the bar and it suddenly seemed as if everyone was with someone except for her. And despite her resolve not to, she searched for Jeff, who was still talking to Clint at the bar. When Jeff laughed, she found herself smiling, but then glanced away. Kissing him had awakened feelings that had been dormant for far too long.

A demanding career that kept her on the road had curtailed her love life in a big way, but that wasn't the whole story. Cat knew she was a bit, well, different. Her unconventional childhood coupled with the kidnapping scare had changed her parents in a good way, but made for a rather odd and sheltered existence. Books and music were her escape and for the most part that still remained true. In high school she'd been tall and gangly but found humor as a way to cope with her insecurity, especially with boys. Her success gave her some hard-earned confidence, but to this day she was still floored when people called her beautiful.

"You look like you're a million miles away," Mia said as she sat down. "Everything okay?"

"I think I'm going to do it."

"You have to be more specific," Mia said with a laugh. "I'm not quite that good at reading your mind," she added, but then her eyes widened. "Wait. You mean Jeff?"

Cat opened her mouth to tell Mia that she was going to quit being a weenie and see where her attraction to Jeff would take her, but then out of the corner of her eye she spotted a gorgeous blonde throw herself into Jeff's arms and to Cat's dismay he hugged her back. If that wasn't enough, she eased up on tiptoe and planted a lingering kiss on Jeff's mouth.

"Don't jump to conclusions," Mia warned her. "Remember that Jeff is a celebrity and women throw themselves at him."

Cat nodded, but then thought that this was yet another complication she wouldn't want to deal with. Oddly, while women tended to go after music stars, Cat had the opposite experience. Men, maybe because they were intimidated by her celebrity status, actually avoided approaching her. So Cat merely shrugged as if her heart hadn't dropped all the way to the bottom of her stomach, making the hot wings take flight. She faked a yawn. "I meant that I should get going. Tomorrow is a busy day." After her fake yawn she forced a smile. "Will you be here for the concert tomorrow night?" Cat asked brightly.

"No doubt." Mia nodded, but Cat could tell that she saw right though her. "Do you want me to head home with you? Slumber party?"

"I appreciate the offer, but I might actually do a bit of songwriting."

"Text me when you get home, okay? I'm going to hang out for just a little bit longer."

"You don't have to stay here and spy for me."

"Of course I do."

Cat managed a slight grin. "You will always be my best friend."

"I will and to prove it I'm also going to get the tab."

"Thanks. I'll get you back next time." Cat scooted back her stool and grabbed her purse. After giving Mia a quick hug Cat walked with long-legged strides, but the front door seemed a million miles away. She knew eyes were upon her and tongues were wagging. Perhaps leaving while Jeff was deep in conversation with another girl made it seem like she was running away, so she willed her legs to slow down when she wanted to sprint. Just before she reached her escape she felt a hand on her shoulder.

"Hey, where are you rushing off to?"

Cat turned around to face Devin. "I have a long day tomorrow and I need my beauty sleep."

"You can't possibly get any prettier." He gave her a charming grin. "Can I get you to have one last drink? I owe you a chocolate martini."

"I'll take a rain check, if that's okay."

"Then I'll pray for rain," Devin said, and then leaned over to give her a light kiss on the cheek.

Pleasant, but no tingle . . . *Damn.* Cat mustered up a smile anyway. She imagined the gossip mill was having a field day.

"At least let me walk you to your car."

"It's Cricket Creek. I'll be fine."

"Then indulge me."

Cat didn't want to be rude, so she nodded. "Okay." Once outside, she breathed deep, air that smelled of late-spring flowers tinged with burning wood, most likely from bonfires. Devin fell in step beside her as they walked to her SUV. When they got there she dug into her purse for her keys and then turned to face him. "Thank you."

"I'm sorry I didn't recognize you earlier."

Cat waved him off. "I don't mind. In fact, I try to remain pretty low key and avoid pictures. I wear a lot of baseball caps," she added with a smile.

"I just wanted to let you know that's not why I approached you. I didn't realize you were Cat Carson until I overheard people talking."

Cat nodded. When he shoved his hands in his pockets she could tell he was suddenly nervous. "I'm pretty down-to-earth. Don't ever hesitate to approach me. I want to be a part of the regular crowd and just have fun like everybody else."

"Well, then, would you like to go out to dinner with me? Just something casual," he added. His smile was chock-full of charm and she wanted to say yes.

"I'm actually pretty busy right now. I'm writing some new songs for an album, so I'm staying to myself pretty much these days." She put a hand on his forearm and squeezed. "But thanks for the offer."

He nibbled on the inside of his lip as if contemplating, but then nodded. "Well, if you change your mind, let me know. And you do have to eat, you know."

"I'll do that," Cat said, and then opened her door and slid behind the wheel. She watched Devin walk away and for some reason felt a lump form in her throat. For a second she considered rolling down her window and calling him back, but she stopped herself. In her life and in her career she'd often done things simply not to hurt someone's feelings. She had a very hard time saying no and it felt liberating to start living her life on her own terms.

But as she drove home to her cabin, the melancholy mood remained. As she turned the steering wheel she spotted the bandage that Jeff had wrapped around her scratch. She touched the cotton with her fingertips. The image of him hugging that girl slipped into her brain and the lump in her throat returned. Cat knew that she had no right to be jealous that Jeff was hugging or kissing another woman. He wasn't her boyfriend. She shouldn't feel the weight of sadness or the hot flash of anger that Jeff had obviously been toying with her earlier on the deck. And yet all of those emotions swirled around in her brain like dry leaves in a windstorm.

After getting out of her SUV, she closed the door harder than necessary but then felt guilty that she was somehow disturbing the solitude of the woods and waking sleeping animals. She thought of the pretty doe and hoped she hadn't startled the poor thing from peaceful slumber, so she walked very quietly to her front door trying to make up for the noisy slam. She knew she was being ridiculous, but that was the kind of mood she was in. When a tear slipped out of the corner of her eye, she gave it an impatient swipe.

"I think I'll go all Taylor Swift on him and write a song," she muttered and started humming "I Knew You Were Trouble." Angry with herself for caring, she stomped her foot and then, to her horror, realized she couldn't find the key to the front door. "This isn't happening," she whispered, digging around in her oversized purse. She swallowed hard and reached over to turn the knob, thinking she must have simply forgotten to lock the door. Cat groaned when the doorknob refused to turn. "Damn it all to hell and back! How in the world did I manage this fiasco?" How could the door be locked when she didn't have the keys? Was it the kind of door that locked automatically? Were the keys lying on the kitchen counter?

"Typical, ADD me . . ." she muttered with a groan. She could have sworn she'd had her keys when she'd left. But then again, she often misplaced her keys, phone, or wallet.

She just bet that Jeff had a key to the cabin. When she saw his car drive up to his place, she started to walk his way but then stopped herself. No, she was *not* going to let him rescue her again. Surely there had to be a way to get inside without his help. "I can figure this out."

Cat started walking around the porch but then heard some scurrying in the bushes and she nearly yelped. Still, she squared her shoulders, determined, and then snapped her fingers. She'd left the bathroom window open a crack to let out the steam from her shower. The window was up pretty high, but if she could find something to stand on she just might be able to break in.

"Aha!" she said and scooted the sturdy bentwood table over from the front porch until it was beneath the window. She gingerly stepped up on top of the table and, careful to keep her balance, went to work. To her delight, she made quick work of removing the screen and then carefully tilted it up against the wall. Then she eased the window up as far as she could, but would have to hoist herself up by her arms and then tilt her body forward.

"Yes!" She felt the thrill of success, even though it was

a bit scary. When her feet pushed off the table, she managed to knock it over. But she was in!

But it was when she was halfway inside that Cat realized she hadn't really thought this whole thing through. She was headfirst, but the window wasn't wide enough for her to swing her leg up and over the windowsill. The whole headfirst thing was a huge mistake and she decided it was time to abort the mission, when she remembered the table was turned over, leaving her several feet off the ground. Was it far enough down to break a bone? No . . . most likely not. And she could ease her body out and dangle there, letting herself down slowly.

Right?

Cat swallowed hard and felt her palms start to sweat.

"Here goes nothing," she muttered. But when she started to ease herself backward, the movement somehow made the window slide down and land across the small of her back. Her heart thudded.

She was stuck.

12

With a Little Help from My Friends

JEFF STARED DOWN AT HIS CELL PHONE WONDERING how long it was going to take Cat to call him for help. When Mia had brought him Cat's door keys, he was so glad to have a reason to escape Cindy Shafer's clutches. The woman had chased him in high school because he was the lead singer of South Street Riot, and now that he was a success, she wanted him even more. During the years in between, when he'd worked on his parents' farm, she'd acted as if he no longer existed. Jeff was slightly amused that she didn't realize he could see right through her actions.

A polite hug was one thing, but when Cindy planted a kiss right on his mouth, he wanted to tell her to back off. Although when he looked across the room and saw the look on Cat's face, he wanted to thank Cindy—because if he wasn't mistaken, Cat was jealous. Then again, he could simply be a victim of wishful thinking.

When Mia had brought the keys over to him, Jeff wasn't

quite sure whether Cat had left them on the table by accident or Mia had lifted them from Cat's purse. Mia had a
little gleam in her eye that said she just might be up to bit
of matchmaking. Not that Jeff cared. The whole getting a
kiss each time he rescued Cat was a spur-of-the-moment
comment but pure genius. While Jeff was usually a thinker,
a planner, when he was around Cat he found himself becoming spontaneous, and damn if it wasn't fun. She brought
out a playful side of him he didn't know even existed.

Jeff couldn't stop thinking about her. He glanced at
his phone and then up at her cabin, wondering what to
do. Maybe she'd left the door unlocked and was already
in the cabin? But still, he had to deliver the keys to her,
right? With that thought in mind he jogged up the road
and hurried up to her front door. He frowned when he
spotted her suitcase of a purse and then with a grin realized that she must be trying to somehow break into the
cabin. He walked over to the side of the porch and spotted her. Well, half of her. "Need some help?"

"No!" was her muffled reply. "As you can see I have
the situation under—*ouch*—control."

"Let go and I'll catch you." He angled his head and
admired her very nice ass. She had somehow lost one
pink cowboy boot and he grinned when he spotted it
near the overturned table.

"Sure you will."

"I can unlock the door and help you in from the bathroom." He jangled her keys.

"No, I don't need your help."

"Sorry about your luck. You might not want my help,
but you do need it." He jangled the keys again.

"Wait." She sucked in a breath. "How did you get my
keys?" She lifted her head, and when she whimpered as
if in pain, Jeff decided he'd had enough of this nonsense.

"Cat, I'm going to grab hold of your legs and then you
can push up on the window. I'll hold up your weight so
you can use your arms."

"If you grunt I'm going to kick you."

"Use the foot without the boot, please." Jeff laughed and then wrapped his arms around her thighs.

"Stop laughing and don't look at my butt."

"You're pretty bossy for someone needing help. And your ass is resting next to my face. Sorry."

She mumbled something and then pushed up on the window.

"I've got you," he said in a more gentle tone. He remembered that she bruised easily and wondered how long she'd been dangling there, and suddenly the situation wasn't quite so funny. When she clung to the windowsill he said, "Now don't get pissed, but I'm going to reach around your waist and set you down."

"Why would I get pissed?"

"You're always pissed at me." He held her tightly and backed up before taking his time letting her feet touch the ground. "You okay?" he asked.

"Yes," she said, but when there was a slight hitch in her voice Jeff turned her around and hugged her. To his surprise she clung to him. "I think. I was actually starting to get a little bit scared."

"Are you hurt?"

She rested her head on his shoulder. "Just bruised, I think."

"Cat, why didn't you call me?"

"I didn't want to have to pay up."

Jeff felt a stab of disappointment. "I won't ask, then." He pulled back and tucked a lock of her hair out of her eyes. "If I kiss you, will you kick me in the shin?"

"No."

"Punch me in the face?"

"No."

"What will you do?"

"Kiss you back."

That was all Jeff needed to hear. He lowered his head and kissed her gently, coaxing her lips apart. Her soft sigh of surrender had him threading his fingers through her hair. He tilted his head and deepened the kiss, loving the sweet taste of her lips and the soft silky heat of her mouth. When she wrapped her arms around his neck, Jeff hugged her closer, needing to feel her body pressed against his. When she tugged on his shirt, Jeff understood. He wanted to feel her warm skin and explore her body. The woman he'd been thinking about constantly was now in his arms, and it felt so damned good. Jeff pulled his mouth away from her lips and nuzzled her neck.

She sighed softly, and the sexy breathless sound had him wanting her even more. "Cat . . ." he said, and she understood.

"Come inside with me," she offered, and it was all the invitation Jeff needed. He stooped and picked up the keys while she scooped up her purse. Moments later they were inside the cabin. The keys landed with a clank onto the counter and Cat dropped her purse with a thud. Jeff pulled her back into his arms and all the reasons he'd told himself to stay away vanished like fog lifting from a lake. He kissed her, not softly this time but with a hungry passion that had his heart thudding. When he tugged at her shirt she tugged at his and a moment later he was touching skin . . . warm, soft skin.

And he wanted even more.

"Cat?" Jeff wasn't bad boy enough not to give her an out, but she answered by running her hands up his back and pressing her body closer. When she lightly raked her fingernails down his shoulder blades, Jeff moaned. In one quick movement he scooped her up into his arms.

"What are you doing? You're going to break something, like your back. We'll have to wheel you onto the stage and—"

He smothered her protest with a hot, hungry kiss and carried her easily.

"I'm impressed."

He grinned when he shouldered the bedroom door open. "You ain't seen nothin' yet."

"Oh, confident, are you?"

"No." He gazed down at her. "This isn't something I take lightly." He put her gently down onto the big brass bed and then traced a fingertip down her cheek and over her bottom lip.

"Me neither."

He sat down. "This will complicate things."

"Like they aren't already complicated? You have really bad timing when it comes to second thoughts."

"I'm an overthinker." He sighed. "I should have kept my damned mouth shut. Can we go back to a couple of minutes ago?"

"You've got to be kidding me." Cat sighed and turned over to her back. For a moment she remained silent. "What game are you playing here, Jeff?" She sounded hurt and it clawed at his gut.

"I don't play games." He lay down next to her and stared up at the paddle fan.

"For the record, you kissed me this time."

"Guilty."

"So, now what?"

"I guess I go." Jeff held his breath, hoping she'd ask him to stay. If she reasoned with him or told him that they could make this work without interfering with their music, then he would be willing to chance it.

"Oh." She sounded sad and confused and Jeff wondered whether he was making a colossal mistake.

Jeff cleared his throat. "So, then, what are you going to do with the rest of your evening?"

"Write a song."

"About me?" he tried to joke.

"Ha." She turned to give him a look. "You wish."

"Cat," Jeff said on a more serious note. "If we don't want this to happen again, we have to make an effort not to . . ."

"Lock lips?" she asked lightly, but her eyes told a different story.

"Yeah."

"Don't worry about it," she said, just a little bit sharply. "I'll make an effort not to get into precarious situations. But I'll be honest—don't expect miracles. Just come up with some other payment like cupcakes or cookies or something instead of a kiss."

Jeff came up and turned to his side but she failed to look at him. He leaned on one elbow and wanted to trace a fingertip down her cheek again, but he didn't chance it. "Well, then let's take a pledge."

"A pledge? Jeff, I don't do things like get lost or stuck in windows on purpose. See, I have ADD and tend to lose things, which, in turn, gets me into, well, said situations. I also do things spontaneously but with immediate regret. Like this . . ."

Jeff chuckled. "No, not that kind of pledge."

"Well, I did take a pledge of some sort when I was briefly a Girl Scout Brownie, but I was politely asked to leave when I failed to follow instructions and do things like sit still."

Jeff laughed. He could imagine her attempting to behave.

She nibbled on the inside of her lip. "Well, I took the pledge not to text and drive and I am proud to say that I do adhere to that one."

Jeff hated what he was about to say. He liked Cat so damned much and, in truth, was probably already falling for her. He wanted so badly to throw caution to the damned wind but he was so afraid it would end in disaster. He saw the vulnerability in her eyes, and the very last thing he ever wanted to do was hurt her. And so he took a deep breath and let it fly. "Let's take a pledge to just be friends, Cat."

A few seconds ticked by when she failed to respond. The only sound in the room was the soft *whoosh* of the paddle fan. Jeff saw her chest rise and fall and wondered what she was going to say.

"Not on your life." She said it softly but with an edge that held a bit of surprise.

"What?"

"You heard me," she said firmly. "I'm so tired of people jacking me around."

"I didn't do that," Jeff protested, and wondered whether he should scramble from the bed and run like hell.

"You—and I mean *you*—kissed me in the woods. You flirted with me at Sully's and acted pissed that I was dancing with Devin." She finally rolled over to face him. "You came up with the whole kissing-as-payment thing." She pointed a finger at his face. "And now you want to take it all back and want to be *friends*?" She said the word as if he'd just asked her to be a devil worshiper and gave him such a hard shove to his chest that he fell over onto his back. Then she stood up. "Go! Just . . . go!" She turned the finger pointing at his face toward the door. "And take your 'this will complicate things' and your stupid pledge with you."

"Cat—"

"I mean it."

When she looked around as if searching for a weapon, Jeff decided he'd better take her warning seriously. He scooted from the bed and was pelted with pillows as he walked toward the doorway. When he braved turning around a stuffed teddy bear hit him in the head. He opened his mouth to explain that he was only trying to do the right thing for them both, but she gave him a little squeal and looked around for something else to throw. Deciding that the weapons might get more lethal, he backed up.

"And the show tomorrow is off! So is the whole duet thing. So you can tell your band they can rest easy."

Jeff stopped in his tracks. "See!" He pointed his finger

right back at her, even though finger pointing was a pet peeve of his. "I knew that getting involved would create this kind of thing. That's why it wouldn't work."

"Don't you point that finger at me unless it's loaded."

"You are pointing at me."

She looked down at her finger and lowered it. "I detest finger pointing." Her chest was rising and falling and she suddenly looked close to tears.

"Cat," he said more gently, but when he took a step closer she picked up a shoe and hurled it at him. When it hit the wall with a loud smack, Jeff raised his hands over his head. "Okay, I'm leaving."

"Good, and I don't care if I am hanging from the top of Mount Everest or dangling from the tip of the moon. I won't even ask you to kill a spider and I have a severe case of arachnophobia."

"You have several phobias, don't you?"

She lifted one shoulder. "A few. But I don't care. I will not call you for help. Ever."

"Don't say that."

"I just did."

"Okay, then." Jeff nodded stiffly, but as he walked out the door he felt a hot surge of sadness wash over him. He wanted to start the night over. He wanted to have her back in his arms and to hell with reason. She was right. He'd led her on and then backed away.

What an ass. Jeff looked up at the sky. He tried so hard not to be an ass and he'd just failed miserably. She had every right to be angry, but, just as he'd thought, if he kept her pissed it would be easier to keep his distance. Because when she smiled at him, he was lost. And if she did call for help, he'd be there in a heartbeat.

When he entered his cabin all he could do was pace and curse. When his phone vibrated inside his pocket, his heart kicked into high gear. But when he looked at the screen, he saw it was Snake.

"What's up?" Jeff asked, knowing he sounded angry.

"Dude, I guess I should be asking you that question. What are you so damned pissed about?"

Jeff sighed. He explained the rescue. "And then I kissed her. It got kinda . . . you know, out of control, and when I was the voice of reason and said we should just be, you know, friends, she went bat-shit crazy on me and started throwing things at me. Seriously. Like a boot and shit."

"You have got to be kidding me."

"No, she really did wing a boot directly at my head." He pointed at his head and remembered he was on the phone.

"No, I meant you really did ask her to just be *friends*? Jeff, once you're in the friend zone there's no turning back. You're stuck there forever."

"Um, I think I'm in the she-hates-me zone. Cat called off tomorrow's show. See, that's why getting tangled up with her is so damned wrong." Jeff looked up at the ceiling. "I might be an ass but I'm right. It messes with business."

"I'd rather be happy than right."

"That doesn't really make much sense but could be the title to a song. I like it." Jeff blew out a sigh. "I didn't want to do the damned duet anyway. This is a blessing in disguise."

"Personally, I don't like my blessings to be in disguise. And when people say that shit, what it really means is that it's a screwed-up situation and you're just gonna have to make the best of it. That's what you've got goin' on here, my friend."

Jeff closed his eyes and sighed. "You wanna jam over at Big Red?"

"It's almost eleven."

"I don't give a damn what time it is. Give the guys a call. I'm heading over there."

"Okay."

"Snake, did I just screw up?"

"Your career or your life?"

"Aren't they one and the same?" Jeff had wanted success for so long that nothing else seemed to matter. But right now all he was thinking about was the look of anguish on Cat's face.

After a moment of silence Snake said, "I would say yeah, but I don't think you're talking about the music. Jeff, man, I've known you for a long-ass time and I've never seen you so tied in knots because of a girl. She means a lot to you whether you like it or not. When you admit it, things will suddenly become clearer. Anyway, I'll make some calls and bring a twelve-pack. See you in a few."

After Jeff hung up he walked over to the window and looked up at Cat's cabin. He knew that Snake was right. But he owed it to South Street Riot to go ahead with the plans they'd made. His involvement with Cat was already creating havoc with his life and his career. His happiness wasn't the only thing at stake. Being nothing more than friends was the smart thing to do—the *right* thing to do. Jeff swallowed hard and shook his head.

Then why didn't it feel that way?

13

You've Got to Hide Your Love Away

"CAT, YOU'RE EARLY. THIS NEVER HAPPENS," MARIA SAID, but then frowned when she saw the look on Cat's face. "Something wrong, sweetie?"

"I can't do the duet."

Maria put her reading glasses down and came around to lean against her desk. She folded her arms across her chest. "You can't be serious. Rick and I are really excited about releasing 'Second Chances' as a duet single. It's not professional to back out of this, Cat, and you know it."

"I'm sorry, Maria. I . . . I just can't work with Jeff. We're like oil and vinegar."

"I happen to like oil and vinegar. And when mixed together it is actually delicious."

Cat rolled her eyes. "Okay, we fight like cats and dogs."

"The fact that you can only come up with tired clichés tells me that"—she grinned—"you're grasping at straws."

"Maria, he gave me the whole 'Let's be friends' speech."

"Ouch." Maria pressed her lips together in sympathy. During songwriting sessions, she and Cat talked about everything under the sun, and she was beginning to care for Cat like a daughter.

"Exactly."

"And this bothers you because you want more than just friendship with Jeff. Am I right?"

"Yes." Cat closed her eyes and nodded. "I'm not even going to try to hide it from you because you've got my number. You and Mia see right through me, so I might as well own up to it."

"Did you tell Jeff this tiny bit of information?"

Cat raised her hands skyward. "Of course not! I've spent a great deal of my life humiliating myself. I'm not adding this to the list. Wait. I already did. Damn!"

"Maybe he needs to know how you feel."

Cat crossed her arms over her chest. "I will suffer in silence."

Maria tapped her cheek. "Oh . . . good song title."

"Why are all of the amazing songs written when you feel like crap?"

Maria looked up at the ceiling and laughed but felt a stab of pain. "I am the poster child for that."

"Seriously, you've suffered for all the years you were separated from Pete? That's where all those amazing heartbreaking songs came from." Cat shook her head. "I should have known."

"Yes." Maria tapped her chest. "From here. I missed him each and every day."

"Why didn't one of you just give in?"

Maria shrugged. "I was waiting for him to come to Nashville and drag me back home where I belonged. But he didn't. It wasn't until a health scare last Christmas that I knew I needed to make the move back to Cricket Creek."

"And so will you get back together?"

Maria shrugged.

"I don't get it."

"I think I've forgotten how to be happy." She snapped her fingers. "Oh . . . lyrics." She tried to smile but failed. After a moment Maria sighed. "I guess the reason I'm telling you this is that if you allow too much time to pass, it gets more and more difficult to repair the damage." She shook her head. "I'm in my fifties now. Sand is slipping through the hourglass."

"So Pete is the love of your life."

"No doubt."

Cat sank down onto the smooth leather sofa and looked at her. "But . . . you're not even trying."

Maria felt startled at Cat's statement and her heart thudded. "Dear God," she whispered and then inhaled a deep breath. "You're right."

"Why?"

Maria looked toward the window and then down at her feet—anywhere but at Cat.

"Maria?"

"I guess I'm scared. I'm just so used to clinging to the pain."

"Well, that's just silly. I mean, cling to hope instead."

"It's not that simple," Maria felt compelled to argue.

"I think it is."

"You're not even thirty yet. How did you get so wise?"

"I'm an old soul."

A laugh erupted in Maria's throat. "Well, old soul, then let's take a pledge, you and I."

Cat groaned. "Not another pledge! Why doesn't anyone understand that I just suck at pledges? Okay, hit me with it."

"Let's drive Pete and Jeff crazy. Make them come after us."

"Ah-ha." Cat nodded slowly. "I really like this plan of action. Go on."

Maria started warming up to the spontaneous notion. She licked her bottom lip and then said, "Oh, make it subtle, Cat. A touch, a sultry look will get the ball rolling. Men are such simple creatures. Show a little leg, a bit of cleavage and they are goners. They just need a bit of help now and then."

"I've got the getting-rescued thing down pat."

Maria chuckled. "Use it. Oh, and play the jealously card, but sparingly."

Cat grinned. "This feels a little bit wicked."

Maria laughed hard. "Doesn't it, though?"

"And takes the whole humiliation factor out of the picture too. Wow, I love this."

"Cat, trust me. Jeff doesn't want to be your *friend*." Maria rolled her eyes. "Come on now."

"You really think so?"

"Absolutely."

"Well, since we're talking about it." Cat scooted to the edge of the cushion. "Pete adores you, Maria. I've seen it in the way he looks at you with a complete puppy dog stare." Cat demonstrated and Maria laughed.

"Like I said, all the man ever had to do was come after me."

"Did you ever consider he might have been scared of getting turned away and never mustered up the courage, so he clung to the pain as well. Makes me think of the two of you hanging on to a piece of driftwood out in the middle of the ocean, when all you had to do was hop into the lifeboat."

Maria chuckled. "Other normal people would think of that analogy as a bit out there, but we're songwriters and that's how our minds operate."

"I wouldn't know how to be normal if it slapped me across the side of the head."

Maria angled her head at Cat. "Would you want to be?"

"No," Cat whispered with a sense of wonder. She blinked at Maria for a moment. "No," she said with more conviction, and then laughed. "Wow, this is liberating. I always longed to be more like, well, conventional . . . to simply fit in."

"Cat, the only thing you need to fit in to is your own skin."

With a whoop Cat jumped up from the couch and held her palm up in the air. "High five."

Maria smacked Cat's hand. "Are we gonna do this thing?"

"Yes!"

"It has to be subtle so they don't catch on."

"Oh . . . I'm not so good at subtle."

Maria laughed again. "You know Rick said that along with taking on the role as your manager, I need to be a mentor. But you are teaching me some things, Cat."

"I hope that's a good thing."

"It is."

"Now what do we do?"

"First we write a song about this whole situation. Then we put our plan into action. You need to make Jeff think you're buying into the whole friends notion. Then you maybe—oh, I don't know—brush up against him by accident." Maria demonstrated and they both dissolved into a fit of laughter.

"I'm likely to knock him over and fail."

"Well, then, a little lick across your bottom lip. Twirl your hair around your finger. Little feminine things that appear natural, but just watch for the reaction you are going to get."

"How do I not laugh?"

"Ah, for you that's going to be hard, but you can do it if you set your mind to it, Cat." Maria rubbed her hands together. "This is going to be such fun."

"Think it will work?"

"Oh, yeah. And the beauty of it all is that they'll never see it coming. Now let's get to work." Maria felt as if she had been looking at the world through dense fog that had just lifted. "From now on we're going to be walking on sunshine."

"And it feels good!" Cat giggled. "My whole life is related to lyrics. I thought I was the only one."

"Oh, no. It's like I have this chip in my brain that scrolls down to a song that's relating to whatever is going on at the time. For me songs are emotion on the page."

"I feel ya," Cat said and smiled. "It's the same way for me too."

"What are you thinking? I see a sparkle in those pretty eyes of yours."

"I'm thinking that I'm so glad that I had the courage to leave Sweetside Records and sign with My Way. It was a tough year but worth it. Cricket Creek is really starting to feel like home."

Maria felt her eyes mist over. "And I'm so glad that I moved back. Let's grab our guitars and head outside and sit by the river. The water always gets my muse going."

"Me too," Cat agreed.

Maria gave Cat a fierce hug and knew that she must miss her mother. "You're a lovely young woman, Cat Carson. And if Jeff Greenfield can't see that, there is something wrong with the boy." She pulled back and said, "You're going to go through with the duet, right? I won't force you and neither will Rick. We don't call this My Way Records for nothing."

Cat nodded. "Yes," she said softly.

"Good, because 'Second Chances' is going to be a smash hit." Maria was rarely wrong about songs and she truly believed that it was going to be another crossover country song that was going to climb up the Top 40 charts too. The only problem was that Jeff might feel he was selling out when that happened. Maria knew that Rick felt the same way she did. Jeff and Cat could become huge if they wanted to combine their efforts and become an official duo. She and Rick had even come up with the name Sweet Harmony. But to achieve superstar status, they would have to give up their solo careers. Cat would probably be willing to do it. But Jeff? Well, he was another story. But for now all Maria wanted to think about was heading out into the warm sunshine and penning a sweet love song.

To hell with heartbreak.

"Let's go write a kick-ass song." Cat gave Maria a fist bump.

"You're on."

"And what will we do with the rest of this glorious day of enlightenment?"

Maria raised her eyebrows. "What any red-blooded woman would do. We're going shopping!"

Cat laughed. "I need to badly. Can we go to Violet's Vintage Clothing? I've heard it's a really cool shop."

"Absolutely. Then we'll go to Designs by Diamante for some unique jewelry. After that we'll have to get a coffee and Danish at Grammar's Bakery. No big malls for us. It's going to be a perfect Cricket Creek day."

"I'm down with that," Cat said.

"Good. Let's do this thing."

14

Day Tripper

JEFF ALL BUT SWALLOWED HIS TONGUE WHEN CAT BENT over to pick up the guitar pick that she'd dropped for the third time in less than fifteen minutes. With every retrieval of the pick, he got a tiny glimpse of the black lace peeking out above her hip, hugging painted-on jeans that flared out at the bottom. Her yellow blouse had flowers embroidered on the puffy sleeves, and she had several colorful bracelets gracing one wrist. Big silver hoop earrings dangled from her earlobes and swung back and forth when she talked. Instead of curls, her long dark hair draped over her shoulder in a simple but somehow oh so sexy braid. Jeff had the impulse to reach over and tug on the braid and then bring the fringy end up to her face and tickle her with it.

And then it hit him.

"You look like . . . a hippie."

"I know. Isn't it cool?" Her sweet laughter reminded Jeff of his mother's wind chimes hanging from the front porch of the farmhouse. The soft, gentle sound always made him smile. "I got these vintage jeans at Violet's.

They're bell-bottoms, and this is called a peasant blouse. I sent a picture to my mother, and she said she wore this very same outfit back in the early seventies." Cat looked down and then tugged it until the material hugged her shoulders, revealing lots of skin. The result was sweet and yet sexy at the same time.

"Are you supposed to do that?" He made a tugging motion with his hands.

"Yeah, but it keeps scooting back up. Violet said it's supposed to be down on my shoulders like this." When she wiggled her shoulders, the material slid back up, making her laugh, but she tugged it back into place.

"Oh."

"Didn't you hear Colin calling out to you a minute ago?"

"Uh . . ." *No, I was too busy staring at your ass and now I want to run my tongue over your collarbone and up your neck.*

"He's waving his hands at you this time." Cat tilted her head in Colin's direction.

"Jeff!" Colin called. "Hey, earth to Jeff! We've got to get this sound check done. Pete is going to open the doors soon."

"I thought you needed to ring the room."

"I did that," Colin called back. "Quit being an asshat and get with the program." He'd agreed to work the sound for them. Even though it was an acoustic set, the sound system still had to be just right.

"You wanna call me that to my face?"

"I just did."

Jeff cupped his hand by his ear. "Oh, sorry. . . . What did you say?"

"Quit being such an asshat and check the cables. Make sure the mic clips are screwed into the stands while you're at it."

"All right!" Jeff grumbled with a good-natured grin. But when he looked at Cat, she was smiling at Colin.

Jeff's grin faded and he felt an unwanted sharp stab of jealousy.

Cat leaned over and said, "Colin Walker is super cute. No wonder they pack Wine and Diner when he sings."

Jeff really didn't like where this was going. Was she going to ask for Colin's number or something? "And here I thought it was his voice."

"Oh, the fact that he can sing is just an added bonus." She snapped her fingers. "Yes! I was trying to think of who Colin looks like and it just occurred to me. Adrian Grenier."

"Who?"

"The actor who plays Vince Chase on *Entourage*."

"I've never watched it so I don't have a clue."

"Oh, well, I'm a huge fan." She flicked Colin another glance, making Jeff wonder who she was referring to: the actor or Colin? He decided he didn't want to know. Cat leaned a little closer. "Are you nervous or something?"

Or something. Jeff wanted to answer, but he was distracted by the sight of her cleavage peeking out over her . . . what was it? Oh, yeah, a peasant blouse. A delicate gold chain with a small heart nestled where he wanted to put his face. "Uh . . . what did you say?"

"Did you suddenly lose your hearing?" She gave him a perplexed look and then licked her bottom lip slowly back and forth. "Or is something wrong?"

Wow, she smelled so good. "I'm just distracted."

"By what?"

By every move you make. "Everything."

"Oh, well, I can sympathize. Welcome to my world."

"What? Oh . . . ." He looked at her because he understood. "That must be tough," Jeff said and meant it. "My sister, Sara, would get into trouble for things like leaving lights on and the garage door open. She was famous for leaving the tub of ice cream out, letting it melt. Since we only got ice cream as a treat every so often, we would all get really pissed at her."

"She didn't mean to do that. Once my attention is on something other than what I'm doing it's almost impossible to return my focus back to the task at hand. It's completely frustrating, but that's how my brain is wired. Losing things is an everyday occurrence."

"We know that now. We didn't then. After Sara did it once too often, Mom wouldn't let her have any the next time we got a gallon of chocolate chip."

"Oh . . . poor thing. That was pretty harsh."

"She'd been warned at least a dozen times, but Mom had had enough."

Cat lifted her chin. "I would have snuck her some."

"I did," he said with a smile.

Cat put her hand on his arm. "You're so sweet."

"Not really. She had to do my chores the next morning," Jeff admitted but then his smile faltered. "Had my mother known what was going on, she would have reacted way differently. My parents thought Sara was slacking off in her schoolwork and didn't care. We didn't realize that Sara would get sidetracked and forget or that taking a written exam was so difficult for her. Once Mom figured it out she did lots of things to help Sara get organized. Today, if you go into Sara's house or car, there's still mass chaos but also sticky notes everywhere to remind her of things she has to do. She has a pegged thing on the wall for keys and now always has a spare of just about everything she's bound to lose. So I get it, and I sympathize."

Cat shrugged. "Well, having ADD makes life an adventure, that's for sure," she said lightly. She also smiled, but there was a bit of a haunted quality in her eyes that told Jeff that she was glossing over something that had to be difficult to deal with on a daily basis.

"You're frowning again. I asked if you were nervous. Do you want to do another run-through?" She reached over and put her hand on his thigh for just a second and then tilted her head, making her hoop earrings dangle sideways. Jeff decided that the soft and sexy hippie style looked good on her but then again anything did as far as he was concerned. "I'm more than willing." She gave his thigh another little squeeze, but just when he thought she might be coming on to him, she pulled her hand away and adjusted the bangle bracelets. He must be imagining things again.

"No, I'm fine. I've played Sully's a million times," Jeff answered in a rather grumpy tone.

"Someone woke up on the wrong side of the bed."

In an empty bed, Jeff thought, and when he realized he was scowling again, he softened his features. "Seriously, I'm *fine* and dandy. Okay, pretend I didn't say the dandy part. My dad says that a lot."

"My dad is fond of saying okeydokey." She gave his shoulder a gentle shove and then ran her hand lightly down his arm. "I think it's cute."

Jeff nodded. "You do?"

"Yes." She sucked her bottom lip between her teeth and nodded. When the full bottom lip popped back out, it remained wet and shiny. "Listen, if you're still worried about the—you know—pledge, I'm totally down with it. That whole thing about backing out of the duet was just . . . low blood sugar or something. I get like that Snickers commercial when I get hungry and I morph into someone else. No worries." She smiled, revealing perfect white teeth. "Okay?" She reached over and gave his thigh a tiny squeeze.

Jeff wanted to shout that it wasn't okay and the friends-only thing was complete stupidity but now that she'd agreed he didn't know what the hell to do. A little growl of exasperation escaped him and he had to try to disguise it with a cough.

"Jeff, you might not be nervous, but you just seem a little . . . out of sorts, I guess."

"I didn't sleep well last night," Jeff admitted and then wanted to kick himself in the ass. Why had he said that

to her? "I had you on—I mean, a lot on my mind."
God . . .

"Thinking about the performance tonight, then?"

Thinking about you. "Yeah, I guess." If Cat reached over
and touched his thigh again, he might grab her and plant a
kiss right on that shiny mouth of hers. "I'm not really nervous, though," he insisted, not wanting her to think he got
stage fright. "This isn't my first rodeo." Jeff wanted to smack
his hand against his face for saying something so lame.

Cat pressed her lips together for a second. "I am."

"What?"

"A bit nervous."

"You get stage fright?"

Cat lifted one shoulder and seemed as if she wished
she hadn't revealed this bit of information to him.

"Cat?" he gently prompted.

She swallowed and then said, "It will pretty much be
okay here tonight at this smaller venue. It's . . . well, it's
mostly that I'm afraid of the dark and I get all jittery
when the lights dim, but I'm okay when the lights come
up." She nibbled on the inside of her lip and then gave
him a little shake of her head. "Silly, huh?"

"No, it's not silly." The thought of her standing there
afraid and trembling bothered him. He suddenly wanted
to reach over and take her hand, bring it to his mouth,
and kiss it, but that was going to break the friends only
pledge that he'd been stupid enough to initiate, so he
gave her a reassuring smile instead. She glanced away as
if she regretted revealing her weakness. Jeff understood.
Sara had been the same way, using humor and wise-
cracks to hide her insecurity. But Sara had an entire family to rally around her. Although the farmhouse could
often be chaos, Jeff couldn't imagine being an only child.
It must have been lonely for Cat sometimes.

"Colin is gesturing for you to go over to him," Cat
said and then stood up. "I have to go and freshen up
before the doors open. He's looking pretty frantic."

"He's such a diva. Okay, I'd better get over there."

"I'll be back in a few minutes. Save my seat."

Jeff chuckled and then watched her walk away, forgetting all about Colin until he felt a hand clamp down on his shoulder.

"I finally decided I might as well come over here and check the mics myself." Colin shook his head and then gave Jeff's shoulder a shove before letting go. "So does she know how you feel?"

"Who?"

"Come on." Colin nodded toward the bathroom. "Cat."

"We took a pledge to remain friends."

"Are you outta your ever loving mind? A *pledge*? Did you raise your hand and shit? Who does that?"

"It's a figure of speech."

"If you say so."

"Cat's cool with it."

"Wait. So you're the one who came up with *being friends*?" Colin pointed an accusing finger at Jeff.

"Yeah," Jeff answered glumly. "It seemed like a good idea at the time." Now it sucked and he regretted it.

"How? I mean, look at her, for one thing. So she must have been interested for you to come up with this insanity."

"Colin, we have to work together. Cat and I need to keep our personal lives separate."

Colin placed his palms on the stool and leaned forward. "You don't have to make out onstage, you know."

"Yeah, but there's more to it than that. I know how the band feels about me doing this with Cat to begin with. Y'all come first. I don't want how I feel about her to influence my decisions along the way."

"Wait. How you feel about her? So . . . how do you feel?"

"It was a general question. Hypothetical." He shoved his fingers through his hair.

"Right, and you are hypothetically full of shit."

"Really? Well, she just told me how super cute you were and that you look like some actor or something," he mimicked in a high-pitched voice.

"Adrian Grenier?"

"Yeah, I think," he said, still in high-pitch mode.

"Are you gonna sing like that? Who are you, Barry Gibb?"

Jeff responded with a shove to Colin's shoulder. "I was imitating Cat."

"She doesn't sound like a Bee Gee."

Jeff laughed. "Great. Now I have 'Nights on Broadway' playing in my head. But she did say you looked like that actor dude."

"I get that I look like the *Entourage* guy once in a while. It's the hair." Colin pointed to his head and chuckled. "I always hated these damned curls. And I get a five o'clock shadow at, like, noon."

"Apparently chicks dig it." One chick in particular.

"Do you *not* know what's going on here?" Colin pushed up from the stool and crossed his arms over his chest. "Seriously, dude."

"When you say it that way, I guess not. So are you going to clue me in?"

"Jeff, Cat is baiting you and you're swallowing it hook, line, and sinker."

"I'm not following."

"She's playing an oh so subtle jealousy card. Cat isn't interested in me, bro. She's into *you* in case you haven't noticed. I don't think she's buying into the whole 'just friendship' thing."

"Now just how in the hell do you know this? She even told me she was cool with it."

"I watch. Listen. Jeff, I play happy hour five nights a week at Wine and Diner. I can spot interest a mile away."

"Really?"

Colin nodded. "I've heard every pickup line on the

planet. Tipsy women are hilarious when they talk about men. They don't hold anything back. And it's hilarious to see a pickup line epic fail. 'I wanna live in your socks, so I can be with you every step of the way,'" Colin said in a fake deep voice. "'I seem to have lost my phone number; can I have yours?' Oh, and here is a favorite: 'Your body is sixty-five percent water and, baby, I'm so thirsty.'"

"And those work?"

"Never—well, unless the level of intoxication is pretty high and the beer goggles are on, making for a pretty intense Coyote Ugly in the morning. Jeff, I've seen drinks tossed in faces and an occasional slap. But I can spot a look, a stare of baby-I-want-you in an instant. Cat has never even tried to make eye contact with me. And, Jeff, she was all over you."

"What?" Jeff said, wishing he'd quit saying that. "I mean, she barely touched me."

"She sure as hell did." Colin chuckled. "I started to know when it was going to happen. She would kind of hesitate just before she dropped the pick or touched your arm like she was nervous. It was pretty cute, actually. I was getting such a charge out of watching your reaction."

"I don't think you're quite as smart as you think you are."

Colin shrugged. "Believe what you want, but years of cocktail lounges and playing bars has me pretty damned astute when it comes to this shit. I could write a book." He rubbed the dark stubble shadowing his chin. "Maybe I will."

Jeff looked at Colin to try to figure out whether he was joking or not. "Are you kidding?"

"No, I truly think I have enough material to write a book. Each chapter would start with a cheesy pickup line."

"I mean about Cat. Do you really think she was trying to get to me?"

"Hell yeah."

"Then what do I do?" Jeff glanced at the hallway, thinking she'd be back soon.

"What do you want to do? Be honest. Do you really want to be her so-called friend?"

"Well . . . no. It's just that—"

"Shut the hell up with all those lame-ass excuses. Look, for the record, Snake and I aren't as opposed to the possibility of working with Cat as Jax and Sam."

"So you've talked about it?" Jeff shoved his hands into his jeans pockets and tried not to feel as if they were talking about him behind his back. When Colin hesitated, Jeff shook his head. "Meaning, you argued about it. Am I right?"

"Kinda." Colin inhaled a deep breath. "Look, other than you, I'm the only one who stayed as connected to music. I might not have gone to Nashville, but I'm making a living singing and I know that even in a small market it's competitive. I'm not opposed to trying new things and not stubbornly digging my heels in about song choices. I won't ever suggest that we do something just to get a hit record, but I'm not opposed to doing something that doesn't sound like classic country. As far as I'm concerned it's okay to mix it up a bit. Look, if this song is a hit, and Rick and Maria think that marketing you and Cat as a duo is the smart thing to do, then why the hell not? We would still be your band and still be South Street Riot. I don't get what the big deal is, Jeff. I really don't."

"But the rest of the guys do think it's a big deal. I can't break up the band because of something I decide to do. This is a group effort. We are a team and decide things together. Don't you see? It's already an issue. We're already divided and it will only get worse."

"Jeff, she's not like Yoko Ono. I think it could be fun to have her around and see how she fits in."

Jeff shook his head. "No. No way. I agreed to do this song and that's it. Period."

Colin looked ready to argue but then shrugged. "I think at this point just see where this song goes. But don't be so closed-minded."

"Colin, our dream is to open for a big name, specifically Shane McCray. That's the path we are on. We have a manager now and Christy told me just this morning that she's getting some interest from Shane's people. Colin, the man is my idol. For us to open for him would be a dream come true. And he is totally old school. He likes our classic sound. Christy said so and that's one of the reasons we're high on the list to open for him. This duet is something that's crossover. I just don't want to get stuck there permanently or screw this up. It's our dream on the line here."

"Shane McCray is an icon. But he's going to retire after this tour."

"Even more reason to open for him *now*. But we need another hit record to be fully considered." Jeff tapped his chest. "Us . . . not a duet with Cat Carson." He sighed. "I'm just afraid that we are going to go in a direction we don't want and then lose ourselves in the process. It's the very last thing I want to do."

"Just chill, Jeff. First of all, this is just one song. Plenty of artists are doing this nowadays. Big stars. Have some fun with this and don't worry about the future, okay? I swear, sometimes you take overthinking to a whole new level."

"I guess."

"But I have to throw this one last thing out there."

"Am I gonna want to hear this?" Jeff gave Colin a level look. "Lay it on me."

Colin laughed while he checked the chords a final time. "Like I said, Cat was using everything she could pull out of her arsenal to get your attention. And it worked. That last time she bent over, you about slid off your stool."

Jeff stood up and stretched his arms over his head. "No, you don't get it. She drops things and does stuff like that all the time. I think you're wrong."

"Bullshit. She was trying to turn you inside out and it worked like a charm."

"Your point?"

"My point is that both of you want the same thing but the other one doesn't know it. It's pretty comical actually but also damned stupid on both your parts."

"I think the radar that you believe you possess is way the hell off."

Colin shook his head. "Granted, I gotta admit that I'm wrong about a lot of things, but this isn't one of 'em."

Jeff adjusted the mic and then looked at Colin. "For the sake of argument, let's assume you're right. What do you suggest I do about the situation?"

"It's pretty simple," Colin advised with a grin. "Give it right back and then some."

Before Jeff could ask Colin exactly what he was supposed to do, Pete Sully came walking his way and handed him a couple of bottles of water. "Thanks, Pete." Jeff unscrewed one bottle and took a healthy swig.

"If you want anything else or something stronger, just let me know and I'll get it." He slapped Jeff on the back. "You ready for this?"

"What do you mean?" Jeff asked.

"There's a huge crowd waiting to get in and this was by word of mouth. Lucky for me I just hired a new kick-ass bartender and another shot girl. I'm gonna have to turn a lot of people away. I probably should have moved this outside to the big stage, but Maria wanted it to be a more intimate setting where she could gauge the reaction of listeners."

"I'll set up speakers so people can at least hear you

outside," Colin offered. "And it would be pretty easy to get the performance up on the big-screen television."

"Great idea," Pete said and smiled when Maria and Cat headed up to the stage.

"The parking lot is packed," Maria said. "Luckily, Rick and Maggie have already arrived."

"I'll make sure your family gets in and gets a seat, Jeff. I've got a table reserved for them," Pete promised.

"Thanks. This is a big night for them. My mom would have a meltdown if she couldn't get in."

"No worries. I'm gonna open the doors in a couple of minutes. Y'all ready?"

Jeff looked at Cat and she nodded. "Bring it on!"

15

In My Life

"SORRY. WE'RE AT CAPACITY," PETE CALLED TO THE crowd waiting outside of Sully's. When a huge collective groan erupted, he held up both hands. "We're going to pipe the music out here, so if y'all head over to the lawn near the outdoor stage we'll bring out tubs of beer and we're trying to get the big television screen up and running," he said and was rewarded with a cheer. "Do you think we can get Cat and Jeff to come back by popular demand?" he asked and then cupped his hand to his ear and waited for the wild cheering to begin. He pointed to the outdoor arena. "Next time we'll do it up right and use the stage." When the applause and whistles died down, he gave a wave and then headed back inside.

Pete paused to greet patrons as he weaved his way through the beehive of activity. He saw Clint hurrying back and forth getting tubs of beer on ice to sell outside. Colin had managed to get a camera set up so the giant screen would broadcast the show. Knowing they would have a rambunctious crowd, Pete had all of his employees working, but they were still having a tough time keeping up with the demand.

Pete peeked inside the kitchen to see the cooks working at lightning speed. But in spite of the barely controlled chaos, laughter rose above the clanking of dishes and shouting of orders. Just the week before Pete had to post job openings in the want ads; after the lean years during the recession, it did his heart good to see his bar thriving and people working. But most of all he enjoyed seeing so many friends out there having a good time. Residents of Cricket Creek worked hard and played hard.

"How you doin', Angie?" Pete asked the cute head bartender he'd recently hired. Angie Wiseman could make a lemon drop martini with perfect precision and her Long Islands were even better than he could mix. And she did it all with a confident flourish.

"I've got everything under control, boss man," Angie said with a quick grin. "Jodi and Kristin are working their tails off getting the beer tubs filled."

"The new girls, right?" Pete was trying to let go of having to be everywhere and let his able-bodied employees do their jobs. "Are they gonna work out, you think?"

Angie nodded. "Jodi is a little bit shy but a hard worker. And Kristin has some experience, so she's good to go. I trained them earlier and they are both going to work out fine. But hey, if you can round anybody else up, even for just tonight, I'll put them to work. It's going to get crazy in here, but I'll keep it under control."

"I'll try to round some extras up," he promised Angie.

"Thanks, boss." Angie gave him a wink and went back to work.

"Hey there, baby face," shouted Noah Falcon, founder of the Cricket Cougars baseball team and the pride of Cricket Creek. He clamped a hand on Pete's shoulder. "Sully's is hopping tonight."

"This is how we roll," Pete said with a grin and then

reached up to rub the beard that no longer graced his cheeks.

"I love it!" Noah said. "Hey, if you need help behind the bar, just let me know and I'll jump right in."

"Actually, I'll take you up on that," Pete said. "At least until the show starts. Angie will tell you what needs to be done."

"Hey there, baby face, quit your chatter and get your tail over here," called Mia, who had stepped in to help out as long as she could have a tip jar set up for Heels for Meals, and of course Pete gladly obliged. "Can't you see we're busy?" she asked with a grin. He watched her open beer bottles with agility and then tucked the opener in the back pocket of her jeans like a pro.

"I'm comin'!" Pete hurried behind the bar and started sliding cold longnecks into outstretched hands. "You sure are getting good at this," he told Mia, and she nodded firmly.

"Much better than my days as a server at Wine and Diner," Mia said.

Pete laughed. "You mean your *day* as a server? When Cam had to come to your rescue and ended up getting in a fight, nearly getting him kicked off the baseball team?"

"Details, details," Mia said and laughed. She rang the bell when she received a big tip. "I just love doing that."

"Hopefully you'll be doing that all night long," Noah commented.

"Well, then work some of your charm, Noah. I want that tip jar filled to the brim."

"I'll try," Noah promised with a grin.

Pete shook his head when he spotted Ava, Clint's fiancée, tying on an apron. "Ava, sweetie, you've worked at the toy store all day long. Have a seat and enjoy the show," Pete said, knowing full well that Ava would have none of it. Having grown up on a farm, she was no stranger to long days and hard work.

"I can watch while I help out," Ava insisted with an easy smile. She pulled her long chestnut hair up into a bun. "My bartending skills are somewhat lacking, but I can pitch in and bus tables," she offered.

Knowing it was pointless to argue Pete went over and gave Ava a kiss on the cheek. The fact that she and Clint rekindled their high school romance made his heart sing. "Thank you, sweetie."

"No problem," Ava answered and went to work.

Pete looked over to where Maria was sitting with Rick and Maggie and he felt a stab of longing. Maria laughed at something Maggie said, causing her rich brown hair to fall forward and caress her cheeks.

How in the hell had he ever been stupid enough to let her go?

As if feeling his gaze upon her, Maria turned her head and their eyes met. She smiled and then stood up and walked his way. Pete stood there and watched Maria weave through the crowd until Mia nudged his arm to give a customer the forgotten beer Pete held in his hand. "Oh . . . right."

Mia winked, letting Pete know she was aware of the reason for his distraction.

When Maria got close to the bar, she crooked her finger for him to come over to her. "I'll be right back." He wondered whether Maria knew that was all it took for him to follow her anywhere. Pete pointed to the hallway leading to the offices, where it would be less rowdy and he could hear her talk. A moment later he met her there.

"Everything all right?" Pete asked and wondered what Maria would do if he pushed her up against the exposed brick wall and kissed her. He looked at her lips, glossed with something rosy, and nearly groaned. He wanted to taste her mouth, feel her body crushed to his.

"Yes, everything is okay. I wanted you to know that we're delaying for a few minutes until the crowd gets settled and to also create some additional buzz before Jeff and Cat make their entrance."

"I think you've got that in spades," Pete observed. He looked down and was startled to see that she wore a pair of red cowboy boots like the ones he'd bought her for her birthday many years earlier. "Are those"—he swallowed emotion and had to clear his throat—"the boots I gave you?"

"I have dozens, and these are still my favorite," Maria admitted with a soft smile, but then seemed a little bit rattled and glanced away.

"Your thirtieth and you were having such a hard time of it. I wanted you to know you looked so damned sexy in those ruby red boots." He paused, then said, "You still do."

"Why thank you, Pete," Maria said, and Pete could swear she was blushing. He didn't think that she fully understood how truly gorgeous she was—especially to him. In his eyes no other woman held a candle to her . . . and never would.

After a deep breath she said, "By the way, setting up the speakers and television screen was genius. It gives me the atmosphere I wanted in here but we are reaching a much bigger audience." She reached over and put a hand lightly on his arm. "Perfect."

Maria's touch, however slight, was more than Pete could take. He reached forward and drew her into his arms. Pete steeled himself for rejection, prepared for a shove at his chest, but when she wound her arms around his neck and tilted her face up, Pete was floored at her silent invitation. . . .

And he gladly accepted it.

Lowering his head, Pete pressed his mouth to her soft lips and it was like coming home after a long time away. He coaxed her mouth open and kissed her deeply with all the pent-up longing he'd felt since she'd walked into the bar. Hell, make that since she'd walked back into his life. He drank her in, molded her body to his, and kissed her like there was no tomorrow.

But there was tomorrow and he intended to have this amazing woman back in his life for good, come hell or high water.

Pete finally pulled back and looked down at her. "You don't know how long I've wanted to do that, Maria."

"About as long as I've wanted you to do it, I imagine."

Pete's heart pounded. The noise in the bar seemed to fade away because he could focus only on the only woman in the world he'd ever loved. He gently tucked a lock of her hair behind her ear, pausing to rub the silky strands between his fingers. "Come back into my life."

She closed her eyes and pressed her lips together.

"I love you, Maria. I've never stopped loving you." He cupped her chin and tilted her face up so he could look into her eyes. "Or missing you. I was a fool to let you go. I should have followed—"

Maria reached up and put a fingertip to his lips. "We can't go back, Pete." She tilted her head toward the bar. "It's hopping out there. Just listen to the laughter and soon the air will be filled with sweet music. Sully's Tavern is part of this town. It's been the place where people come to forget about their problems, the stress of everyday life. Had you shut this bar down and moved with me to Nashville, Cricket Creek residents would have missed this place."

Pete shrugged. "Someone would have bought it."

"It wouldn't have been the same," she insisted with a shake of her head. "You make people feel welcome. Anyone else owning this place . . . well, it would just somehow be . . . wrong. I know that now. I guess I knew it then, but I didn't want to admit it."

"It's just a bar."

"No, Pete, it's much more than that." She put her palms on his chest and rubbed back and forth. "I didn't need to dig in my heels. We were both so stubborn, wanting our way."

"No, I should have supported your dream. I was dead-ass wrong and totally selfish."

"I won't argue that point," Maria said with a small smile.

"Looking back, I think I was so afraid that your success at songwriting would change us . . . maybe change *you* and that you'd leave me for someone better. Funny that what I feared most happened anyway."

"I never really wanted fame or to get rich." Maria fisted her hands in his shirt. "I only wanted to help. And, Pete, music is in my blood. Part of who I am. I should have made it clear, talked to you instead of getting angry. You simply didn't understand. Ah, we broke each other's hearts, Pete. You weren't the only one at fault. Stubborn, foolish pride tore us apart."

"Can we pick up the pieces?" He ran a fingertip down her cheek and held his breath, waiting for her answer. She hadn't said she loved him still, but he could wait until she was ready.

"No," she replied, and disappointment slammed him in the gut like a sledge hammer. But when he started to pull his hand away, she reached up and held her hand to her cheek. "We need to sweep away the pieces of our broken hearts."

"And then what?" he asked gruffly.

"We begin again."

"I would say that sounds like a line from one of your songs but it smacks of hope rather than despair. Damn, but you wrote some sad-ass songs."

Maria laughed and Pete loved the sound. "You're so right. Cat and I were talking about this earlier. I think it's about high time to write some happy songs."

"Then I need to work on making you happy," Pete said and meant it with every fiber of his being.

Her smile trembled and went straight to his heart. "I like that plan. Let's take this one day at a time. I need to go slow." She swallowed hard. "Because I'm scared,

Pete," she admitted in a voice so soft that Pete could barely hear her above the sound of the crowd.

Pete cupped her chin in his big hand. "Well, if you leave me again, I'll pack up my things and go with you, just so you know."

Maria laughed. "Did you know that's a line from a Toby Keith song?"

"No. But it's a brilliant idea. You can't shake me this time."

"Ah." Maria pressed her lips together. "Now there's a song title. 'You Can't Shake Me This Time'! I need to write that down. These days I think of something amazing and then can't remember for the life of me."

"Don't worry." Pete leaned in and gave her a soft, lingering kiss. "I won't let you forget. Now, we'd better get this show on the road before the buzz turns into feet stomping in protest."

"You're right, baby face."

"I have a feeling I'm going to be called that now forever."

"I think it's cute." Maria smiled up at him and cupped her hands on his smooth-shaven cheeks. "The plan was for me to try to entice you all night long and try to work you into a frenzy."

"You had a plan to get to me?" Pete laughed. "Baby, all you had to do was show up."

Maria closed her eyes for a second and then smiled at him. "For the record, I've never stopped missing you either." She dropped her hands and turned around, leaving Pete standing there for a minute wondering whether this really had just happened.

Did he really have Maria back in his life? If she missed him, she must still love him . . . right? "Yes, she must." Pete stood there with a silly smile on his face. He would give her all the time she needed, but he knew one thing for sure. He would not let Maria Sully out of his life ever again. "Ain't no way, no how."

Just when he'd come to his senses and realized he needed to get back into the bar, Maria came rushing back into the hallway.

"Are you okay?" Pete asked when he saw the look on her face. "What's wrong?"

Maria folded her hands together as if in prayer. "I just had this kind of wild idea. I'm going to need your help."

"Name it."

"You're going to have to get Jeff out there onstage and then I have to get Cat and stop her."

"From going onstage?"

"Yes." Maria nodded vigorously. "I want him to think he's flying solo."

"But he's not?"

Maria nodded. "I'm going to have Cat make her entrance with the cordless mic and make her way through the crowd."

"Why would you do such a thing to Jeff?"

"To let Jeff feel like he is truly better off with Cat than without her. He will be feeling the impact of the lyrics when Cat starts singing her part. I'm going to text Colin and tell him what I need him to do. Are you with me?"

"Of course."

"And I need you to go out there and introduce Jeff."

"The audience is going to be totally confused."

"And what's going to happen will knock them naked," Maria said.

"If you say 'naked' again I might have to take you into my office and get you that way."

Maria laughed. "Wow, you're frisky tonight. I guess I should wear these boots more often." She leaned in and gave Pete a kiss that held more than a hint of promise. "Now go and get the crowd stirred up. I've got to get to Cat before she heads out there to join Jeff."

"You don't think he's going to be pissed not knowing what's going on?"

"Yeah, but he'll get glad again." She grinned. "Now go! Hurry!"

"Okay." Pete shook his head, but he was willing to do anything Maria asked of him. And he just bet that whatever she had up her sleeve was going to be amazing. But he couldn't wait to find out just what that was.

16

If I Fell

"**W**AIT." CAT PUT A HAND ON MARIA'S ARM. "JEFF HAS NO clue what's going on? I . . . I think we should tell him."

"The element of surprise will be better. I just came up with this on the spur of the moment. Only Colin and Pete know—not even Rick. I simply think the song is perfect for this little bit of drama. I know the concept will make an awesome music video. Are you ready for this?"

Cat nodded, but her stomach churned with an odd mixture of nervousness and excitement. Maria was right. This entrance could be really dramatic. Hopefully, the crowd would do as predicted and part, giving her the opportunity to sing her way over to Jeff. Otherwise the performance could turn into one hot mess.

Cat took the cordless mic from Maria and stood in the shadows while Pete introduced Jeff. Since the stage was raised a couple feet off the floor, Cat could see Jeff from where she stood. He appeared a little bit confused as he sat down on the stool, but he remained professional and smiled at the cheering crowd. Did he think that she'd dipped out on him? Cat really didn't like the thought of disappointing him even for a minute and she had to wonder whether this was part of Maria's plan as well. Emotion was so much a part of singing, of performing and selling the lyrics. It wasn't just about entertaining but having the audience connect to the song rather than just listen. Cat put a hand to her chest and closed her eyes. A moment later, Cat heard Pete's booming voice and the noise suddenly died down. Oh boy . . .

"Hey, y'all, I wanna thank you for comin' out to Sully's tonight to support our very own Jeff Greenfield. We also have the amazing Rick Ruleman from My Way Records in the house!" he said, making the crowd erupt with applause. Rick stood up and waved. "And thanks to y'all chillin' outside too! Is this exciting or what?"

Cat felt her heart start beating rapidly when she spotted the slight frown on Jeff's face. She saw him try to get Colin's attention but Colin refused to even glance his way.

"I think we can get Jeff to sing 'Outta My Mind with Lovin' You' in a bit, but he's got a current single getting some airplay called 'Second Chances.' Jeff, you ready to play your new song?"

Jeff nodded and then glanced over at the empty stool. A bit of buzz rippled through the crowd. Rick and Maggie bent their heads together, making Cat look over at Maria, who gave her a thumbs-up that was meant to be reassuring but wasn't. A moment later Jeff strummed the first chord of the song and started singing: "All I want is a second chance. I'll even settle for a second glance."

Cat stepped into the room and sang: "But you left me crying when I needed you. Why should I believe that your heart is true?"

Jeff sang the next two lines while scanning the crowd for her. At first she was hidden from him but as predicted people parted, giving Cat a direct path to the stage. And then he spotted her. Jeff homed in on her progress and she could tell that he was angry at being kept in the dark and he poured his emotion into the lyrics.

Cat lifted her chin and gave it right back. "When I needed love you turned me away. So tell me why I should come back to stay?" The crowd ate up the drama, the emotion that hung thickly in the air. Heads turned, craning to watch Cat approach Jeff. She paused halfway, bent forward, and belted out the heart-wrenching lyrics. "I had to leave you, couldn't read you!"

"I said I'm sorry, but it wasn't enough. I'm on my knees begging you, please. Give me a second chance," Jeff countered. "I'll even settle for a second glance."

Cat started walking but kept her eyes on Jeff. They bantered back and forth and when Cat stepped up onto the stage Colin piped in the instrumental track so Jeff could put the guitar down. He grabbed the mic and faced Cat. "Show me you need me. Give me a second chance. Just get me started with a second glance."

Singing the lyrics, Cat turned her back on Jeff, refusing to look at him. The audience was eating it up, waiting for the next line, the reconciliation that might not come. Jeff's voice became gruff with emotion, begging her to give in, but she remained with her back to him while she sang her heart out.

They drew out the last note. Cat bowed her head and raised her fist skyward but just before the song ended she turned and gave Jeff the second glance he'd been begging for the entire song.

The crowd erupted with applause. Jeff was right. The song was about hope, about having tomorrow to make things right. Cat felt sudden emotion well up in her throat and when she turned all the way around she could see some of the same in Jeff's eyes. He'd felt the power of the music too.

And so did the audience.

Cat glanced over to where Pete stood near the stage

and she saw him swipe at the corner of his eye with the
heel of his hand. He looked over to where Maria sat and
Cat saw them exchange a look filled with meaning. *Love
is worth a second chance.* After a deep breath Cat let the
applause die down and then said, "That song was written
by Jeff Greenfield and Colin Walker." She pointed to
Colin, who inclined his head, and then she extended her
arm toward Jeff. "It is an honor to sing it."

Jeff gave her a nod and a smile but Cat could see that
he was still a bit miffed at not knowing what was going
on. She couldn't blame him really, but he needed to get
over it and go on with the set. He leaned in close and
gave her a kiss on the cheek but said in her ear, "Don't
ever do that to me again."

"'Outta My Mind with Lovin' You'!" someone shouted,
and Jeff nodded. "You got it. Cat, want to sing along?"

Cat knew the song well and jumped in with the harmony. The edge to Jeff's voice spoke volumes but Cat
gave it right back to him. They ended the song face-to-
face. A muscle jumped in his jaw but Cat didn't back
down and raised her chin. She was done with bowing
down, holding back, and being told what she could or
couldn't do.

"'Sail-Away Summer'!" shouted someone else.

Jeff gave her a nod and sat back. It irked Cat that he
either wouldn't or maybe couldn't harmonize because he
didn't know the words. Or was it beneath him to sing one
of her beach-themed hits? With a huge smile Cat reached
behind her and picked up her guitar and started singing.
Before long the audience was singing along and she forgot all about sulky Jeff Greenfield. He needed to get
over himself. Seriously. No, she needed to get over him.
She shot him a look hoping she'd feel pissed off and
nothing else, but of course she felt a hot shiver of attraction. *Damn . . .*

Cat looked over at Maria. They were supposed to do
only a few songs, but the crowd was clamoring for more.

Jeff leaned closer to her. "You know any Johnny Cash?" he asked with the arch of an eyebrow.

"Of course."

"You know 'Jackson'?"

"Absolutely." Cat nodded. "I love me some Johnny Cash. Let's do it." She'd show him!

Jeff jumped right into the song and Cat jumped right with him. He even stood up and did some classic Johnny Cash moves that had the audience eating it up with a spoon. Cat tossed some sass right back at him and at the end of the song the audience jumped to their feet, giving them a standing ovation.

Cat looked over and Maria gave them the cutoff sign. Cat understood. That performance was great and she knew Maria wanted everybody to be talking about it. Leaving them wanting more could be a very good thing.

A moment later Pete stepped up onto the stage and swung his big hands in Cat and Jeff's direction. "Let's give Cat Carson and Jeff Greenfield a big round of applause," he shouted, although he didn't need to because the whistles and clapping seemed to go on forever without any need for encouragement. Pete finally had to raise his palms for silence. "Would y'all like to see these two out on the outdoor stage sometime soon?" Pete looked at Cat and Jeff and grinned. "I think they want y'all back," he shouted into the mic. "And I just bet South Street Riot will join them," he added, to the delight of the crowd.

With one last wave to the crowd Cat picked up her guitar and stepped down from the stage. As she walked over to the hallway leading to the offices and dressing room, she could feel tension radiating from Jeff. Even the heels of his boots sounded angry. Cat opened the door to what was considered the greenroom at Sully's. After carefully placing her guitar in her case she picked up a bottle of water and took a swig, bracing herself for whatever was to come. She wondered whether Maria and Rick were going to join them to critique the performance and hoped that they would, to put a buffer between her and Jeff.

"Just what the hell was that all about?" Jeff wanted to know.

"My delayed entrance was Maria's brainchild, Jeff. I was only following orders."

"Don't you think it would have been nice for me to have a heads-up instead of sitting up there next to an empty stool feeling like a complete jackass?"

Cat sat her water bottle down so hard that liquid sloshed out of the opening. "Take it up with Maria, not me."

"You knew, Cat. You could have clued me in."

"The element of surprise enhanced the emotion. You have to agree."

"So you would be cool with this happening to you?" He angled his head to the side and waited. "Come on, this was bullshit. Admit it."

Cat would have agreed if he wasn't forcing her to. "I don't answer to you."

"No, you don't, and I don't answer to you either, which is why I don't want to be a damned duo. Because of this kind of crap! And I wasn't about to sing—" he began, but then caught himself.

Cat saw red. She walked—no, *marched* over and in her boots stood only a couple of inches shorter than him. She stopped directly in front of Jeff and tilted her head up in challenge. "Oh, let me guess, my shitty beach song that everyone in the audience could sing along to but . . . *you*." She poked him in the chest. "Because you're better than that?"

"Don't poke me again," he warned.

So of course she did. Harder.

Jeff nodded slowly. "See, this is where your having siblings would have warned you that you really shouldn't have poked me in the chest again."

Her gaze clashed with his. She slowly pulled her hand away and widened her eyes as if in fear. And then she poked him, twisting her finger around for good measure.

Jeff inhaled a deep breath, making his nostrils flare. He swallowed calmly and then said in a low tone, "You're really going to regret that."

"Not in this lifetime." Cat felt a ripple of nervous excitement that had nothing to do with fear and stood her ground. "Do I look scared?"

"Yes." He took a step closer.

"I'm not."

"You should be." He stepped even closer until she could feel the heat from his body. The top three mother-of-pearl buttons on his dark blue shirt were undone, giving Cat a glimpse of tanned skin. She longed to reach up and tug, making the remaining buttons pop open so she could splay her hands on his bare skin. "I'm just giving you fair warning." He arched one dark eyebrow and licked his bottom lip as if in anticipation.

"I could take you with one hand tied behind my back," she boasted, but the thought of being tied up sent a hot shiver down her spine. Cat's chest rose and fell while she contemplated poking him once more. . . .

Or pulling his head down for a much needed, much wanted, oh so hot *kiss*.

Cat opted for a quick poke and pivoted on the heel of her boot in hope of a hasty retreat followed by a quick escape. But before Cat could turn away Jeff grabbed her and spun her back around. The whole spinning thing made Cat wobble and she teetered into the buffet table behind her, causing a plate of chocolate chip cookies she had been eyeing earlier to slide to the opposite edge before stopping. Water bottles fell to the floor with loud smacks and rolled away as if trying to escape.

"That was a mistake." Jeff stood between Cat and the table, trapping her. He reached over and picked up her braid, wrapped it around his fist, and then tugged her forward with just enough force to have her fall against him.

And then he crushed his mouth to hers in a hot, hard kiss.

Cat kissed him back, leaning against him. When his tongue touched her, a flash of heat traveled through her body with enough intensity to make her gasp. Never in her life had she wanted a man more than she wanted Jeff Greenfield. She reached in and tugged at his shirt, loving the sound of the snaps popping open. She splayed her palms on his chest, exploring smooth skin, silky hair, and sexy contours. His mouth found her neck and he kissed, nibbled, and licked until she felt as if she were melting from the inside out.

When he suddenly let go and walked away, Cat felt slightly stunned but before disappointment could settle in she realized that he was locking the door. With long strides he crossed the room and pulled her back into his arms and a moment later they were lying on the leather sofa. He kissed her deeply and when his hand cupped her breast Cat wrapped her legs around him and urged him on. She arched her back wanting more and when he tugged the peasant blouse over her shoulders she didn't protest. His mouth found her shoulders and he rose up to begin a trail of light kisses over her bare skin to the top of her lacy demi-bra.

"God, I want you."

"What about just being friends?"

"A moment of insanity."

She laughed.

"I want to make love to you, Cat. But not here. I want you in my bed, where I can do this right. Where I can do this all night long."

"I . . . like that plan," she answered in a voice so breathless that she almost laughed at herself.

"We can escape out the side entrance, where my truck is parked, okay?" He rubbed his thumb over the swell of her breasts, making her forget what he'd asked, but she nodded—at this point she would agree to make love to him on the roof of the building. He stood up and reached for her, tugging her to her feet. Of course, true to form, she stumbled against him and suddenly they were kissing and kissing . . .

And kissing.

Cat could feel the beat of his heart beneath his smooth, warm skin. She pulled her mouth from his and then pressed her lips against his bare chest. "I want to lick you like you're one giant ice cream cone."

Jeff chuckled and then lifted her head so she had to look at him. "Now that's an offer I can't refuse."

"Good, because otherwise saying that would have been super embarrassing."

Jeff laughed again. "I want to lick you everywhere too," he said. "So what are we waiting for?"

"Christmas?"

"No way . . . much too long of a wait. I want you now."

17

Love Me Do

JEFF TOSSED HIS HEAD BACK AND LAUGHED AGAIN. *GOD, I love you* slammed into his brain and nearly slid out of his mouth, but he caught himself just in time. It dawned on Jeff that he did love Cat, or at least he was falling hard. Being with her was like being on a runaway train that he was unable to stop. But he realized he didn't want to. "Grab your purse and your guitar," he said and then grabbed her free hand.

"You're awfully bossy."

"You like it."

"I do not," Cat insisted, but followed him down the dimly lit hallway. When she clung to his hand he remembered that she was afraid of the dark and he pulled her closer to his side. Once they were outdoors they jogged over to his truck. He opened her door and took her guitar, placing it and his own in the extended cab behind them. "Hop on in."

Cat laughed when Jeff made gravel fly in an effort to go fast. "Trying to impress me, country boy?"

"Not yet, but that will happen soon enough."

"Right." Cat made a scoffing sound but held on tight while he sped off down the road but turned away before the front entrance.

"Where are you going?"

Jeff grinned her way. "Taking a little shortcut."

"Little shortcut?"

"Big shortcut."

She lifted her hand to point out the front window. "But . . . there's no, you know . . . *road*."

"This truck is four-wheel drive, city girl. Just hold on tight."

"You don't scare me."

"Ha," Jeff said and did a donut in the middle of a field.

Jeff laughed when Cat squealed and clamped one hand on the dash and the other on the armrest.

"Really?"

"Really."

"You want more?"

"Give it to me, baby," she boasted, but he figured he would find fingernail marks on his dash the next day.

"You know I can't resist a dare." He took her across bumpy terrain, over hills and splashing through a shallow creek bed. At one point she bounced up so far from the seat that she bumped her head on the roof and yelped. "You need me to take it easy on you?"

"Never!"

"Are you gonna get sick?"

"Maybe." She laughed but Jeff took it easier the rest of the way. Still, they ended up at his cabin in half the time it should have taken them to get there. Jeff ran around to her side, helped her down, and grabbed her hand. They jogged up to his front door, which was unlocked, and they all but tumbled inside his cabin. He dipped his head and kissed her, pedaling backward and turning sideways, nearly taking out a lamp. They somehow made it to his bedroom. He tapped the round light switch on the wall, turning it to bathe the room in a soft glow.

Still kissing, they fell onto the bed in a tangle of arms, legs, and locked lips. When they fell apart, Cat laughed and the throaty, sexy sound made Jeff's pulse pound even harder.

And suddenly he wanted to slow things down and savor each little detail. Jeff rolled to his side and propped himself up on his elbow. "How's your broken finger?"

"Still broken, I think," she said, and he kissed it.

"All better now?"

"No . . . kiss it again," she said in a husky voice filled with emotion.

He traced the outline of her lips with a fingertip and then trailed his fingers lightly down her chin and over her neck.

"When you touch me, I melt," she said with a shiver. "Is it some kind of superpower you have?"

"I hope so. With you, anyway." He played with the elastic of her peasant blouse, dipping his finger beneath the edge until he felt the lace of her bra. She sucked in a sharp breath, arched her back, and when he tugged the soft material downward off one shoulder Jeff had to lean in and taste her skin. He kissed and then nipped, tugging the material down inch by inch until he exposed part of her black lacy bra. "You're gorgeous, Cat." He looked into her expressive green eyes and was surprised to see a question.

"Am I?" she whispered.

"Surely you know . . ." Jeff replied, but when he expected a flippant remark or a joke she lowered her lashes and swallowed.

"Funny—I spent a lifetime longing to fit in, but I was always gangly, awkward . . . forgetful and so insecure. I never really thought anyone would find me beautiful . . . only funny."

"Well, think again."

She looked at him and smiled. "Maria told me that the only skin I needed to fit into was my own."

Jeff traced his finger over her collarbone and over the swell of her breasts. "I agree. Now, that being said, I fully admit that I've never known anyone remotely like you."

"You mean that in a good way, right?"

"Mostly."

She slid a glance his way.

"I wouldn't change a thing," he said. "Not one damned thing."

Cat raised her hands and cupped his cheeks. "Kiss me, Jeff. Just kiss me."

"Ah . . . Cat." He lowered his head and captured her mouth in a tender, lingering kiss. He wanted her to know that this was more to him than a quick tumble in his bed. He cared about her, worried about her. "If anybody even looks at you wrong, there would be hell to pay."

"Are you going to start beating your chest?"

"Maybe."

Cat chuckled low in her throat. "That's actually quite a turn-on."

"Good, that's my goal," he said, but he looked at her with serious eyes. "But I mean it."

"I know," she answered softly. "You make me feel safe and that's no easy feat," she said. There was something in her eyes that made him want to know more, but she smiled and gave him a long, lingering kiss.

And after singing "Jackson" with her tonight he knew they had something unique onstage. They had chemistry. They clicked. He couldn't deny that they had potential to become something special, lasting. He just didn't know what to do about it. For now he just wanted this amazing woman in his arms in his bed and hopefully the rest would find a way to fall into place. Jeff pulled back and ran his tongue over her wet bottom lip. "I want to make love to you all night long."

"Do you think that's possible?"

"I hear a challenge in that question."

"Are you up for it?"

Jeff glanced down and nodded. "Definitely," he said with a laugh. "Ah, but first take your clothes off for me, Cat. I want to see all of you."

"Okay," she said softly. She scooted off the bed and stood up. She took off her boots and kicked them to the side, then turned to him. "Help me," she said, raising her arms above her head. "I'm a little . . . shaky."

Her soft admission was like a zip line going straight to Jeff's heart. He found her honesty sweet and so genuine. He scooted to the edge of the bed and tugged her blouse over her head. Leaning forward, he reached around her back and unclasped her bra and when her breasts tumbled free he sucked in a breath. He cupped the fullness, and when he rubbed his thumbs over her nipples her head tilted to the side and she moaned.

"That feels . . . delicious."

Jeff took a nipple into his mouth, licked and then sucked. When he nipped lightly she cried out and threaded her fingers through his hair, offering him more. "Tastes delicious too," he murmured. Jeff put his hands on her ass and pulled her even closer and then, while feasting on her breasts, first one and then the other, he found her belt buckle and made quick work of sliding her hip-hugger jeans down, revealing a black lace thong. "I wondered all damned night after you teased me with peeks, but dear God . . ." He toyed with the lace and then slipped his finger beneath the patch of satin, finding her oh so wet. "Were you teasing me on purpose?"

"Yes. Did it work?"

"You know the answer. Colin told me to give you a taste of your own medicine."

"Is that what this is all about?"

"Yes."

"Well, I'm not cured yet so keep going . . . Ahhhh . . ."

Jeff laughed. He wanted to flip her onto the bed and sink into her silky heat but when she sucked her bottom lip into her mouth he was powerless to stop stroking her flesh. Cat grabbed his shoulders, digging in her fingers while he caressed her through the black satin. And then with one quick movement he tugged the thong down and kissed her there. She gasped but then moved seductively against him. Jeff held her close and licked her sweet, silky hot core until she threaded her fingers in his hair and moaned.

"You . . . That's . . . Oh!" Cat cried out and her knees buckled. When she fell against him he turned her over onto the bed. He tugged her thong all the way off and tossed it over his head before pausing to drink in the sight of her lying in his bed. She looked up at him with eyes that were a little bit dazed. With her flushed cheeks, heavy-lidded gaze, and wet mouth, she looked so damned sexy that Jeff heard himself groan. Her body, while toned and fit, had an abundance of curves rather than bones and sharp angles. She was truly perfection in his eyes but it went beyond the physical. He simply liked being with her and when he wasn't with her all he did was think about her. Cat Carson was never far from his mind.

"I want to take your clothes off but I'm not sure I can move just yet," she admitted, making Jeff grin. She came up to her elbows. "No, I'm serious. I don't think I can move. Even this was difficult. What did you do to me?"

Jeff's grin widened. "Rocked your world and I plan on doing the same thing over and over in many different ways."

"Dear God . . ." She fell back onto the bed and moaned up at the ceiling. "What next?"

"I think there was mention of licking your body *all* over. Are you ready?" Jeff asked as he tossed his shirt over his shoulder. After he tugged off his boots, the rest of his clothes joined the pile.

"I'm ready."

"Me too," he said and joined her on the bed. He ran his hands over her body until he felt goose bumps and a little shiver. "Cold?"

"Yeah, warm me up, would you?"

"Gladly." When he caressed her breasts, she sucked in a breath and he knew she was ready for him once more. After rolling on a condom he covered her body with his and kissed her deeply. And then, threading his fingers with hers, he raised her hands above her head and entered her in one sure stroke.

"Oh!" Cat curled her fingers over his and held on while he moved in a slow and steady rhythm. She arched her hips as if wanting more of him . . . all of him, and he gave it to her. When she wrapped her long legs around him, Jeff stroked harder, deeper, loving the feel of being inside her sweet, silky heat. Jeff held back until he felt her body shudder, and then he let go, feeling pleasure erupt in a long, hot explosion.

Jeff stayed there, buried deep, and kept Cat flush against his body. He could feel the rapid beat of her heart and when she kissed his chest Jeff felt a warm rush of tenderness. He rolled to the side and held her against him.

"That was . . ." she trailed off, and Jeff smiled.

"Nice?"

"Mmm, yes, very nice. No—better than nice. I would elaborate but my mind is blown right now."

Jeff laughed. He loved her candor, her willingness to be honest. "And we're just getting started."

"I need a moment . . . to regroup."

"I understand. I'll be right back," he said and headed for the bathroom. When he returned Jeff pulled Cat next to him and held her closely. With a sigh, she snuggled against him, and when she put her head on his shoulder and laid her hand on his chest, he felt relaxed and content. He'd never been a one-night stand kind of guy, so this was a game changer and she needed to know it. After a few minutes he said, "I can't fight how I feel about you any longer, Cat."

"Me neither." She kissed his neck and started drawing little circles on his chest. "So what are you saying?"

"Let's give it a shot." Jeff's heart thumped while he waited for her answer.

"Okay, but not tequila, because it makes me crazy and I throw up."

Jeff chuckled but then kissed the top of her head. "This won't be easy. There are complications."

"I know," she said softly.

"But I want to get to know you more. I . . . I already care about you, Cat."

The circle drawing stopped and she propped up on her elbow. "Well, then, we should all *drift*."

"What does that even mean?"

"Well, when I went white-water rafting last year there were some pretty intense level four and five rapids. After coming through them to the calm waters, the guide would tell us to lift our paddles out and . . . *all drift*. To relax and let the current take us forward."

"Ah, so we should all drift and see where this takes us?" Jeff asked.

"Precisely. There will be some rough water. We already know that going in, but if we can make it through, then we'll be fine." She rubbed her fingertip over the stubble on his cheeks.

"We'll make it through," Jeff said firmly and then gave her a light kiss. He pulled back and looked at her. "So I have to know. How did the white-water rafting excursion pan out for you?"

"Oh, I fell in twice and had to be rescued with a rope at one point. Apparently that's rarely done."

Jeff pictured the situation and chuckled. "That's why you have to wear the helmet?"

"Are you surprised?"

"Nope. Just how did you manage to fall in?"

"Apparently you're not supposed to stand up and point to a bald eagle."

"You saw a bald eagle?"

"Well, no, but I thought it was one. But I did see one

later when the guide pointed it out. Excitement over-took me and, well, cue my second big splash." She grinned. "But hey, I survived, didn't I?"

"You did, and made the excursion more memorable for everyone involved, I imagine. And by the way, I would have jumped in to save you."

"Ah, then you would have broken one of the many rules imposed upon us. Rafters are only supposed to ex-tend their paddle if someone falls overboard and not jump in and attempt rescue."

"I don't care," Jeff said firmly, almost dropping an *I love you* but caught himself again.

"I believe you." Cat snuggled closer and whispered, "All drift, Jeff . . ."

A moment later he felt her breathing soft and evenly and knew she'd fallen asleep. He smiled, thinking he'd let her rest for now. And then he planned to make sweet love to her until the roosters starting crowing.

18

Here There and Everywhere

PETE DID A THREE-SIXTY AND THEN LOOKED AT CLINT
and Ava. "Well?"

"You are a handsome devil," Ava assured him with a
grin. "Maria is going to simply swoon." She gave Clint a
nudge with her elbow. "Right, Clint?"

"I don't think Mom is the swooning type," Clint said
with a chuckle.

"There's always a first time." Ava made a face at Clint.
"If she swoons I want to know. Text me, okay?"

"Do I make *you* swoon, Ava?" Clint wanted to know.

Ava gave Clint a dreamy look and then put the back
of her hand up to her forehead. She tossed her hair over
her shoulder. "I declare," she cooed in a slow Southern
drawl. "I'm . . . I'm . . ." She started fanning her face.
"Glory be, I'm feeling a bit light-headed."

"Ha ha, very funny," Clint said glumly.

Ava grabbed him around the waist with both arms.
"Come on now, you know you make my heart go pitter-
patter as soon as you walk in the room." Ava gave him a

squeeze. When she tilted her head up, Clint planted a light kiss on her nose.

"Enough of that ooey-gooey stuff," Pete complained, but in truth he loved seeing Clint and Ava fawning all over each other. It had taken a team effort to get those two back together last Christmas, but having Ava back in Clint's life had been the best gift ever. "Seriously, love-birds, do I look okay?" Pete adjusted the cuffs of his starched white shirt, glanced down at his dark blue dress pants, and examined the shine on his best boots with a critical eye. He would have gone all out with a suit and tie, but Ava said that would be overkill at Wine and Din-er's patio. Pete was secretly glad because he wasn't sure he could last very long wearing a tie, although he'd wear a clown suit and a big red nose if Maria wanted him to.

"You look perfectly groomed." Clint gave him a quick, firm nod but then angled his head. "You're sort of glowing."

"I used a loofah in the shower," Pete explained.

"A what?" Clint asked.

"You know . . . one of those . . . Oh hell—tell him, Ava."

"A long, spongy, scrubby thing. I have one. You exfo-liate with it."

"Really, Dad? When did you go all girly on me?"

"It was in a *men's* grooming package that I got for Christmas a while back." Pete had to grin. "I guess some-one gave me that for a reason." Pete saw Clint's lips twitch and he pointed a finger at him. "Don't laugh."

Clint's eyes widened as he raised his hands. "I wouldn't dare," he promised, but then of course he tossed back his head and roared with laughter. "Sorry. . . . I'm just trying to picture you exfoliating."

Pete shook his head and had to chuckle. "Look, I ex-foliated, brushed, flossed, trimmed my nails, plucked my eyebrows, and put some product in my hair that the stylist insisted I buy this morning when I got a trim. I've never put goop in my hair in my whole, entire life."

"It looks good, Pete. You have really nice, thick hair," Ava told him.

"Thank you, Ava." He ran a hand down his face. "I tried on three different shirts and had to decide if these pants made my butt look big." He turned around and pointed.

"They don't," Ava said with a giggle.

"Did you shave your legs?" Clint asked and was rewarded with another elbow from Ava.

"Clint Sully, would you give your daddy a break?"

"Now what fun would that be?"

Pete didn't mind the teasing. Having his son back in his life after so many years apart was worth any little bit of ribbing. In fact, Pete got a kick out of it.

Pete lifted one pant leg. "Should I?"

"No!" Clint and Ava said in unison.

"I think you look perfect," Ava said. "And the bit of stubble on your cheeks is just right."

"I was getting tired of being called baby face." Pete rubbed his chin. "I put on the aftershave you suggested I buy, Ava. Boy, that smell-good stuff costs the earth."

"Oh, but the results are worth it," Ava told him. "I think Maria might actually swoon in spite of what Clint says. Now, you'd better get going before you're late. Never keep a lady waiting."

"How come women are the only ones allowed to be late?"

"I'm not late."

Clint gave her a pointed look. "Um, I seem to recall you almost missing riding in the sleigh with me in the Christmas parade because of your tardy arrival."

"Only because of a last-minute customer at the toy store!"

"Do I need to give a dozen more examples?" Clint teased. "Even back in high school you had to run to your locker to get there before the bell."

"We can be late because we're worth it," Ava replied. "Right, Pete?"

"I don't mind," Pete said with a soft smile, "waitin' on a woman, just like the Brad Paisley song."

"Oh, that song makes me cry every time I hear it," Ava admitted with a sigh. "And the video with Andy Griffith waiting on that bench in heaven?" Her eyes misted over and she put a hand to her chest.

"Aw, Ava." Clint reached for her hand and brought her palm to his mouth for a kiss.

Pete looked at his watch to check the time. Like everyone else, he didn't need to wear a watch because of cell phones, but he wore it because Maria had given it to him on their tenth wedding anniversary. He inhaled a deep breath. "Would flowers be overkill? Too much?"

"Absolutely not," Ava said, but Pete looked at Clint for guidance as well.

"Mom loves flowers."

"I just don't think your mother looks at this as being a date. She thinks it's all about business."

Clint shook his head. "Dad, I think you're wrong."

"You do?" Pete felt a giddy flash of hope. "Why?"

"I just do."

Ava glanced at Clint and then grinned. "I wasn't supposed to tell you this but I ran into Maria at Violet's up on Main Street, and if Maria wears the dress she bought she definitely thinks this is a date." Ava raised her hands in surrender. "But you didn't hear it from me. Now skedaddle." Ava shooed him with her fingertips.

"Are you staying here for a while?" Pete asked.

Clint nodded. "I want to sit on your front porch and enjoy the evening. I'm trying to talk Ava into us buying a house instead of living in the flat above the toy store."

"But it's such a short commute to work," Ava reminded him.

"True, but I want a yard. Don't you?" Clint asked.

Pete hoped Clint wanted a yard for children. He was looking forward to grandbabies.

"Of course. Let's get Maggie to start looking for us," Ava replied. "She can also start searching for someone to lease the flat. But I want to stay here in town so we can walk everywhere. Oh, Maple Street is lovely, don't you think?"

"Or we might consider building on some land down by the river near your family's farm," Clint suggested.

"Oh, Clint, that idea has merit as well. I'd love to have a garden. But I really do love it in town."

Pete smiled when he looked back at Clint and Ava sitting on the front porch deep in conversation. He and Maria used to do the same thing so many years before, often with her head resting on his shoulder. Pete dearly hoped that she might someday sit on that porch with him once again and live in the home where they had shared so many good memories. It was funny how the happy times were crowding out all the heartache.

Pete rolled down the windows of his pickup truck, thinking he'd like to buy a sweet little convertible to tool around in on evenings like these. He pictured Maria sitting next to him with the wind blowing in her hair and a big smile on her face. Yeah, he needed to put that plan into action. Pete realized that for a long-ass time he'd been running on cruise control, never really enjoying what life had to offer, but he suddenly wanted to make up for lost time and then some. Angie and his new bartending crew were doing a bang-up job, and it was high time he took a break from Sully's.

He no longer indulged in simple pleasures like sitting on his front porch watching the world go by. Sully's Tavern could get along without him always being there and he damned well knew it. He just needed to hire a few more people, maybe even someone to manage and free up time to relax. When was the last time he fired up his gas grill on his back patio and had friends over for the evening? And vacation? Forget it. But his heart started beating faster when he thought of taking a cruise or heading to the beach. And he knew why: because he wanted Maria by his side. Maybe they'd even walk hand in hand down the streets of London or Paris. Pete had never been out of the country and it was about damned time he started expanding his horizons. "I'm not gettin' any younger," he mumbled, but then grinned. "But it sure as hell feels like it."

Pete turned on the radio and sang along with George Strait as he drove up the hill to Wedding Row and parked in front of Flower Power. The gorgeous row of wedding-related shops had been there for only a few years, but with the gas streetlights and brick storefronts, they blended in with the old-fashioned look of downtown Cricket Creek. The spectacular view of the Ohio River added to the overall appeal. He hoped that he could open Sully's South on Restaurant Row, the second phase of the development Maria wanted as a haven for song-writers, like the Bluebird Cafe in Nashville, and Pete thought it was a great idea, especially if it meant working together.

Pete paused in front of the bridal shop and sucked in a breath at the sight of the wedding dress displayed in the big picture window. The simple yet elegant gown reminded Pete of the one Maria had worn on their wedding day and he found himself staring. They'd had a small church wedding with an understated reception in the church undercroft. The honeymoon had consisted of a long weekend in the Great Smoky Mountains, a popular destination for newlyweds. Next time around he wanted to go all out and take her somewhere exotic. "Whoa, down, boy," Pete said with a chuckle and reminded himself to go slow. First things first, he thought. Like a date, for instance.

But when he walked away Pete looked over his shoulder and read the awning above the bridal shop. "From this moment," he said softly, and then started humming the Shania Twain song and stopped in his tracks. *From this moment,* Pete decided, he would let go of the past and all the mistakes, misunderstandings, and most of all . . . the pain. Pete chuckled as he thought of what Ava had said to him when they were shopping for clothes. "When the past comes calling, let it go to voice mail," he repeated. Great advice.

Pete opened the door to Flower Power and chuckled when he saw cute little Gabby Goodwin working on a flower arrangement. Well, she was Gabby Marino now. She came from humble beginnings living in the local trailer park and lost her mother to cancer way too soon. Marcie Goodwin had worked as a server at Sully's, and Pete had made damned sure there was always food on their table. Pete used to cringe when some sweet-talking man would come on to Marcie. She always seemed to fall for some jerk, but she was a wonderful mother and loved Gabby dearly. Pete hoped that Marcie was watching down and knew that Gabby had married Reese Marino, a good man who treated Gabby like gold.

Gabby wore earbuds and bobbed her blond head to the beat of whatever she was listening to, so she didn't hear Pete enter the shop. Pete looked around and smiled. The flower-filled shop oozed charm, and after a slow start was doing well, but then again residents of Cricket Creek took care of their own.

Gabby looked up and squealed when she spotted him. "Pete!"

"Gabby!" Pete braced himself for Gabby to come flying across the shop and throw herself into his arms. He wasn't disappointed. She had to dodge the rack of cards and nearly clipped a display of sunflowers, but she made it to him without incident.

"What brings you here?" Gabby tugged on the earbuds and had to crane her neck to look up at him. She put a hand to her chest. "Oh . . . nobody . . . passed, did they?"

"No." Pete had to chuckle. It was rather sad that the only time he ordered flowers was for a funeral. Well, that was going to change. Maria was going to have fresh flowers at least once a week. Maybe twice. "I'm here for a bouquet of something special."

Gabby gasped. "You have a date? Oh my gosh, please tell me it's with Maria."

"It's with Maria," Pete said and was rewarded with another happy squeal.

"Nice, because otherwise I was going to have to punch you."

Pete laughed. He doubted that Gabby had ever taken a swing at anyone in her life. "Good to know."

"So what do you want? Roses?" Gabby asked while tapping her cheek. "No . . . too ordinary." She nibbled on the inside of her lip and then brightened. "How about a spring mix?" She rushed over and showed Pete the bouquet.

"Perfect."

"Lots of color and it will last a long time. Just have Maria clip off the ends and change the water daily."

"Will do. I hope to keep her in fresh flowers, if she allows it."

Gabby's eyes welled up with tears. "I don't know why you two split up, Pete, but you're the best. The very best," Gabby said and gave him a big hug. "If you want this to work out, it will. I know it." She stood back and looked at him. "And don't you just look totally handsome!" But she shook her head.

"What?"

"You're more than handsome. You're hot!"

Pete laughed. "For an old coot I clean up well, I guess."

Pete gave Gabby a kiss on the cheek. "I love you,

short stuff. Give that man of yours a hello from me, okay?"

"I'm heading over to the pizza parlor as soon as I close up here. Reese made some Italian cream cake and he promised to save me a slice. You should bring Maria in sometime soon. Reese and Tony will treat you like royalty."

"Excellent idea. Hopefully there will be a date number two."

"I'm sure of it," Gabby said. "But keep me posted, okay? I'm a busybody just like everybody else in Cricket Creek."

"I will do that," Pete promised, and was whistling when he walked over to his truck.

The pieces of their broken hearts had been swept away. Tonight was going to be filled with flowers, wine, laughter, and hopefully a kiss or two.

But most of all this was a new beginning.

19

All You Need Is Love

WHEN MARIA HEARD THE KNOCK AT THE DOOR, HER heart nearly flipped over in her chest. Biting her bottom lip, she gave her reflection a critical once-over. Pete loved her in deep red lipstick, but was the eyeliner too dramatic? Was the little black dress a bit much for the patio at Wine and Diner? Was it too tight? Too short? Did it show too much cleavage? She glanced down and swallowed hard. Were her strappy heels overly sexy? And did wearing the pearls Pete had given her on their tenth wedding anniversary say too much? Would he notice? Maria put her hand to her throat and felt a tug of emotion as she stroked the smooth pearls warmed by her skin. She hadn't worn them since the divorce, but tonight it just somehow felt right.

When the doorbell chimed this time, Maria knew she was going to have to just go with it. Still, she tugged at the hem as she hurried to the door. Inhaling deeply, she turned the handle and tried for a casual smile.

"Hello, Maria."

"Oh . . . my." She stood there dumbfounded and

nearly toppled sideways in her spiked heels. That old Brooks and Dunn song started playing in her head: "Ain't nothing 'bout you that don't do something for me." From his neatly trimmed salt-and-pepper hair to the sexy stubble on his cheeks to the spit-polished boots and the dress clothes in between, Maria loved it all. And he was holding a bountiful bouquet of beautiful flowers.

"May I come in?"

Maria blinked at him for another moment and then came to her senses. "Oh . . . Oh, of course." When she stepped aside, Pete walked past her, leaving the clean, spicy smell of his cologne in his wake.

"These are for you," Pete said, but instead of his usual booming voice he sounded a bit shy. "From Flower Power."

"Oh, how is sweet little Gabby doing?"

"Well, she threatened to throttle me if these weren't for you."

"That's my girl." Maria laughed. "I just adore her." She accepted the bouquet. "Thank you. They're lovely! I'll just go and find a vase," she said. When he followed her into the kitchen, she hoped that her butt didn't look big in the tight dress. She located a glass vase and hoped that Pete didn't see the slight tremble in her fingers as she removed the tissue paper and snipped the ends with her kitchen shears.

"Gabby said to trim the ends and change the water, but it looks like you already know that," Pete said, then cleared his throat. "Maria . . . you . . . you look amazing. And smell good too."

"So do you. Who knew you had such good taste?"

"I have a confession." Pete grinned. "I had some much needed help from Ava."

"Ah, she's such a wonderful girl." Maria felt a school-girl blush steal into her cheeks at the thought of Pete trying to impress her. "Well, Ava did a good job."

"Thank you. Gabby said I look hot. Do you think so?"

"Yes, Pete, you do." Maria's hands went to the pearls and she caught the look in his eyes.

"Tenth, right?"

Maria felt emotion clog her throat, so she merely nodded. When Pete held up his wrist she saw the gold watch and had to swipe at a sudden tear.

"Maria?" He took a step toward her. "I . . . Damn, did I do something—*say* something wrong?" His stricken expression had Maria giving him a watery chuckle.

"No." She shook her head slowly. "Not at all. In fact, you're doing everything right."

"That's a first," he said with a chuckle. "Then . . ." Holding her gaze, Pete walked over to where she stood and pulled her into his arms. "May I . . . kiss you?"

"Since when did you become so formal?"

"I think it's the clothes. I've been transformed."

Maria laughed and then tilted her head up. "Yes, you may kiss me," she said breathlessly. When his mouth covered hers Maria wrapped her arms around his neck. He might be all dressed up, but Pete was still her Pete no matter what he was wearing.

And, God, how she'd missed him . . .

When his tongue tangled with hers, Maria felt a tug of longing that had her pressing closer. With a groan Pete slanted his mouth and kissed her deeply. He always was a damned good kisser and she reveled in the feel of his lips, the taste of his mouth. When he slid his hand down her bare back, a hot shiver slid over her body and it had nothing to do with the hot flashes that plagued her.

It was all about Pete Sully.

When he finally pulled back, he inhaled a breath as if to catch his breath. "I'm going to be so proud to have you on my arm tonight."

"Well, that's too bad because I'm not going anywhere with you."

The stricken look returned and Maria laughed low in her throat. "Unless you count going to bed," she said boldly, trying to keep a huge blush at bay. But then shyness evaporated like sunshine hitting fog. This was Pete. Her Pete. And when the stricken look slid into a smile she put her hands on his shoulders.

"Works for me," Pete said.

"Mmm . . ." She ran her hands over his wide chest and arched an eyebrow. "I suddenly feel like ordering in. How about you?"

"Yes, but later." He scooped her up in his arms and she gave him a throaty laugh. He added, "Much, *much* later."

Maria linked her wrists around Pete's neck and rested her head on his shoulder. He was such a big, strong teddy bear of a man and he carried her into the bedroom with ease. Because she'd left the bathroom light on, the room was bathed in soft light. When they reached the edge of her king-sized bed he let her slide down his body until her feet touched the floor. "I need your help."

"Name it."

"Help me out of this dress."

"Gladly."

With a pounding heart Maria turned her back to him so he could unzip her dress. The sound seemed loud in the stillness. In fact her senses felt heightened and when his fingers grazed over her skin she felt a ripple of excitement. When he reached for the pearls, Maria shook her head. "Leave them on," she told him, and then let her dress slide off her shoulders and pool at the floor. When she felt the heat of his mouth on her back, Maria let her head fall to the side, giving him access to her neck. He brushed her hair away and kissed his way to her earlobe, sending tingles everywhere. Oh . . . and then he reached around and cupped her breasts with his big hands. His thumbs rubbed over the swell of her skin just above the satin of her push-up bra, sending a hot thrill all the way to her toes. "You're making me go up in flames."

"That's the plan."

"Mmm, I like the way you think." Maria released a soft sigh while letting the pleasure of being held against him wash over her. She felt the cotton of his shirt brush her bare arms when he moved to unhook her bra. She let the satin slide to the floor and then leaned back so he could caress her breasts. Knowing what she liked, Pete placed lingering kisses on her neck. The stubble on his cheeks against her skin both tickled and felt mildly abrasive, making her breath catch. "And I love the way you feel," she said, then gasped when he slid his hand lower and touched her through the silk of her panties. He hooked his thumbs in the lacy sides and pushed the material downward until it slid to her ankles. There was something vulnerable yet so very sexy about being naked while Pete remained fully clothed.

"I want to look at you," Pete said in her ear.

Maria felt a sudden flash of insecurity about her body. She'd resisted nips and tucks, and it had been such a long time since Pete, or any man for that matter, had seen her naked. But she squared her shoulders and shook her negative thoughts off. The stretch marks on her tummy were from having Pete's child. *They are stripes of honor and nothing to be ashamed of*, she told herself.

"Maria?" Pete asked gently. "Do you want this?"

"Yes, oh, yes." She nodded and then turned around. "It's just been a while," she said honestly. "And I'm . . . older."

"And stunningly beautiful. I'm a lucky man to have you in my arms." He put a hand on her cheek. "I always was. We have a past. We have a son, but this really is our new beginning, Maria. I was going to wait, but I'll just go ahead and say it once more. My love for you is stronger than ever and I want to have you back in my life. I want to grow old with you," he said and then grinned. "Well, *older*. I don't want you in this high-rise. I want you to come home. Sit on the front porch."

"Pete—"

He put a gentle finger to her lips. "I know it's too soon for you to move back. I just want you to know what I want, so there's no mistake. I'm gonna lay it all on the line right here, right now. Maria, we might have gotten divorced, but I never stopped thinking of you as my wife. I've not . . . laid down with another woman. It never even crossed my mind. You're all I ever wanted and I want you back for good."

"We can't start over, Pete, but we can start fresh. Just give me time."

"I'll give you anything you want, anything you need. Just ask," Pete said.

Maria reached for him. "Right now all I want is you in my arms."

"You don't have to ask twice."

"But first things first." She reached for the buttons on his shirt. "For once in your life, Pete Sully, you're way overdressed. I need to fix that little problem."

Pete laughed and Maria loved the deep, rich sound. She felt the troubled past get nudged away by happiness. She knew she had to go slow and get her footing. True, they'd lost so many years, but that only made what they had left even more valuable, and she intended to let the past slip away and treasure each day forward.

20
Glad All Over

"ARE YOU SERIOUS?" CAT STOOD UP AND YELLED. "THAT was low and inside, Blue!" When Cat raised her hands skyward in protest, Jeff reached up and tugged on her Cricket Creek Cougars T-shirt, which she'd bought at the stadium and insisted upon instantly wearing.

"You're gonna get kicked out of the ballpark if you keep riding the umpires like that," Jeff warned with the shake of his head.

Cat sat down with a thump and nudged him with her elbow. "Am I embarrassing you?"

Jeff glanced left and right. "Yeah, kinda."

Cat laughed. "Good, then I'm going to keep it up. You should have said no." She reached for his soft pretzel and pulled off a big chunk.

"Why do you keep refusing food and then eating mine?"

"I feel less guilty eating bad-for-me food if you order it instead of me. It's like it doesn't count."

Jeff adjusted his baseball cap and gave her a look. "That is the craziest thing I've ever heard."

"Ah, but the day is early. I've got more where that came from, so stay tuned." She cupped her hands around her mouth and yelled, "We need a base hit!" When she reached for his pretzel again, he pulled it out of her reach, but when she gave him a pout, he sighed and handed it to her.

"Anything else you want me to order?"

"Nachos with extra jalapeños."

"I thought you said spicy food bothers your stomach."

"It does, but I'll worry about that later. Sometimes you just have to live in the moment."

"You know you're crazy, right?"

"So you keep telling me." She nodded and he thought she looked so damned cute in her baseball cap and ponytail swinging out of the back. "You say that like it's a bad thing."

Jeff laughed. They had decided to go to a Cougars game when Mia gave them box seats behind the home plate up in the second deck, away from the crowd. She'd pretty much insisted that they attend and Cat was glad to get a break from the studio. With sunglasses and baseball caps they tried to keep their attendance on the down low, but when Cat started yelling, that blew their cover all to hell and back. They'd been seen around town the past week and Jeff knew people were talking, but he didn't care. He was even starting to warm up to the whole Sweet Harmony thing, but Jax and Sam were still adamantly against the idea. Jeff refused to think about that right now and just enjoy a rare day without being in the studio. "I think that's a great idea."

"What? I thought all of my ideas were great."

"Really? I seem to recall you trying to crawl through a bathroom window."

"It was a great *idea*. I didn't say that they all work out as planned."

"It was a terrible idea," Jeff told her. "But I do like your living-in-the-moment plan. I've never been very good at that one. Farming is all about planning for the future."

Cat tilted her head and looked at him. "I was allowing others to plan my life for me. This is so much better. I like being in control for once," she said in a rare serious moment. "Even if it doesn't go as planned, it will be my choice, my mistake. I won't get pushed around again."

"Good for you." Jeff didn't like the idea of anyone taking advantage of her, but her good nature and trusting attitude meant that she was a prime target. No one would ever be able to do that again as long as he was in the picture. "I think you're a lot stronger than you give yourself credit for, Cat."

"I'm getting there," she said with a smile and then turned her attention to the game. "I think we need a bunt to move the runner into scoring position, don't you?"

"I'd rather see him swing away," Jeff said, just to get her going. "I never did like playing small ball, but who am I to question whatever Ty McKenna decides to do? I was such a fan of his as a kid."

"And you must have been so thrilled when Noah Falcon came back here and built this stadium."

Jeff nodded. "Noah came back here to star in the local theater after he was killed off that soap opera he was on for a few years after his baseball career ended. The women of Cricket Creek all watched. Even my mother."

Cat laughed. "I watched once in a while. Noah was a horrible actor."

"That didn't seem to matter," Jeff said with a laugh. "No one thought he'd settle back down here, but he fell for Olivia Lawson, his costar in the play." Jeff shook his head. "I know he wanted to help save the failing economy here in his hometown, but I think he built this stadium to impress Olivia."

"A pretty grand gesture," Cat said. "But hey, if you build it, they will come, right?"

"Apparently," Jeff replied. "But it brought this town back to life." He hesitated and then asked, "Do you like living here, Cat?"

"Oh, yes. I haven't been this relaxed in years. I knew I had to make some changes in my life and when I drove to the cabin I immediately felt it was the right choice." She looked at him and smiled. "Sometimes you can just know when something is right."

Jeff felt a measure of relief. He wondered whether at some point Cat might get bored with small-town life and decide to head back to Nashville or even Chicago.

"It's the bottom of the lineup with no outs. We need a sac bunt."

Jeff leaned in close to her ear. "Do you know that it's damned sexy that you know baseball so well?"

Cat grinned. "I watched tons of baseball with my dad. We are die-hard Cubs fans."

"So you went to Wrigley Field a lot? What an awesome stadium."

Cat's grin faded. "No, we watched on television. My . . . my parents didn't like to go out much when I was a kid." She looked out over the baseball diamond as if she didn't want to elaborate.

Jeff nodded, but he didn't really understand. He knew there was something in Cat's past that she didn't talk about, but he didn't want to pry. He supposed she'd tell him when she felt the time was right. But he wanted to know. "Well, it's on my bucket list to go to Wrigley Field. Will you go with me?"

"Yes!" When she nodded and gave him a bright smile, he put his hand over hers. Jeff got the feeling that, although she came from wealth, Cat Carson had lived her childhood cut off from the rest of the world.

"I even promise to order bad food and let you eat it."

"Even better. And we have to get pizza at Giordano's."

"Chicago-style, I'm guessing?"

"The best stuffed pizza pie on the planet and always

voted the best in Chicago. Yeah, the cheese is on the bottom and the sauce on top. One slice will fill you up."

"Not likely," Jeff said. "This country boy can eat."

"So can this city girl," she said and ate the last of the pretzel. "Sorry."

"No, you're not."

She wrinkled her nose. "Not really," she admitted and then turned her head back to the game. A moment later the second baseman laid down a perfect bunt, advancing the runner to second. "Now do we pinch-hit for the pitcher?"

"It's only the fifth inning and he's still got some heat. I'd leave him in."

"I agree," Cat said with a slow nod.

"That's a first," Jeff said.

"Well, you softened me up with the Wrigley Field offer."

"When will your parents be back in town?"

Cat sighed. "I'm not sure. I was able to text them last week, though."

Jeff wanted to know more, but when the pitcher managed to get a rare hit Cat jumped to her feet and cheered. The man on second was being waved on by the third-base coach. "They're sending him home! We're going to have a play at the plate!" She tugged at Jeff's hand until he stood up with her. When the runner slid headfirst and was declared safe, Cat started jumping up and down. She turned and gave Jeff a chest bump, making him laugh.

Jeff had never had more fun with any other girl. "You are one of a kind," he said and pulled her in for a hug.

"I get that a lot. Wait. You mean that in a good way, right?"

"No," he said, and when she gave him a shove he grabbed her hand and held it, not caring one bit who noticed.

"Liar. Hey, do you want some peanuts?"

"No, but I'll pretend so I can eat some," Jeff said with

a laugh and then flagged down the peanut guy to come to their private seats just below the press box. When he looked at her and she smiled, Jeff felt a strong pull of something warm and amazing. In that moment he knew he couldn't picture his life without Cat in it and it hit him that he was absolutely in love with her. He knew it must be love because she was always on his mind. He'd dated and had a couple of serious relationships, but no other woman had ever occupied his thoughts the way Cat did.

He had to admit that being in love felt pretty damned good. While Jeff considered himself a private person, he wanted to stand up, point to Cat Carson, and shout, "I love this girl!" Or better yet, put it up on the scoreboard. Have it written across the sky. The peanut vendor needed to know. Everybody did. His parents . . . his dogs.

"What in the world are you smiling about?" Cat asked.

"Just that . . . Oh my God, Cat . . . duck!" Jeff shouted after he saw the pop-up shoot up over the backstop.

Of course Cat, true to form, looked up instead of ducking. With a little squeal she put her hand up to catch the baseball before it landed on her face. At the last second she decided that her catching plan wasn't smart and ducked her head to the side but kept her hands raised as if by some miracle she might still catch the ball. Jeff lunged for the baseball and caught it just before it smacked her hard. The crowd cheered.

"You can open your eyes now."

"Did you catch it?"

"Yeah, I did."

She opened her eyes and snatched the ball from him. "Awesome!" She raised it above her head while the crowd kept looking their way while cheering.

"You stole my pretzel—now you've stolen my baseball and my thunder!"

"Sorry," she said with a not-sorry shrug.

"Now it's my turn."

"What are you going to steal?"

Jeff moved the bill of her baseball cap to the side. "A kiss," he said and pressed his mouth to hers. When the crowd cheered louder he looked up and saw that they were on the big screen.

"Oh, no—busted." Her eyes widened at Jeff. "Now what? Should I slap you to throw everybody off?"

Jeff felt a pull of disappointment, but then realized she was joking.

Cat pointed a finger at him. "Ha, gotcha."

"No, you didn't."

She tossed a peanut at him. "I certainly did."

"Okay, you got me. A first."

"Ha! Not the last."

"But you should know that having us kissing in public will spread like wildfire in this little town. In less than five minutes my mother will be calling to invite you to Sunday dinner, but not until she complains that she's always the last to know everything." He looked down as his phone beeped.

"Your mom already?"

"No, it's Sara texting me. She's with mom down at the reception barn planting flowers. She says that mom wants to know why she is always the last to know everything. Can I call it or what?"

"You know your family well."

"And I want you to get to know them, Cat. Are you ready to meet the Greenfields?"

Cat popped a peanut shell open. "You want to know a secret?"

"Yes."

"I've wanted to meet your family and see your farmhouse for a while now."

"Really?" Jeff accepted the peanut that she put in his mouth.

"I've been all about you since the moment you saved me from the evil suitcase."

Jeff felt a grin slide across his face. "Really?"

"Stop saying 'really.' Yes."

Jeff reached over and took her hand. He rubbed his thumb over her knuckles and felt a strong pull of longing. "How bad do you want to see the end of this game?"

"Pretty bad."

"Oh . . ."

Cat grinned and then leaned over and whispered in his ear, "But I want to be naked in your arms more."

"Dear God . . . if you keep talking like that I'm going to have to put my baseball cap over what you're doing to me."

Cat laughed.

"It's not funny."

"Yes, it is."

Jeff squeezed her hand. "But it's more than that, you know."

Her smile faded and she looked into his eyes. "Tell me."

Jeff leaned closer, glad that there wasn't anyone sitting next to them in their box seats. "It's more than just caring about you, Cat. I'm falling for you."

She dropped the peanut she was holding but didn't seem to notice. "Like, falling in *love* with me?"

"Yes . . . *No*—I take that back. I'm not falling, Cat."

She frowned. "I wish you hadn't. That was a quick turnaround."

Jeff grinned. "I'm not falling. I've been doing that since the night of the suitcase attack. I'm *in love* with you."

"Then say it."

"Damn the complications." Jeff took her hand. "I love you, Cat. There's no doubt about it."

"I love you too."

"I didn't mean you had to say it back."

"No one makes me do anything. Those days are done." Cat smiled. "You had me at 'Are you hurt?'"

"I still think I need to wrap you in bubble wrap."

Cat laughed. "You just have to shadow me. Save me from the big, bad world of suitcases and baseballs and clowns."

"Clowns?"

"Yeah, don't let one near me."

"I'll do my best."

"That's all I can ask."

"So are you ready to leave?"

Cat grabbed his hand. "I'm ready."

21

I Feel Fine

"YOUR PLACE OR MINE?" CAT SAID AFTER THEY HURRIED to Jeff's truck. "I've always wanted to say that—kinda like 'Follow that car' when I get in a cab."

"I have a feeling you'll say that someday just for shits and giggles, as Sara would say."

"You're getting to know me pretty well." Cat laughed. "And you're still hanging around? Amazing."

"I'm not going anywhere. We're stuck like glue, like the Sugarland song."

Cat started singing it. "But not like the video. I'm not quite as crazy as Jennifer Nettles in that one."

"You're my kind of crazy."

"Oh, you're so sweet," Cat said with a laugh. "Just like the Brantley Gilbert song?"

"You have songs for everything in life, just like me. So I guess I'm kinda crazy too."

"We're such a cute crazy couple," Cat said.

When they stopped at a red light, he looked her way. "Are we?"

"Cute? But of course," Cat said, knowing full well what he meant.

"A couple?"

"I think it's time to make it Facebook official," Cat said with a chuckle but then reached over and put her hand over his. "Yes, Jeff. I want to see where this takes us. And I'm so excited to meet your family," she added, but felt a little flash of insecurity.

"Wait. What's that look?" Jeff asked as he turned down Riverview Lane.

"I guess I'm not used to big family dinners."

"Cat, you and Sara are two peas in a pod, as my mom would say. You'll bond instantly. My brothers Reid and Braden are as nice as they come, and Cody, Sara's husband, is like a brother to me too. Addison is Mia's cousin, so you already know her, right? Plus the grandkids Katie and Leah will take center stage. You'll be fine, trust me."

"I know." Cat rolled her eyes. "Funny that I can sing before thousands of people but something like a Sunday dinner makes me nervous. Am I weird or what?"

"Yes, and before you ask it, I mean that in a good way. Mostly," he added.

Cat pulled a face but then laughed. "I won't deny it. I have some odd insecurity issues."

"And phobias."

"Hey, who isn't afraid of spiders and bats?" She shuddered. "And clowns."

"Me."

"So what are you afraid of, tough guy?"

Jeff shrugged and appeared to consider her question. "I don't know. Growing up on a farm, I had to face just about every kind of animal and insect and lots of snakes. Oh, and big green hornworms on tobacco leaves are pretty gross."

"They sound horrid."

"Sara hated hornworms and so of course I liked to

toss them at her. She was so happy when our mom decided that we would no longer grow tobacco on the back forty. It was a great cash crop, but she hated that it was so harmful so we stopped growing it. We used to hang tobacco in the barn that I turned into the practice studio."

Jeff pulled in front of the cabin and killed the engine. "Cat, I know you had an unconventional childhood, and if you ever want to talk about it just say the word. But my family is going to love you. Just like I do." He reached over and ran a fingertip down her cheek. "You're weird and crazy. You're funny and smart. Gorgeous. And super sexy. And have an amazing voice. I can't get enough of you."

"Ah . . . you say that now."

Jeff rubbed his thumb over her bottom lip, making her toes curl. "I know one thing: I'll never be bored with you around."

"We can agree upon that one," Cat said and waited for him to come around and open her door. The one time she didn't let him Jeff complained that his mother would have his hide. When he opened the door she missed the step down and tumbled into his arms. "I meant to do that."

"And I mean to do this." Jeff tossed both of their baseball caps to the side but she didn't complain. He pushed her up against the truck, bent his head, and kissed her.

Cat put her hands on his wide shoulders, loving the sturdy feel of his muscles. But Jeff's strength went further than physical. When he pulled back, Cat cupped her palms to his cheeks. "You're a good man, Jeff Greenfield."

Jeff smiled. "And remember that a good man is hard to find."

Cat tilted her head to the side. "I thought it was the other way around."

"What?" Jeff asked and then grinned. "I've got ya covered on that one too."

"I was hoping you'd say that," Cat said, and Jeff thought it was adorable when her cheeks turned a pretty shade of pink.

"Well, how about a soak in the hot tub? I do have some rib eyes in the fridge that we can grill and cold beer or wine or I can even make you a martini. Whatever you like. I plan to wait on you hand and foot all day and all night if you'll let me."

"I'll have to think about that one."

"Me waiting on you hand and foot?"

"Are you kidding. That's an offer I can't refuse." Cat squeezed his shoulder. "Oh, I'm down with that. I was thinking about what drink sounded enticing." Jeff took her hand, but Cat held back. "Oh, I don't have a bathing suit here." She pointed up to her cabin. "I should go and—"

"No bathing suits allowed," Jeff interrupted, tugging her forward. "It's against house rules, at least if your name is Cat."

"Or Jeff."

Cat followed Jeff inside and couldn't keep a smile off her face. "This day is so relaxing, so wonderful. Like that Bruno Mars song—'Today I don't feel like doing anything.' It's a total all-drift day." She did a little dip and wave with her hand.

Jeff pulled her into his arms. "Oh, no, that doesn't quite fit. I can think of a couple of things to do, starting with this." He kissed her until Cat clung to his shoulders for support. She felt the ripples of muscle beneath her hands and moaned. She couldn't wait to get him out of his shirt. "So . . . I get to order you around, huh?"

"Definitely." He sucked her earlobe into his mouth, making her shiver. "Your wish is my command."

"Mmm, just like a genie in a bottle?"

"Like that, but you get more than three wishes."

"Off with the shirt!" she ordered and clapped her hands.

Jeff reached down and tugged the T-shirt over his head. "Done."

Cat splayed her hands on his chest and then explored warm skin until she came to the belt buckle of his cargo shorts. She felt his ab muscles clench, and it was a heady feeling to know that she turned him on too. "You're a beautiful man."

"I prefer ruggedly handsome," he said but sucked in a breath when she dipped her fingers beneath his belt, toying, teasing. "Are you going to order me to take off my shorts, I hope?"

"No, I'm going to take them off for you."

"Ah, even better."

"But first let's get the hot tub warmed up. And I decided I want a super-chilled martini."

"You're getting into this bossing-me-around thing, aren't you?"

"You've created a monster." She leaned in and licked a nipple.

"God . . . Cat . . ." he said, but when he reached for her, she took a step backward and he came up with air. "You're killing me."

Cat only laughed. She wanted to work Jeff up into a frenzy, making the anticipation last for both of them. This was the first time in so long that she simply felt free of any obligation and could have a rare day of just having fun. Although she loved the music industry, it could be overwhelming.

"There are big towels in the linen closet in the master bathroom. I'll do as ordered and join you in the hot tub after I make you a kick-ass martini. If we time it right we can watch the sunset and then cook dinner." He arched a dark eyebrow. "Unless you can think of something you want me to do first, like make sweet love to you, for example. Just a suggestion, of course. You're the boss."

Cat gave him an impish grin. "Maybe."

"I'll take that as a yes," Jeff said, but when he took a step in her direction she sprinted for the bathroom, laughing over her shoulder.

Cat's resolve faltered when she took a look at Jeff's big bed sitting there mocking her. She swallowed hard, thinking about calling him—no, *ordering* him to come in and make love to her, but she lifted her chin. "No, anticipation is the word of the day!" she announced and started humming the Carly Simon song. "Is making me wa-a-a-a-a-i-t."

With one last look at the bed, she went into the bathroom and almost shrieked when she looked at her reflection in the mirror. "That just can't be accurate." She reached up and tried to tidy her messy ponytail and wished she had her makeup bag to fix her faded lipstick and eye shadow. "Ew." She had a mustard stain on her shirt that she tried to get out with a damp washcloth, without much luck. "I am such a slob."

A knock on the door made her jump.

"Yes?" She tossed the washcloth down and reached up to smooth her unruly hair.

"Can I come in?"

Cat gave her reflection a frown. "Okay . . ."

Jeff stepped into the bathroom and seemed to fill the small space with his bare chest. "What's taking you so long? Did you find the towels?"

"I haven't looked yet." Cat pointed to her reflection. "Check this out. I'm one hot mess."

Jeff tilted his head and smiled. "You got the hot part right."

"Really?" Cat met his eyes in the mirror. When she saw the admiration, the longing, she felt a warm rush of love for him.

"Are you fishing for compliments?"

"Totally." She waved her fingertips toward her chest. "Have at it."

Jeff wrapped his arms around her. "I love everything about you. I wouldn't change one thing." He kissed her neck but then shook his head. "Wait. There is one thing. . . ."

"My boobs?"

He cupped them in his hands. "Nope, perfection."

"My butt?" She tried to glance over her shoulder but he held her tight.

"Hell no." Jeff shook his head. "You have one sweet bum."

She pointed to her mouth. "My lips? Do I need to have an injection?"

"You'd better not!" Jeff looked so horrified that Cat laughed.

"I wouldn't do that." Cat shuddered at the thought of a needle. "So what, then?"

"You're wearing way too many clothes. I want you naked. In my hot tub. Or in the kitchen. It doesn't matter where."

"I thought I was the boss today?"

"You are." When his hands went beneath her shirt, Cat felt goose bumps and sighed.

"Then take my shirt off." When she clapped her hands twice, he frowned at her in the mirror. "I need to lose the hand clap, right."

"Please."

"But it's so much fun."

"I'll show you fun." A moment later her shirt landed on the tile floor. But Jeff didn't stop there. With a flick of his wrist her bra joined the shirt. His hands, tan against her pale skin, caressed her breasts. Cat watched in the mirror, and when his thumbs circled her nipples her breath caught. "You're right—this is . . . Oh . . ." He kissed the tender part of her neck, driving her wild with his warm mouth, strong hands. "Fun."

And she watched.

Unzipping her shorts, he was able to tug them over

her hips, revealing her new pink-and-black thong that she'd worn for him. With one hand still on her breast, he toyed with the pink lace, moving his fingers beneath the black triangle but staying just above, where she wanted him most. "Are you getting back at me?" she asked, her voice a hot whisper. "For the hand clap?"

"Yes," he said, toying, teasing, until Cat arched her hips in silent invitation.

"You're so mean . . ."

"Raise your arms up and hook your hands around my neck."

"I'm the boss," she protested, but did as she was told. He slid her thong to her thighs and she was fully exposed in the mirror. Her heart thudded and she watched while he touched her, caressed her, dipping his middle finger into her folds. She pressed her head into his shoulder and when he suddenly stopped her entire body throbbed with the need for him to continue. "Jeff . . ."

He raised his head and met her gaze in the mirror. "I want to watch you," he said, and Cat knew he wanted to see her when she climaxed. This was so intimate, so erotic, and when he so slowly, just barely caressed her, it felt as if every nerve ending in her body craved release. He kept up the featherlight tease until her heart hammered, her blood pulsed, and when he finally dipped his finger deep and then stroked her harder in small circles, Cat gasped. "Jeff!"

Her mouth parted and her orgasm washed over her in hot waves of pleasure. She clung to his neck but then he wrapped his arms around her for support. "That was . . . I can't . . . Oh God . . ."

Jeff's low chuckle vibrated against her skin.

"I feel like I'm made of liquid," she said, and her eyes fluttered shut. "Seriously, don't let me slide down the drain."

He chuckled again and nuzzled her neck. "I love you."

Cat opened her eyes and when he lifted his head she

gave him a shaky smile. "I love you too. More than I thought was even possible. I've had people taking advantage of me for a long time and I know I can trust you, believe in you. You make me feel so loved and so very safe. With you I feel like I can be my crazy self and you accept me as I am."

Jeff kissed her cheek and held her tightly. "You can put your trust in me, Cat. I won't let you down. I promise."

"I believe you." She turned around and wrapped herself around him. He held her and then tilted her head and kissed her sweetly.

"Are you ready for that martini?"

"After you make love to me in that big bed of yours."

"Is that an order?"

"Do I have to clap?"

"No!" Jeff laughed and then scooped her up in his arms.

When he gently placed her on the bed, she smiled up at him and then tilted her head to the side.

"What are you thinking, Cat?"

"Just that this past year was so trying, so difficult, but it's led me to being here with you, right here, right now."

Jeff joined her in the bed and gently tucked a lock of hair behind her ear. "Tell me about it, Cat. I want to know your story. I want to know everything about you."

She inhaled a trembling breath. "I was being pushed around, forced to do things I didn't want or believe in. I trusted Matt Stanford, and all he cared about was money. I felt pressure because so many people's livelihood depended upon my success. But I just couldn't live a lie anymore."

"I'd like to kick his ass."

"I still feel guilty sometimes."

"Don't. Cat, I did the same thing when I felt I couldn't leave the farm. You have to be true to yourself. You have to go where you want to go in this life and not where others want you. It isn't fair. And in the end those who love you want you to chase your dream and be happy. Anything else just won't work in the long run."

Cat nodded. "I know. And it's funny, but I wouldn't be here right now if Mia hadn't landed in Cricket Creek. She had to find herself too. I guess we all do at some point."

"This is a special town with hardworking, caring people."

Cat nodded. "I do miss my parents but Cricket Creek feels like where I belong."

"Once they come for a visit maybe they'll move here too. It seems to happen a lot. But if not, we'll have to visit."

"You just want some deep-dish pizza and to go to a Cubs game," Cat teased, but she felt a tug of emotion that he'd said *we* instead of *you*. She smiled, then said, "I command you to remove your pants."

"And if I refuse?"

"Like that's gonna happen," she said and he laughed.

"Good point." A moment later his shorts hit the floor. Cat sighed when Jeff slid his naked body against hers.

"That was a good sigh, right?"

"Of pure bliss," Cat said. "I don't want this day to end," she said and snuggled against him.

"We've got tonight," he sang in her ear and Cat sang the next line.

"Wow, I would love to do that song with you. Dolly Parton and Kenny Rogers did an amazing version. It's timeless. I love it."

"Let's bring it up with Rick and Maria," Jeff agreed, making her wonder whether he was warming up to the duo idea too. Could she possibly be lucky enough not only to fall deeply in love, but to fall in love with someone who could share both her life and her career?

Cat certainly hoped so. But for right now she was going to live in the moment, and as moments went, this one rocked . . .

22
She Loves You

JEFF PULLED OPEN THE DOOR OF MY WAY RECORDS AND was greeted by the smiling face of Teresa Bennett, the receptionist Rick had recently hired.

"Hello, love," Theresa said in her English accent, which never failed to make Jeff grin. "Rick is on a conference call but he'll be with you in a couple of minutes." Teresa also had a great voice and filled in as a studio backup singer when needed. She and Rick went way back to his rock and roll days and Jeff just bet that Teresa had been a bit of a wild child. "Can I get you anything? Coffee?"

"No, thanks." Coffee would only jack up his nerves even more. He inhaled a calming breath and glanced out the window.

"Lovely day outside, don't you agree?" Teresa asked.

Jeff nodded, although in truth he'd been too distracted to notice.

"Am I boring you with my chitchat, love?" She arched one eyebrow and waited.

"Teresa, you know I could listen to that accent of yours all day long," Jeff said and relaxed just a little bit.

"Ha, like you don't have one yourself."

"Not as cool as yours," Jeff said and smiled. "How do you like living in Cricket Creek?" he asked, glad to get his mind off his meeting.

"I need a London fix once in a while but just adore this little town. I'm so glad that I took Rick up on his offer to work at this studio," Teresa said.

"You've got an amazing voice. We're lucky to have you."

"Ah, I go way back with Rick." Teresa shook her head. "Had you asked me fifteen years ago if he and I would end up in Cricket Creek, Kentucky, I would've laughed my ass off. We had some crazy times back then, but it feels good to put down roots and settle in," she said, then picked up the phone. "Rick is ready for you, darling." She gestured toward the door. "If you need anything, let me know."

"Thanks, Teresa."

Jeff opened the door and walked across the plush carpet.

"Hey, Jeff. Thanks for coming in on such short notice. Have a seat."

"No problem." Jeff shook Rick's hand and then sat down in the chair in front of his desk. He knew what this meeting was going to be about, and it made his heart thump hard in his chest.

"Can I get you anything? Water? Soft drink?"

"Teresa already offered." Jeff blew out a sigh. "But is it too soon for a shot of bourbon?"

Rick chuckled. "There was a time in what I like to call my previous life when I would have said hell no and tossed back a shot with you, but those days are done, I'm afraid."

"Well, then, I think I'm good," Jeff answered.

"I guess you know what this is all about."

"Yes." Jeff nodded. "It's decision-making time."

"I'm afraid so." Rick sat up straighter and nodded.

"So here are the facts. The 'Second Chances' duet hit the country *Billboard* charts at ninety-one with a bullet. You and Cat have a hit on your hands and it's starting to get some airplay on Top 40 radio stations, just like Maria and I thought it would. So congratulations. We've got interest in having you two on CMT Insider and Second Cup Café. We're really pumped, Jeff."

"Thanks."

"As you also know, we released the single as Cat Carson and Jeff Greenfield, but as we discussed we're prepared to make you two a duo as Sweet Harmony. Simply put, this can be a onetime release or even an occasional collaboration between you two, and you keep your separate careers . . . or we make Sweet Harmony official."

"What are your thoughts?"

"I think you know, but I'll say it again." Rick leaned forward and pressed his fingertips together. "You are both great artists on your own, but you two have the potential for something really special together. We spotted that from the beginning and nothing has changed. Not to mention, this industry is ready for a hot male-and-female duo right now. The timing is right, Jeff, and that doesn't always happen. This isn't just about talent. You're in the right place at the right time."

"But South Street Riot is divided. It could break the band up if I do this." Jeff felt so torn that it had been keeping him up at night.

"It shouldn't break you up, but I understand strong personalities and ego all too well."

"I can't really blame them," Jeff said. "I brought these guys back together with a definite plan in mind. And you know that Christy has interest from Shane McCray for us to open for him, but as Jeff Greenfield and South Street Riot, not Sweet Harmony. Rick, it's our dream and the goal we've been working toward. Shane McCray has been my idol all my life. How can I turn my back on that, especially with this being his farewell tour? But you know all of this already."

Rick scrubbed a hand down his face. "Yeah, I do. That's why we're having this conversation." He paused and said, "And it's no secret that you and Cat are seeing each other."

"It's not."

"I'm just going to ask point-blank because we're family around here. Are you in love with her?"

"Yes, I am." Jeff no longer felt the need to hide it.

"That raises additional complications. I don't mean to be a Debbie Downer, but if things happen to, well, go south, it can really get dicey trying to work together, especially on the road. I've seen it happen."

"No doubt." Jeff couldn't even fathom ending his relationship with Cat, but the cold, hard reality was that it could happen.

"I guess you have to weigh your options and think about how much of a risk you're willing to take. Individual careers are the safe way to proceed. And maybe a collaboration here and there. But you don't seem like a play-it-safe kind of guy."

"You're right, and I have the scars to prove it."

"And would you take the chances all over again?"

"That's how country boys roll," Jeff admitted. "But this is different."

Rick shrugged. "In some ways. With big risks come big rewards."

"So have you talked to Cat about this?"

"Yes."

"So, can I ask what Cat's answer to this is? I mean, when we first met we discussed how we both wanted control of our careers. This opportunity was so unexpected."

"Honestly, that's how this industry works. Sudden opportunities. A door opens. Rascal Flatts is an example.

Jay and Gary are from Columbus, Ohio, and by chance they met up with Joe Don from Picher, Oklahoma, while playing a gig at a club in Printer's Alley in Nashville. They immediately knew they had something special and the rest, as they say, is history. Of course, song choice certainly helped. Tyler Hubbard and Bryan Kelley of Florida Georgia Line met through mutual friends while attending college in Nashville. They skyrocketed to stardom with the crossover hit 'Cruise.' That song is the best-selling digital country single ever. Those guys simply exploded onto the scene. I think you and Cat have the same kind of potential because you have old-school appeal but with a fresh, young twist. And you have chemistry."

"It would really help to know how Cat feels so I know what to expect when I approach her with this decision. We really haven't talked about it all that much. I suppose we should have but I guess we were afraid that it might come between us and so we pretty much tabled it for the time being. But I guess we always knew that time would run out. While I know it's mutually beneficial, like you said, if it's not what we ultimately want, it could destroy us in more ways than one. Can you give me a hint?"

Rick shook his head. "It might not seem fair not to answer about Cat's reaction, but I want you to be honest with yourself. And I also want you to be selfish right now. I know it doesn't seem like it, but this is about what you want, Jeff, not what your band members want or even what Cat wants."

"I don't know how I can separate those considerations. I care about my band, my friends. And I love Cat."

"Well, you know my story. I made the decision to do what everybody wanted me to do years ago and it was flat-out wrong. The old saying goes that if you try to please everybody, you'll please nobody. Please yourself. Go with your heart and *your* gut."

"Yeah, but the problem is that my heart and gut are

conflicted. That's why I resisted getting involved with Cat to begin with. I mean, I'll just be honest."

Rick stood up and walked over to the window. He gazed at the view for a moment and then turned around. "Then I'll be honest too. I don't think your heart and gut are conflicted, because the two are connected. I think you're feeling guilty that this is tearing your band apart."

"Rick, we've been friends all my life. We started South Street Riot back in high school. They're like brothers to me."

"I get that. But I want to be clear. This isn't about money or fame either. Trust me, neither of those things will make you happy. You don't want to play a role in your life and look back and wonder who in the hell that person even was. My choices ruined my marriage and nearly destroyed my relationship with my son. And the cold, hard fact is that you can't go back and get what's already gone."

"You're not making this easy." Jeff really wanted that shot of bourbon.

"Because it isn't easy. And unfortunately I can't make you any promises or give you any guarantees, no matter what road you choose. But you have to give me an answer."

Jeff closed his eyes for a moment and then rubbed his damp hands on his jeans. "You also have to know that this will affect my relationship with Cat, no matter what I decide."

"Yes." Rick chewed on the inside of his bottom lip and then said, "You know, people envy those of us who are in the arts because we get to do what we love for a living. And they would be right. But the downside is that, because it's a passion, part of who we are, it's never gone from our brain. There isn't any real downtime. To do something that's all-consuming, you have to love it. If not, you should run like hell."

"My parents are like that with farming. They could

have sold out to a big corporation or sold the land to a developer and not had to work another day in their lives, but farming is in their blood."

"It's not easy to love something so much," Rick said. "Or someone . . ." He paused to look out the window again. "Look, take the rest of the day to make a decision."

"What should be the defining factor? If I knew what Cat thought about all this, it would be easier. I mean, what if I decide to go for Sweet Harmony and she's not on board? Can't you give me some direction? A hint?"

"Sorry, Jeff, but this is all you. Hey, if you want to talk to her about it, go ahead. But know what you want first. Then talk to Cat and your band."

Jeff stood up and then shoved his fingers through his hair. "Well, this is clear as mud."

"I think it's clearer than you know right about now."

"Care to elaborate?"

"Well, I built this recording studio in Cricket Creek because I fell in love with Maggie McMillan."

"And Noah built the baseball stadium. Mitch Monroe built Wedding Row for Nicolina. You guys are a hard act to follow."

"When you love somebody with all your heart, you'll move mountains to be with them."

"Or hike up a mountain to save her," Jeff said.

"Cat?"

"She finds herself in crazy situations on a regular basis," he said with a soft chuckle.

"Let me guess . . . and you like coming to her rescue? Don't even try to deny it. It's written all over your face."

"I've been getting that a lot lately."

"Because you're in love. It's pretty damned hard to hide."

"Yeah, I like coming to Cat's rescue." Jeff walked over to gaze out the window with Rick. He grinned when he spotted Maggie sitting on a bench reading a book. "Ah, so that's the scenery you've been looking at?"

"I'm lucky to have Maggie by my side. It sure took me a long-ass time to get it right. And now that I have my son Garret back in my life, everything else is just gravy."

Jeff looked at Rick. "I haven't seen Garret in a while."

"He's in Nashville scouting for talent."

"Pretty cool job, making someone's dream come true. I remember singing for tips and wondering how I was going to pay the rent. But there was something fun about playing to small crowds and just having a blast without all of the pressure."

"Yeah, I agree. Some of my fondest memories were just playing for friends." He sighed. "Once you have to go on the road it's hard to keep the magic. When all of the business crap gets in the way and you wake up not sure what city you're in, remember the joy your music brings to people and you'll never get burned out. I can't imagine a day without music and neither can most people. Remember that, okay?" He clamped a hand on Jeff's shoulder. "And I'm always around for you to bend my ear, day or night."

"Thanks, Rick." He reached over and shook his hand.

"Now you've got some thinking to do."

"I'll get back to you later."

"Fair enough."

After Jeff left the studio he thought about heading to his cabin but ended up sitting on the front porch of his parents' farmhouse. He thought of Miranda Lambert's song "The House That Built Me," and realized it was so true. No matter how lost or confused he was, sitting on this front porch somehow cleared his head and brought him answers.

Jeff sat down on the swing and moved slowly back and forth, waiting for a sense of peace to settle over his jumbled emotions. He looked out over the front yard and smiled at the big oak tree that he'd climbed as a kid. The tire swing was still there waiting for the grandchildren to get big enough to use. He inhaled a deep breath of air filled with his mother's flowers mixed with the rich, deep scent of turned-up earth.

When he heard the screen door creak open, Jeff looked up and smiled at his mother.

"Well, I heard a truck pull up, but I didn't expect to see you, Jeffrey." She wiped her hands on her apron stained with something red. "I was in the middle of making some strawberry freezer jam."

Jeff stood up and gave his mother a kiss. "Don't let me leave without some of Susan Greenfield's legendary jam."

"I won't. I'm glad to see you, but you looked troubled. Everything okay?" She sat down in the white wicker rocker and looked at him expectantly.

"I've just got some career decisions to make."

"Ah, can't help you there." She smiled. "But I can tell you that we're all so very proud of you, Jeffrey."

"Thank you, Mom."

"Ah, sweetie. I wish we had encouraged you sooner."

Jeff shook his head. "No, I'm glad that I stayed and worked the farm when you needed me most. Don't give that another thought." He moved his arm in an arc. "I was just thinking that my family, this farm, made me who I am. I don't have any regrets and I don't want you to either."

Her eyes filled with tears and since he mother rarely cried Jeff felt the impact of her emotion. "Thank you for that. Your father and I have felt a sense of guilt for a while."

"Well, then look at it this way. Because I waited, I ended up with My Way Records right here in Cricket Creek. So see? Everything worked out for the best."

She sniffed and then shot him a bright smile. "And you met Cat Carson. You're bringing her to Sunday dinner, right? I think I'll make a nice pot roast."

"Yes," Jeff replied. "And she's a little bit nervous."

"What? Of us?"

Jeff swung back and forth. "Cat and I are from way different backgrounds. She's an only child. A bit sheltered, I think."

His mother shrugged. "*Pfft.* We're all just people." She played with the hem of her apron and then said, "I'm guessing that this visit has a lot to do with whether you team up with Cat or stay a front man with South Street Riot. And you're trying to understand how loving her fits into the equation."

"Wow . . . you just nailed it."

"It wasn't all that hard to figure out."

"How do you know I'm in love?" Jeff asked and then raised his palms. "Wait. Are you going to tell me it's written all over my face?" He really had to do something about that face-reading thing.

"No, Sara told me. She and Reid might be twins, but I think she understands you more than anybody does. And of course nobody understands Braden."

"Have he and Ronnie been butting heads again?"

"Braden says she spends too much time working at her candy store. The girl is trying to build a business! He can be so hardheaded sometimes. If he's not careful, he's gonna lose her and she's a keeper as far as I can tell."

"Braden just needs to grow up a little bit. He's the baby, Mom. We all spoiled him."

"True. But hey, we were talking about you. Have you made a decision?"

"No. So what do I do, Mom?" He looked across the yard and over to the barn. "I have so many what-ifs running through my brain it isn't even funny."

"Sorry, but you get the worry gene from me. Your father is a more go-with-the-flow kind of guy."

"That's why you complement each other."

"Ah, and why we butt heads. Relationships aren't easy. Love isn't easy. Life isn't easy, for that matter." Susan lifted her palms upward. "And farming sure as shootin' isn't easy."

"I won't argue."

"You boys never did argue with me. Ah, but Sara argued enough for the rest of you put together."

"So do you have any motherly advice?"

"Of course I do." She reached over and patted his knee. "Make the choice that means the most to you."

Jeff blinked at his mother. "Say that again."

Susan smiled. "Make the choice that means the most to you. Not the easy one." She tapped her chest. "The one that touches you right here."

"So it's that simple?" It sure didn't feel like it.

"You have to consider everything very carefully. But in the end, yes. Yes, it is." She brushed at another rare tear. "Your father and I were faced with some tough decisions about this farm. We could have sold it, Jeff, and we could be sitting in Florida basking in the sunshine fishing and playing shuffleboard. That was the easy choice."

"I know."

"But now we have Old MacDonald's, where Sara and your father get to teach children about the importance of respecting the land. And Sara has the beautiful barn weddings, which are such a blessing for this town." She pointed to the tire swing. "And soon I'll have grandbabies big enough to play in the yard. This old farmhouse might be a money pit but I simply love it." She put a hand to her chest and closed her eyes. "And I'm so glad that we held on to it all. It wasn't the easy choice, but it was the one that meant the most to us."

"So if I choose what means the most to me, the rest will fall into place?"

Susan shook her head. "No, sorry. It's not nearly that pain-free. Once you make your choice you have to work at it, fight for it, and *put* everything in its place, Jeffrey. The key to a fulfilling life is waking up every day with a sense of purpose. A goal." She waited to let him digest her comment. "So, what is your goal with this singing career? Is it making money? Having a number one song?"

"Well, that's high up there on the list," Jeff said, but he knew full well where his mother was going with this.

"When I watched you and Cat sing at Sully's, I looked around the room and saw the joy on the faces of the audience. Everyone was having such a good time. And you have the ability to do that for people. It reminded me of when you'd get your guitar and sit here on the porch and play for us and your friends after a hard day's work."

"I was just talking to Rick Ruleman about how I loved those good ol' days."

"You're too young to have good ol' days," she scoffed, but then her eyes misted over. "Oh, I do miss those days, though. Sometimes it seems like it was just yesterday when you were in diapers. And you used to like to chase bees, you silly thing."

"I always did like to flirt with danger."

"And now you flirt with Cat Carson."

Jeff chuckled. "Like I said, I like to flirt with danger."

"Cat doesn't seem dangerous."

"No, but she likes to get into dangerous situations." As Jeff recounted Cat's failed attempt to break into her cabin, his mother was in stitches.

"Oh my. Well, never a dull moment with that one. She reminds me a little bit of Sara."

"You're right."

"I usually am. Just ask your father."

Jeff laughed. "I'm so glad I stopped by. I knew you would help."

"I miss you, sweetie. Like I said, time has just flown by, it seems. I woke up one day and you were all adults." She raised her hands skyward. "How does that even happen?"

"Time flies when you're having fun."

Susan grinned. "More like time flies when you work your tail off. But music . . . songwriting and singing? It's a gift you have. Use it wisely." She tipped her head to the side. "I don't know where you got it, though. Neither your father nor I can carry a tune in a bucket."

Jeff laughed. "I love you, Mom."

"Even if I can't sing?"

"Unconditionally."

"Oh, Jeffrey, I hope I helped if only a little bit." She put her finger and thumb an inch apart. "It was much easier when I could fix your problems with a Band-Aid and a purple Popsicle."

"You helped me more than you realize," he said and felt a warm rush of emotion.

"Just know that we love you and we will always be here for you. You can count on that if all else fails."

"I know. And believe me, that helps too." Jeff stood up. "But I'll never turn down a purple Popsicle." He stretched the kinks out of his neck. "I need to get going."

When his mother stood up, Jeff pulled her in for a hug. She smelled like strawberries and felt like the warm love that only a mother could give.

"I'm so glad you stopped by. Your dad is going to be sorry he missed you. Of course, he would have been quiet and nodded while I chattered away. I might be a firecracker, but that man is a rock."

"I knew where I needed to come. No matter where I go, it always feels good to come home." He chuckled. "How come I didn't know you were so smart back when I was a teenager?"

She pointed at him. "Good question. I could have saved you a lot of trouble." She laughed. "Of all the children, you really are the daredevil." She pointed a finger at him. "You always had to learn the hard way, as your father would tell you."

"I'm a hands-on kind of learner." Jeff kissed his

mother on the cheek. "I'll be here on Sunday with Cat. And save me some of that jam."

"Will do."

Jeff left the farmhouse chock-full of the sense of purpose his mother talked about. He loved Cat. And he couldn't imagine not choosing to team up with her for Sweet Harmony. After all, Rick Ruleman and Maria Sully were legends in the music industry. He needed to listen to them. The thought of singing, recording, and traveling with her made him smile.

But it wasn't going to be easy telling the band his decision. The very thought made his stomach churn. "Choose the one that means the most to you," Jeff repeated. When he got in his truck he realized he'd left his phone sitting on the middle console. The screen blinked with a missed call from Snake. Jeff thought about calling him back, but he didn't want to clutter his brain with anything else before talking to Cat. Snake could wait.

Jeff pulled his truck into his own driveway and then walked up the road to Cat's cabin. He raised his hand to knock on the front door, but then he heard her singing. Jeff followed the sweet sound around the porch and then stopped in his tracks. Cat sat cross-legged in the middle of the deck, strumming on her guitar. She wore faded jeans, a white tank top, and as usual her feet were bare. The messy bun perched on top of her head slid a little bit sideways when she tilted her head and strummed a few more chords. With a sigh she picked up a notepad and wrote a few lines and then bent her head back to her task.

And then she sang.

Her voice, pure and sweet, washed over Jeff like warm summer rain. Closing his eyes, he lifted his face as if to catch the beauty of the words sliding across the breeze to swirl around him. Soft and sultry, she sang about love lost but then found somewhere on the edge of the ocean. Jeff swallowed hard and suddenly realized that she was combining her love of the sand and the sea with something deeper and meaningful. He could feel her passion, hear her emotion, and he smiled. Cat Carson was finding her true voice.

Jeff shook his head, pissed at himself for dismissing her talent as fluff and unworthy of his listening. What a snob he'd been. And how damned stupid was Matt Stanford for letting such talent go? But then with a grin Jeff thought he should give the man a call and thank him, because his stupidity had brought Cat to Cricket Creek and to the cabin next to his.

Jeff took a step forward but Cat started singing again. Afraid of interrupting her creative moment, he stood still and listened. In his head, he harmonized with her.

Sweet harmony.

Yes.

When she bent her head forward, she exposed the gentle curve of her neck. Jeff wanted to put a kiss on that vulnerable spot. And he wanted to kiss her bare shoulder. He wanted to make love to her, outside, on the deck with nature all around. He wanted her soft sighs to blend with the breeze while she wrapped her legs around him. . . .

And a groan escaped his mouth.

Cat raised her head and their eyes met. She put her guitar to the side and watched him approach. Neither of them spoke when he sat down next to her and pulled her onto his lap.

When she wrapped her arms around his neck, Jeff kissed her, and passion ignited like a match dropped in dry straw.

Their tongues met, tangled, dipped, tasted, and savored. Jeff kissed her hotly, deeply. He wanted her with an intensity that blew him away. They spoke, but not with words.

A quick gasp.

A low moan.

A soft sigh.

Cat threaded her fingers in his hair and leaned back, giving him access to her breasts, free from a bra. He licked through the thin cotton, making the material wet, and when her nipple pebbled beneath his tongue he sucked it into his mouth. He cupped her other breast in his hand and when he heard her breath catch he nibbled lightly. With a little cry of pleasure she pressed his head closer and then moved seductively against him.

Needing more, Jeff tugged her shirt over her head and then slid his tongue against her soft, warm skin until she gasped. "I want you naked."

"I want me naked." She fumbled with the snap on her jeans, laughing breathlessly until he helped. She turned sideways, knocking over her glass of tea but letting it roll.

Leaning over, Jeff helped her shed her jeans and made quick work of removing his own clothes. An instant later she straddled him once more. He arched upward and she sank down, gasped, and their moans blended together. She gripped his shoulders and Jeff let her set the slow and steady pace that had his heart pounding. He understood. She wanted to make this last, let the pleasure rise, build like the crescendo in music.

As she moved faster, Jeff braced his hands on the wooden deck and then leaned back so he could watch the play of emotion on her face. When she bit her bottom lip and moaned deeply, Jeff thought he'd never seen a more beautiful sight. Leaning forward, he wrapped his arms around her while pleasure ripped through him.

Her thighs trembled and she collapsed against him, putting her head on his shoulder. Jeff held her tightly, thinking he never wanted to let her go.

Finally, she spoke. "Jeff, I didn't expect . . ." she began, but he put a fingertip to her lips.

"Don't worry—it's totally private here. And that was amazing. You're amazing." He smiled. "Let's go inside. I want to ask you something."

She nodded but then leaned her head against his chest. "There's something I want to tell you too." Her voice, though muffled, against his chest sounded emotional. He pulled back and looked into her eyes.

An odd feeling settled in Jeff's stomach, but he nodded. "Okay."

Cat leaned in and kissed him softly, sweetly, but her smile trembled at the corners. He knew he must be overreacting, but the kiss felt like . . .

Good-bye.

23

Ticket to Ride

CAT TUGGED HER CLOTHES ON AS QUICKLY AS SHE COULD manage with shaking fingers. She could feel Jeff's confusion radiating off him but she shook it off. She shouldn't have fallen into his arms, but she just couldn't help it. All it took was just one kiss. She'd rehearsed what she was going to say, but now the words seemed to stick in her throat. But she knew she was doing the right thing. Wasn't she? Then why did it hurt so much?

"Can I get you something? Water? Sweet tea?"

"Bourbon?" His smile appeared strained.

"Actually, I think I have a bottle." She looked in the pantry on the shelf where she kept liquor and reached for a bottle of Buffalo Trace. "You want it neat? Over ice? Mixed with Coke?"

"Southern boys don't mix good bourbon with Coke," Jeff said. "Two fingers and a couple of cubes of ice, please."

"Coming right up." Cat nodded, then poured one for him and one for herself. They each took a sip in silence.

"So I guess what you're going to tell me has something to do with the suitcase sitting in the living room."

Cat took another sip, licked her bottom lip, and nodded. "I have some business out of town."

Jeff nodded to a formal dress draped over the back of
the sofa. "Doesn't look a lot like business."

Cat shrugged but didn't want to elaborate. The fact
that she was going to sing at a wedding for a woman who
might not live to see her first anniversary was neither
here nor there where all this was concerned. In fact, letting him think the worst might help the situation right
now. The stormy look in his eyes made her heart clench,
but she pressed forward knowing that this was breaking
them up. But she'd rather do it now than later, when he
missed his band and blamed her for it. Plus, Jax was right.
Opening for Shane McCray was a huge honor and their
dream until she'd waltzed into Cricket Creek and threw
a monkey wrench into the whole plan. No . . . she had to
do this. Inhaling a bracing breath, she took another sip
of the bourbon and then said, "I had a talk with Maria
and Rick this morning about our collaboration."

Jeff looked at her in silence. "And?"

Cat took a bigger swallow of bourbon, letting the
burn slide all the way to her stomach. "I . . . I know that
'Second Chances' is shooting up the charts, and I'm so
thrilled." She inhaled a shaky breath, unable to get the
next words past her lips.

"Me too. Go on," Jeff prompted.

"In spite of that, I've given it careful thought and I've
decided that I want to keep my career separate," she
said, wondering how she kept her voice from cracking.

Jeff looked down at his glass and then back over at
her. "Why?"

Cat hesitated. "You know why."

"I think you need to enlighten me."

"Okay." She was so damned bad at lying, but she
couldn't tell him that when she started to walk into the
studio for her meeting with Rick and Maria she'd overheard Jax Pike telling the rest of South Street Riot that

hell would freeze over before he would become part of Sweet Harmony. He'd gone on to say he'd rather dig ditches, which quite frankly she thought was going a bit overboard. Snake started arguing and Colin had to come between them and break up what looked like it could turn physical. She replayed the exchange in her head once more:

"Shane McCray wants Jeff Greenfield and South Street Riot, not some lame-ass Sweet fucking Harmony. I mean, seriously? We're dudes," Jax had nearly shouted. "Who has a name like that?"

"Well, Sugarland and Lady Antebellum are names of successful bands that come to mind," Colin had pointed out. "And we would still be South Street Riot, Jax."

"So, you suggesting we turn Shane down?" Jax argued. "It's our dream. Well, it *was* our dream until Cat Carson came along. I mean, I have nothing against her. In fact, I like her. I just don't want to do this. I *won't* do this."

"Are you forgetting about the megahit record they have right now?" Snake said. "That we have right now?"

"Yeah, well, we could have sold out a long time ago with some pop-sounding crap but we stuck to our guns. I'm still sticking to mine," Jax said flatly. "All I want to do is what we set out to do. Why am I the bad guy here?"

Cat's heart pounded just thinking about it again. She wasn't about to be the reason that South Street Riot broke up. The thought that Jeff could later hold her responsible made her feel almost ill.

"Cat?" Jeff prompted, drawing her back to the present. "Are you going to answer me?"

Cat wished she could be honest and tell him what she'd overheard, but that would likely cause even more internal drama. No, she needed to bow out before all hell broke loose. She tucked a lock of hair behind her ear, hoping he didn't see her fingers tremble. "I already did. I want to be Cat Carson. Not . . . not Sweet Harmony."

Thank God she got that out without bursting into tears—once she started crying, it was always quite the event. "And I have to . . . um . . . get going soon, so . . ."

"Are you kidding me?" Cat saw a muscle jump in Jeff's jaw. "What just happened out there on the deck, Cat?" He shoved his fingers through his hair.

Cat's mouth moved but no words came out.

"I thought we loved each other. I just told my mother I was going to ask you to Sunday dinner."

Cat felt as if her heart was physically getting ripped from her chest. "I'll be out of town Sunday."

"Where are you going?"

"To a wedding."

He glanced over at the dress that she was going to sing in. "Wait. . . . so do you have a date?"

"I . . ." She tried but faltered.

"I guess that means yes? God. I'm such a flaming idiot. So was this just fun and games to you? Are you even staying in Cricket Creek?"

"I . . . I don't know." She hadn't thought past not wrecking his career, his dream. "Jeff, don't you see that this is easier this way?" She wondered why he didn't mention the offer to open for Shane McCray.

"Wow." Jeff tossed back the rest of the bourbon. "Well, you sure had me fooled." He slammed the glass down with a hard clink and then turned toward the door. He stopped when his hand was on the doorknob. If he turned around Cat knew she would fly into his arms and deal with the consequences later. But he twisted the handle and walked out the door.

And out of her life?

Cat stood there, stunned. She knew this was going to be hard, but the pain that ripped through her was more than she could bear. And then, with a soft cry of complete anguish, she sank to the floor. With her head cradled in her hands, she started sobbing. Had she lost her ever loving mind? She loved Jeff so completely, but changing the course of his career, crushing his plans and the chance of a lifetime just wasn't something she could do. And she could not—*would not*—come between him and his band, his best friends. So she needed to let him think the worst. She shouldn't have made love to him, but she wanted that in her memory bank to fall back on on days when she missed him the most.

Cat raised her head and swiped at her tears. She was a noisy, messy, *leaky* crier, but she decided she needed to get up and get herself under control. She had a wedding to sing at in Nashville tomorrow night and she should hit the road soon. Maybe after that she should keep heading south until the map turned blue. "Yes, the beach will help cheer me up," she said, inhaling a shaky breath, but in truth she knew that nothing could cheer her up. She had just pushed the man she loved out of her life.

She wiped her eyes with the edge of her T-shirt and winced when she saw tracks of mascara. But when she looked at the suitcase, it reminded her of the night she and Jeff had met, and she started blubbering all over again.

A moment later she heard pounding on her front door. Her heart skipped a beat. Was Jeff coming back? "Dear God, I am one hot mess. He can't see me like this!"

Cat tried to scramble to her feet but she failed and sort of stumbled toward the door, which suddenly swung open.

"Cat?" Maria hurried over and grabbed Cat's arm. "What's wrong? You smell like bourbon. Are you drunk?"

"No, but that's a dandy idea." She sank to the floor in a fresh heap of tears and Maria sat down beside her.

"Oh, sweetie, what's wrong?" She patted her on the head and the kind gesture made Cat cry even harder.

"I . . . I . . . I . . . told Jeff that I didn't want to do Sweet Harmony because I wanted my career separate"—she paused for three short sniffs—"and that I was moving aaaaa . . . waaaay."

"Why on earth did you do such a thing?"

"Be . . . because his band was going to break up over the whole thing and on . . . on . . . on top of that, Shane McCray wants Jeff and South S-Street R-Riot to o-open for h-him." She raised her head from her knees and looked at Maria. "I—I h-had no choice," she said in a voice filled with doom and lots of gloom.

"There are always choices."

"N-never the right ones."

"Okay, you have to stop."

"Making the wrong choices? I knoooow."

"No, I mean you have to stop crying so we can figure this out."

"I c-can't. I g-get like this wh-when I cry. It's m-messy." She looked at Maria but then sat up straighter and gulped. "Wait. Maria, are you . . . Have *you* been c-crying too?"

"*Pffft.*" Maria waved a dismissive hand. "Of course not."

"Really?" Cat narrowed her eyes and looked closer. "Yes, you have. Your mascara is smeared and you are always, like, perfect."

"I had something fly into my eye. A bug or something—" Maria insisted but her comment ended with a tiny sniff giving her away.

"What?" Cat brought her knees up to her chest and let out a shaky sigh. "Tell me."

"This requires a little nip of that bourbon of yours," Maria said, but when Cat made a clumsy attempt to stand up Maria put a hand on her shoulder. "Stay here. I'll get it."

"'Kay."

A moment later Maria returned with the glasses of bourbon. "Do you want to sit on the sofa instead of leaning against it on the floor?"

Cat didn't even consider it. "No, this is the position of

sadness. When I have a crying jag I have to do it some-
place uncomfortable. It's usually on the bathroom floor
so I don't have far to go if I have to pee."

"Smart thinking," Maria said with a tired half chuckle
and then joined her.

Cat took a sip of her drink. "So, Maria, what's wrong?"

"Pete asked me to marry him. He even had a—" She
swallowed and then said, "A ring."

"Ohmigosh! So those were happy tears? I love happy
tears." Cat put a hand to her chest. "That's wonderful.
Let me see," Cat said, but then frowned at Maria's empty
ring finger. "Oh . . . you said no? Are you serious?"

"Yep." Maria looked at the amber liquid in her glass
and then took a healthy gulp. She coughed and nodded.
"Sure did."

"But you love him."

"I do."

"And he obviously adores you."

"Yes."

"Then I don't get it. Why not make it official? You
wouldn't even have to change your name," Cat said with
a small smile.

Maria crossed her ankles and leaned against the back
of the sofa. She looked up at the ceiling as if trying to
find a way to explain. After taking another sip of bourbon she said, "It's not getting remarried to him that is the
issue." She sucked her bottom lip in and then sighed.
"It's moving back into the house—*our house*, as Pete
calls it. We sort of argued over it and I left."

"Why?" Cat asked, even though she already kind of
understood. But she wanted Maria to be able to talk this
out.

"Because Pete hasn't changed hardly anything since
the day I left. It's like walking back in time. I mean, Cat,
it brings back so many memories and some of them are
so painful. And the good memories? Where do I file
those?"

"So did you tell Pete this?"

"Yes, and he said that it's our home and it's his dream to have me come back and live there. Cat . . . I just *can't*."

"Well, surely that's not a deal killer, though, right? I mean, move somewhere else."

"Pete loves that house."

Cat put her hand on Maria's knee and squeezed. "I think he loves that house because it reminded him of you. When you were gone he still had bits and pieces of you everywhere. But, Maria, now he has you back, so he doesn't need the house. He probably doesn't realize that. I mean, did you talk this out or did you just get girl-crazy emotional on him?"

"A little bit of the first part and a lot of that last part."

"Like, storming-out girl crazy?"

"Yes." She closed her eyes and blew out a bourbon-scented sigh. "But why didn't he come after me, Cat? I mean, why doesn't he just come after me?"

As if on cue the front door opened.

And Pete walked in.

24
I Need You

"I SOLD THE HOUSE," PETE ANNOUNCED AND WATCHED FOR Maria's reaction.

"Wh-what?" Maria blinked at him and then looked at her glass, as if wondering whether she'd heard him correctly.

"I sold the house to Clint and Ava," Pete explained. "They are thrilled."

"When did this happen?"

"On my drive over here. I followed you after you left, and, by the way, you drive like a maniac. I'm just sayin'."

"I was in a mood—"

"That's no excuse to have a lead foot. You need to slow down."

When Maria opened her mouth as if to argue, Cat said, "He's right."

"Yes but you—"

"Maria, just hear the man out, for Pete's sake . . . Ha-ha, get it?" When he saw Cat's discreet nudge with her elbow he almost grinned.

"And you, Pete? Are you thrilled about *selling* the house?" Maria asked.

Pete walked over to where Maria sat with Cat, who watched them back and forth like a Ping-Pong match. "Yes," Pete stated firmly. "Our house stays in the family, but I know they will remodel and make it their own. And if Clint and Ava hadn't bought it, then I would have called Maggie to list it."

"You would?" She craned her neck to look up at him. "Why?"

"For you, Maria. Because I love you more than that house and more than Sully's Tavern. I love you more than anything."

"Oh, Pete . . ."

"I will live in a damned igloo if you want to."

"Well . . . no."

Pete grinned. "Well, that's a relief."

"Although with my hot flashes an igloo holds some appeal. Why didn't you say this earlier?"

"Um, maybe because you stormed the hell out. Like this—" Pete jutted his chin out, puffed his chest, and made his boots click on the floor.

Cat giggled and got a look from Maria. "Oh, come on, that was pretty accurate, I'm guessing."

"It was spot-on." Pete walked closer and offered his hand to Maria. "I'd sit down with you but it might take a crane to hoist me back up."

Maria grasped his hand and then stood there with her hands on his chest. "I don't know what to say."

"Tell him that you love him," Cat advised from her seated position.

"More advice from the peanut gallery?" Maria asked.

"Hello—apparently you need it," Cat said.

"Apparently I do," Maria agreed and then smiled up at Pete. "I love you, Pete Sully. But I want to start fresh. And when we started to argue, it brought back fear—and losing you all over again isn't something I could deal with."

"You won't ever have to." Pete shook his head and then cupped her chin. "Maria, we will disagree. And I can be a pain in the ass. But I won't let you run out of my life ever again. I will pack up my bags and come with you just like we talked about. So if you run away, I'm running with you."

"Can I come too?" Cat asked. "Will we go to Mexico and ride donkeys? Wear big floppy hats?"

Maria laughed.

"I'm not kidding," he said and felt his eyes mist over. "I will follow you to the ends of the earth." There was a time when he would have suppressed tears, but not now. He let them slide down his cheeks. "I am dead-ass serious." He pulled her in for a hug. He kissed the top of her head and said, "We need to call Jason Craig and have him design our dream house. Maggie can start looking for some land down by the river not far from the studio." He reached in his pocket and pulled out the diamond and sapphire ring. "And I want you to marry me, Maria. Please say yes. It's the third time I've asked. Hopefully it's the charm."

"Yes!" she shouted and started crying too. When he slipped the ring onto her finger she put her hand over her mouth and then turned to show Cat.

"Finally, happy tears!" Cat swiped at her eyes too. "I love happy tears!"

Pete reached down and helped Cat to her feet. "Group hug," he said gruffly. "And now, Cat Carson, we need to fix whatever is making you so sad. Tell me about it." He gestured to the sofa. "But we have to discuss it while sitting on real furniture."

Cat held up her empty glass. "I need a refill and then you can help me straighten out the mess I've made of my life. Or we can switch to ice cream. I'm clumsy enough without getting tipsy."

"Coming right up." Pete nodded. "I think I'm the poster child for messing up. But it's never too late to fix things. Isn't that what the hit song of yours is all about? Second chances?"

The mention of the hit song seemed to bring upon distress. "I'll go search for the ice cream."

"Just bring pints and spoons," Maria suggested.

A few minutes later Pete was sitting on the sofa next to Maria while Cat sat cross-legged on a big overstuffed leather chair.

"Rocky road." Cat pointed to the carton and shook her head. "Oh, the irony of it all." She dipped her spoon and took a big scoop. "You tell Pete what's going on, Maria. I need the ice cream fix. But this stays between us, okay?" She twirled her finger in a circle.

Pete nodded. "Of course." He listened to Maria as she explained Cat's dilemma.

"Well?" Cat asked. "It's that whole rock-and-a-hard-place kind of thing."

Pete had opted for bourbon over the ice cream. He didn't indulge often but this was a special circumstance. After a sip he said, "Are you kidding me? The answer is so simple."

Cat shoved her spoon into the ice cream, making it stick straight up in the air. "Go on."

"You know who Shane McCray's idol was, right?" He gave Maria a look and her eyes widened.

"Ohmigod . . ." Maria gasped and then looked over at Cat.

"The suspense is making my ice cream melt," Cat said. "Pul-*ease*!"

"Johnny Cash," Pete answered.

Cat frowned as if not really following, but Maria waved her spoon in the air. "Oh, Cat!"

"What?" Cat asked. "I mean, I know I'm kinda distracted by the rocky road but I really don't get where you're going with this."

Pete scooted forward and put his drink on the coffee table. "Cat, I have the tape of you and Jeff singing 'Jackson.' I mean, your single 'Second Chances' is doing well, but to be honest, over at the tavern I still hear people talking about you and Jeff singing 'Jackson'; it reminded them so much of Johnny and June."

"Ohhhh . . ." Cat's eyes widened.

"And Shane is a good friend," Maria added. "I've written half a dozen of his number one hits."

"So you can call in a favor?" Pete asked.

Maria nodded, and they high-fived.

"I sorta get where this is going but I'm not sure what you have in mind." Ice cream forgotten, she looked at them.

"Just step away from the ice cream and go get a notepad, Cat," Maria said with a smile. "We're about to put a kick-ass plan into action. Jeff Greenfield isn't going to know what's hit him."

25

Yesterday

JEFF PUT HIS GUITAR AWAY AND THEN POPPED OPEN AN-
other beer that Snake handed to him, but he wasn't
even sure he wanted it. They were going to fire up the grill
later and throw on some steaks but he wasn't in the mood
to eat. He hadn't been in the mood for anything since Cat
went away. He glanced up at Cat's cabin and sighed.

"How many times are you gonna look up at that
damned cabin and let out a big-ass sigh?" Snake asked.
"It's dark inside there. She's not home."

"I know," Jeff answered glumly. "It's just she's been
gone for several days and I'm kinda worried."

"Worried? You said she had a date for a wedding and
the date wasn't you." Snake shook his head. "You're a
better man than me, bro."

Jeff cracked a slight grin. "Well, that goes without saying."

"Call her."

"Not gonna happen."

Snake reached into the cooler for another beer. "Call
Mia, then. I bet she'll know where Cat is."

"No way," Jeff said and continued to drink his beer. But after looking at the cabin again, he kind of warmed up to the idea. "I mean, that would be kinda ballsy."

"Then grow a couple. Do you have Mia's number?"

"Yeah, I showed her the cabin for Maggie a few months ago."

Snake blew out a low whistle. "All right, then, you forced me. Dude, I dare ya."

"Fuck." Jeff ground his teeth together. "Good thing I'm three beers in." He scrolled through his phone book and, before he could lose his nerve, he called. But as it was ringing he forgot to put a reason for calling in his brain. *Damn* . . .

"Hey, Jeff. What's up?"

"Mia!" He shrugged over at Snake, who was grinning from damned ear to ear. "Hey, um, do you happen to know where Cat is?" *Think fast!* "The cabin needs, um, to be sprayed for, um, bugs."

"Oh, gross. Bugs, you say? What kind?"

"Big ones." He winced and looked over at Snake, who chuckled silently up at the sky.

"Well, Cat was singing at a wedding in Nashville. Then I think she was going to visit with Amy Peterson, her former assistant."

"Oh, cool . . . Wait. Singing?" Jeff stood up from where he was leaning against the railing.

"Yeah, for a fan who is in remission from leukemia. It was a surprise from her husband. I heard it was amazing. But then again Cat is always amazing," she said and then grunted. "Ouch!"

"You okay?"

"I just bumped my shin."

"Oh . . ."

"You mean you didn't know?" Mia asked, but there was something in her voice that told Jeff she wasn't supposed to be telling him this, but that never stopped Mia. "Yeah, she went to a prom a while back with a sweet kid going through chemo treatments. Cat does a lot of that kind of thing but keeps it on the down low. That's how she rolls— Ouch! Sorry. I keep bumping into the darned table."

"So, do you know when she'll be back? You know, so I can spray for big bugs."

"Why don't you call her, Jeff?"

He heard scuffling in the background, making him wonder what was going on. Maybe Cam was home. "I, um . . ."

"And don't even tell me you've tried," Mia said in a slightly scolding tone.

"She left me, Mia. Changed her mind about everything. I'm sure you know that already."

"Things aren't always as they seem," Mia said in a more gentle tone. "That's especially true with Cat. And that's all I can say. Cat would have my hide if she knew I told you any of this, but meddling is a way of life in Cricket Creek so I feel okay about it. Mostly. Stop it!"

"Stop what?"

"Nothing."

"Hey, thanks. I'll keep my mouth shut. I promise. I owe you one."

"Oh, I'll get a favor in return, trust me. Maybe singing some stuff for Heels for Meals? An acoustic set at a Cougars game?"

"Done."

"Sweet, now go take care of those 'bugs.' You know, Cat is deathly afraid of creepy-crawly things. And she should be home later tonight . . . and she would be super scared," Mia said in a voice filled with intention. "I'm just sayin'."

"And I hear ya loud and clear," Jeff said with a chuckle. After he ended the call he took a swallow of beer before relaying the information to Snake.

"That sounds like the Cat we know and *you* love," Snake said. He gave Jeff a pointed look. "And it sounds like Mia might be trying to tell you to booby-trap Cat's cabin."

"Really? Are you serious?"

Snake grinned. "Okay, maybe it's just what I would do. At any rate, I like that girl. Too bad she's already taken by Cameron Patrick."

"Yeah, like you'd ever settle down with one girl."

Snake shrugged. "Maybe if the right one came along."

"Think that will ever happen?"

"Fat chance," Snake admitted, but there was just a hint of sadness in his reply.

"Well, I can't believe that Mia was suggesting that I booby-trap the cabin so Cat has to call for help."

"What? It's brilliant. Let's get a porcupine."

"You've had too many beers."

"Not even close. Okay, then, how about a mouse?"

"Like I would stoop that low."

Snake raised his beer can and tapped it to Jeff's. "Ah, that's what friends are for."

Jeff sat back down on the edge of the railing. "Look, Cat might have been singing at a wedding, but she still backed out of Sweet Harmony." He snapped his fingers. "Just like that. Why would she do that and make me think the worst? It doesn't make a lick of sense."

"Beats my whole hand." Snake looked at Jeff for a long minute. "Wait—whoa—what kind of car does Cat drive?"

"A white Lexus SUV."

"Holy shit." He shook his head and took another slug of beer.

"Okay, you can't stop there. What are you thinking?"

Snake shoved his fingers through his hair, making it even messier than it already was. "Jeff, I think Cat might have overheard Jax and Colin arguing about you two becoming Sweet Harmony in the parking lot of the studio. I mean, it got really heated. Typical Jax, he flew off the handle and said some really stupid shit."

"So what are you getting at?"

"Come on. Think about it. She bowed out to save the band from breaking up. She was making it easy on you, Jeff."

"Easy? How the hell is this easy? I love her and I thought she felt the same way."

"And she must love the hell out of you to back away. Don't you get it?"

Jeff's heart thudded. He turned around and gripped the railing. It was starting to make crazy but perfect sense. "And she must have known about Shane McCray's offer before I did or I might have put two and two together sooner. Damn, Cat knows how much that meant to me and to the band. She didn't want to screw it up for us so she took Sweet Harmony off the table."

"Yeah."

"Wow." Jeff felt emotion squeeze his chest.

"She's one helluva woman. Not a selfish bone in her bangin' body."

Jeff shot him a look.

"Sorry."

"So now what the hell am I supposed to do? I mean, the answer seemed so simple. My mother said to make the choice that means the most to me." Jeff looked up at the sky, hoping he'd see the answer written in the stars.

"Jeff, I've known you forever and I've never seen you so strung out over a girl. This is the real deal for you. I love you like a brother and I love the band, but you've got to go after her. You'll never be happy, even if we win a damned Grammy and become rich as fuck."

Jeff looked over at his best friend. "Yeah, but could Cat ever be happy knowing she broke us up or ended our dream? How would the guys treat her?"

"They'd get over it. But if Jax would get his shit together, we won't have to break up. He always did have a hard head. I don't have a problem with South Street Riot being the backing band for Sweet Harmony instead of just you. I never really did."

"Yeah, but you're forgetting about Shane McCray. How can we turn that down?"

Snake inhaled a breath and blew it out. "There's got to be a solution."

They stood there in silence until Jeff's cell started ringing. He looked down. "It's Rick Ruleman calling."

"Answer it."

"Hey, Rick. What's up?"

"Sorry about the short notice but I'm on my way over, if that's okay?" Rick asked.

"Sure, I'm on the back deck drinkin' a few cold ones with Snake."

"Sweet, have one ready for me. I'll be there in a few."

"Holy shit," Snake said. "I wonder what this is all about."

"We're about to find out."

"I need another beer for this." Snake shook his head.

"I know sometimes I still find it pretty wild that he ended up in Cricket Creek of all places. And I'm glad that Rick reconciled with Garret. I don't know what I'd do if I wasn't close to my dad. But I guess being a mega rock star and being on the road constantly is tough on a marriage and kids. If we make it big, I hope I can find balance. I mean, it's why Garth Brooks dropped out of the limelight. I wonder if Rick wishes he'd done the same thing."

"Sometimes when I'm listening to classic rock and one of Rick's old-school head-banging songs comes on, it's hard for me to picture him in leather and all that spiky-ass hair. And you're right—it is wild that he's living in Cricket Creek married to a real estate agent. Crazy sauce."

"Somebody say crazy sauce?" Rick asked when he walked toward them. "Snake, reach in there and toss me a beer."

"Comin' right up."

Rick deftly caught the beer and cracked it open. After guzzling some of it he looked at them. "You're not gonna believe what I'm about to tell you."

Jeff gripped his can so hard he thought he might crush it.

"And before I tell you, I want this to stay right here — well, within your band anyway. This can't get leaked to the public."

Jeff and Snake nodded.

"Pete Sully had a tape of you and Cat singing 'Jackson' sent to Shane McCray," Rick said to Jeff. "He was blown away and he wants Sweet Harmony to open for his farewell tour along with South Street Riot."

"That's amazing," Jeff said.

"There's more," Rick said. "And this is when you're going to have to keep this under your hat. Maria called in a favor and asked if Shane will kick off his tour with a little sneak preview at Sully's outdoor stage. It will be filmed as a teaser for the tour."

"More crazy sauce," Snake said slowly and looked over at Jeff.

"He also likes Jeff Greenfield and South Street Riot. He wants you to do 'Outta My Mind with Lovin' You' and a few more songs."

"How will that work? Is Cat going to keep her career separate and do a song with me here and there?" Jeff didn't like the idea of going on the road for months on end while they did their own thing. No, this wasn't the solution he wanted.

"You have to talk to Cat about that part and work things out," Rick replied.

Jeff angled his head at Rick. "So you already know what she's decided?"

"Yeah." He nodded slowly. "You really need to talk to her face-to-face."

Jeff felt a little flash of anger. He was damned tired of

her making decisions without him. "That's kind of hard to do since she skipped town."

Rick nodded up toward Cat's cabin. "She should be arriving home in a few minutes. Hopefully you two can work this out."

Snake pushed up from the railing. "That's my cue to go too. Rick, would you mind driving me home? I've had a few."

"No problem. I'm glad you asked."

Snake walked over and clamped Jeff on the shoulder. "If you need to talk or anything, call me, okay?"

Jeff nodded. "Thanks. I will," he said and then extended his hand to Rick. "This is amazing news. I can't thank you enough for everything you do."

"It's for the love of music but it goes deeper than that. I care about all of you. And so does Maria. We want what's best for you as artists but as people too. Never forget that we are in your corner no matter what."

"I won't," Jeff promised. He stood there for a minute after they left and tried to process all of what Rick had just told him. He loved Cat more than he thought possible but he also knew that decisions needed to be made together. Otherwise this wasn't going to work.

Staring at the ground, he let out a sigh, and when he looked up he saw headlights.

Cat was home.

26

Silly Love Songs

WHILE DEEP IN THOUGHT ABOUT LYRICS TO A NEW SONG, Cat opened the hatch of her SUV and reached for her suitcase handle.

"Can I help you with that?"

"*Eeek!*" Startled, Cat backpedaled but forgot to let go of the suitcase handle. She stumbled and, feeling an odd sense of déjà vu, let go and braced herself for the impact, but Jeff dove forward and, like a linebacker in a football game, tackled the suitcase just before it slammed into her legs.

Wow. That was impressive. Wide eyed, she watched Jeff land on top of the luggage. He grunted, then rolled to the left and tumbled into the grass. "Well, that hurt like hell. You really need to stop packing bricks."

"Jeff!" Cat ran over and knelt down beside him. "Are you okay?"

"Define *okay*," he said with a slight grin.

"Okay as in, is anything broken?"

He blinked up at her for a moment. "Only my damned heart, Cat." With a groan, Jeff sat up and looked at her.

"Oh, Jeff." She glanced away.

"Are you ever going to include me in these decisions you keep making? I think my vote should count for something."

She reached out and put her hand on his cheek. "I'm so sorry."

Jeff closed his eyes and then let out a sharp sigh. "Seriously, Cat. You have to talk to me. Don't keep me in the dark."

"Yeah, I hate the dark," she tried to joke, but he didn't even crack a smile. "Let's go inside."

"Good idea." Jeff nodded and then glared at the suitcase before picking it up.

Trembling fingers made unlocking the door a task until he took pity upon her and did it for her. Cat had rehearsed what she was going to say to Jeff all the way from Mia's, but butterflies in her stomach were making her forget the entire speech. She was going to have to wing it, which was nothing new, but still . . .

Cat flicked on the light and then turned to Jeff. Her smile trembled a bit. "Can I get you anything?"

"Just an explanation will do."

"Okay, well, I need a bottle of water. Have a seat on the sofa and I'll join you in a second," she said and then headed into the kitchen. She took a swig of water, letting the cold liquid slide down her dry throat, and then joined him on the sofa. While trying to piece together her scattered thoughts, she grabbed a pillow and hugged it to her chest while playing with the gold fringe.

"You can start anytime now."

"I love you." She put a hand over her eyes and then peeked through her fingers at him. "That part was supposed to come last but I had to say it. You know, to break the ice." When he didn't respond, she continued. "Not that broken ice is always a good thing, I guess. There was that time when I was ice-skating—"

"Cat, I love you too," Jeff gently interrupted. "But

that doesn't fix everything. We need to talk, communicate. Look, I understand what you did and why you did it. Snake said that you overheard Jax and Colin arguing. I get that you were trying to make my life easier and your selfless act blows me away. But it's not the answer. Running away is never the answer."

"Unless you're being chased by a bear. Then run away. Or is it play dead?" Cat knew her jokes were an attempt to mask her nervousness, but she couldn't stop herself.

Jeff reached over and cupped her chin. "But you weren't being chased by anything."

Cat looked at him with serious eyes. "But I was, Jeff. I was being chased by fear. I didn't want to burst into your life and wreck your dreams and all that you've been working toward. I didn't want to come between you and your best friends. I couldn't be *that* girl."

"So what's the answer? Having separate careers? Cat, I wouldn't be able to stand being gone from you for weeks, or even days on end for that matter. I've looked up at this cabin a million times watching for you to come home. You know what Snake said? He said that we could win a damned Grammy and it wouldn't make me happy if you weren't in my life." He rubbed his thumb over her bottom lip. "And he's right. Now talk to me. Please."

Cat put her hand to her mouth when she was hit with a wave of emotion. She knew she had to keep her tears at bay in order to tell him everything that needed to be said. "When I sang at the wedding this weekend . . ." She had to pause and swallow hot tears welling up in her throat. "Some things became clear to me. Kelly, the bride, is fighting cancer. She had no idea I'd be singing when she walked down the aisle. I will remember the joy on her face as long as I live. Jeff, her hair was just growing back in and she was so thin and frail, but I'd never seen anyone as beautiful or radiant. Or happy. And who knows how long she has with her amazing husband? Will she live to have his babies? Be a grandma?" Cat put her hand to her chest and swallowed. "And then it hit me . . . hard and all at once."

Jeff reached over and took her hand. "Tell me, baby."

"I realized that I miss my charity work so much. It means more to me than performing. I want to bring happiness in the form of music to those battling cancer. Whether it's at a wedding or prom or in a hospital room, I want to heal and help if only for a little bit. I want to call it Sweet Harmony. I'll get other artists on board and make it happen."

"I love that idea."

Cat smiled and leaned her cheek into his palm. "Rick and Maria are on board with it too. My Way Records will play a big part in the project."

"Rick and Maria are amazing people."

"You're right. I was so thrilled with their response. And I hope to get my parents involved so I can keep them home, maybe even get them to move to Cricket Creek."

"I know you must miss them."

"And that's not all. Jeff, after writing with Maria I know that's where my real love of music lies. Songwriting. I think I've always known that."

"Wait. . . ." Jeff frowned. "So you don't want to tour?"

"Yes, *with you*, but I'll get to that part in a minute." She bit her bottom lip. "But first, I have a confession to make."

"Okay."

With her heart pounding Cat tossed the pillow aside and scooted around to face him. "I . . . I spent the day with your mother yesterday. At your family farm."

Jeff's eyes widened. "You did?"

"She gave me a tour on a big green tractor and at one point let me drive, which was a mistake because I almost ran into a fence post—but I'm getting sidetracked. Sara came over with little Katie and I held her. And, well, I want babies." She gave him a shy smile. "Your babies."

"I'm glad you clarified that part," Jeff said and she laughed.

But then Cat looked over at the stone fireplace, swallowed, gathered her courage, and turned to him. "And I told your mother that I wanted your babies—like, blurted it out like I do sometimes." She looked up at the ceiling and shook her head. "And then wanted to die—well, not die, but have a trapdoor open up and swallow me. Or maybe have a giant pterodactyl swoop down and carry me away. You get the picture."

Jeff laughed. "So what did Mom say?"

"That I needed to marry you first and then I said okay, I like that idea." Cat inhaled a deep breath. "And then Sara and your mom laughed. And so did little Katie, even though she didn't know why."

"Did Mom say anything else?"

Cat gave him a soft smile. "She said that you told her you loved me."

"I did." He shook his head. "Knowing you, Sara, and my mother, I can actually picture this happening." Jeff shook his head. "I knew the three of you would get along. And be trouble. Looks like Katie is going to be following in her mother's footsteps. So then what?"

"Sara said I should do it. Apparently you Greenfield boys are a little bit slow on the uptake when it comes to asking your girl to marry you."

Jeff chuckled. "Sara speaks her mind. She was instrumental in bringing Reid and Addison together. They are true steel magnolias. Beautiful, strong Southern women."

Cat shook her head in wonder. "Yeah, the fake wedding that was real . . . I'll never forget it. I couldn't believe that something as crazy as that could be pulled off."

"Only in Cricket Creek." Jeff shrugged. "I was so bummed when you left and didn't stay for the reception. I wanted a slow dance with you," he added with a chuckle.

"Really? Well, I remember you looking so handsome in your tuxedo." Cat nibbled on her lip for a moment and then said in a rush, "And speaking of that . . . Jeff Greenfield, will you marry me?"

Jeff stopped in midchuckle. "Cat . . . are you . . . Wait— are you serious?"

"For once in my life, yes. Totally. Will. You. Marry. Me?" Her heart pounded so hard that she thought she might pass out and not hear his answer.

"Yes."

"Yes?"

"Um, *hell* yes."

"He said *yes*!" Cat jumped up and spun around in a graceful move.

"That was beautiful."

"I have my moments. Well, not many, but that's what makes them special."

"Every moment with you is special, Cat."

"You say that now," she said and then tossed her head back and laughed with pure delight. She smiled and held out her hands to him.

Jeff took her hands in his and pulled her into his arms. And then he kissed her over and over until she was breathless and giddy with happiness.

"I love you, Cat Carson. And I want to marry you."

"Well, this is good news because Sara is already planning a big barn wedding. It's such a gorgeous setting."

"You will be a stunning bride."

"I just hope I don't trip or something."

"I'll catch you if you fall." He pulled her in for another long kiss. "I'll always be there for you. You know that, right?"

Cat nodded.

Jeff suddenly angled his head sideways. "Wait. I have to ask you something."

"Okay."

"So were you with Mia earlier when I called?"

"Yes—*and* she told you things she shouldn't have, and I kept kicking her, but Mia can't be stopped when she is on a mission."

She scooted to face him and then sat cross-legged.

"Since moving here to Cricket Creek and living out here in this cabin, I started to feel a sense of peace like I've never known before. You see, when I was a child I was kidnapped."

"Oh, Cat," he said as he reached out and took her hands in his. "Dear God."

"I don't remember really, only that I was in a dark and scary place, most likely the trunk of a car. I . . . I still get a sick feeling sometimes when I smell exhaust fumes."

"And the fear of the dark." He squeezed her hands. "God . . ."

"My mother told me that she prayed and prayed for my safe return, telling God that she would devote her life to good works if I was returned to my parents unharmed."

Jeff reached up and wiped a tear from her cheek with his thumb.

"Understandably, they became overprotective and my childhood was sheltered."

"Ah, that's why you watched the Cubs on television rather than go to the games."

Cat nodded. "I was always dropped off and picked up from school and I was never allowed to stay the night with anyone. So I developed a love of reading and music, being on my own so much. It wasn't until I found out that I could make people laugh that I came out of my shell. And then it wasn't until I met Mia at a charity event that I rebelled and started traveling and seeing the world with her. College wasn't for me but I knew I wanted to sing and, well, you know the rest of the story."

"So, Cat, what now?"

"We get married in that big red barn and live happily ever after."

"Well, that's a good plan."

"I thought so."

"But surely you're not going to quit singing?"

"Jeff, I really love singing with you. I want to perform

with you but on a more limited basis. Release a single here and there. Pick and choose our songs together carefully. I want to travel with you on the Shane McCray farewell tour and perform and write songs, but I want to take a big step back from the limelight and leave time to raise a family someday. When we record something together I want it to be something amazing."

He nodded.

"And I want to do the charity work that I've missed so much." She raised her hands up in the air. "Like that Keith Urban song, 'I just want a little bit of everything.'" She looked at him and smiled softly. "So how do you feel about all of this?"

"I think having it all is a very sweet plan."

"Sometimes I surprise myself in my infinite wisdom."

"So do you want to hear *my* plan?"

Cat leaned closer and wrapped her arms around him. "Yes."

"I want to make you happy. Everything else is just gravy."

"I like your plan. In fact, I think it's the best plan ever in the whole history of plans."

"I had a feeling you would." Jeff smiled but then his eyes turned serious. "I told my mother what was going on with the band and how much I love you. She advised me to choose the path that means the most to me. You mean the most to me, Cat. I don't want love to just be in the songs that I sing but in the life that I live."

"Just no sad songs, then, okay?"

"Okay." Jeff pulled her into his arms. "Just silly love songs, like the Paul McCartney song."

"Oh, there's nothing silly about love songs. In fact, I think we should write one together." Cat tilted her head up for a kiss. "But first, I need a little inspiration."

"And you will get it." He gave her a soft, lingering kiss. "I plan on loving you today, tomorrow, and always."

"That's all the inspiration I'll ever need."

Epilogue

And I Love Her

JEFF PACED BACK AND FORTH BACKSTAGE UNTIL SNAKE grabbed him by the arm. "Would you pul-*ease* stop that?"

"I can't," Jeff answered. "I'm too damned nervous."

"Jeff, Cat already said yes," Colin reminded him, and the rest of the band nodded in agreement.

"No . . . *I* said yes. This is different." Jeff reached into his jeans pocket for the millionth time and touched the felt box. "We decided not to make our engagement official until I had a ring, but she has no idea I'm going to do this today."

"You gonna get down on one knee?" Snake wanted to know.

"Should I?" Jeff felt another surge of panic and looked at his band members for help. Again, they all nodded their agreement.

"Okay." Jeff shook his head and reached into his pocket again.

"Do you really think that ring is gonna jump out of your jeans?" Colin asked with a laugh.

"Just chill, man," Sam told him. He slid his guitar to the side and gave Jeff a quick guy kind of hug.

"This is gonna be epic," Jax agreed. "Hey, Jeff, I'm sorry for all the shit I put you through. Cat is a super cool chick. I really regret being such an asshat."

"Yeah, you were kind of an asshat." Jeff gave Jax a shove. "But looking back, I think everything had to happen the way it did for Cat to figure out what she really wanted. We're gonna record some sweet-ass songs together, but she will have the time to do what's important to her." He shook his head up to the sky. "And damn, I love her."

"Where is she?" Sam asked. "It's almost time to go on."

"Last-minute wardrobe change. She spilled sweet tea on her white jeans," Jeff said with a chuckle.

"Does she have any idea of your surprises?" Colin asked.

"Neither one," Jeff replied and felt his heart thump.

"Can I see the ring?" Sam asked.

"No!" Jeff said.

"Just a quick peek before Cat gets back?" Sam insisted.

"A quick peek at what?" Cat asked.

"Nothing!" they said in unison, but Jeff made the mistake of putting his hand over his pocket. His eyes met hers and she smiled.

"So . . ." Cat tilted her head to the side. "What's in your pocket?"

Jeff cleared his throat. "Cat . . . I don't—"

"No," she interrupted softly. "Perfect timing, actually," she added and Jeff understood. These guys were going to be like brothers to her and it suddenly felt right to include them in this special moment. Cat stepped closer and, knowing what was going to happen, the band formed a protective circle around her and Jeff, hiding them from any onlookers.

Jeff reached in his pocket, pulled out the ring box, and knelt down on one knee. Flipping the lid open, he said, "Cat Carson, I love you with all my heart. Will you do me the honor of becoming my wife?"

Cat put her hand to her chest and nodded. "Yes!" She held out her hand for him to slip the ring on her finger. "Oh!" She gazed down at the delicate solitaire.

He'd chosen a ring that was perfect and unpretentious, just like her. Jeff got up to his feet. "You like it?"

"I love it. I love you!" Cat threw her arms around his neck and hugged him hard.

Jeff kissed her and then grinned when she stepped back and spun in a slow circle showing off the ring.

"Snake, are you crying?" Cat asked.

"Hell no!" Snake shook his head but then laughed and swiped at the corner of his eyes. "Aw, damn," he said and then pulled Cat in for a bear hug. Each of the guys hugged her in turn and Jeff watched, having trouble keeping his own emotion under control.

"Can I announce our engagement onstage?" Jeff asked.

"Yes, absolutely," Cat said and then threw herself into his arms again, nearly knocking him over.

Colin peeked his head around the wall and ducked back. "They couldn't have fit one more person on that lawn. This is crazy."

"I'm still floored that Shane wanted to open the tour here in Cricket Creek," Sam said.

"Maria wrote six of his number ones," Cat reminded them. "And she's got one more amazing song for Shane up her sleeve that she enticed him with." Cat leaned in closer. "You didn't hear it from me, but Rick is trying to get Shane to retire here in Cricket Creek," she said, just loud enough to be heard above the crowd. "Apparently Shane is an avid fisherman and Maggie has a huge log cabin for sale with a private dock overlooking the river."

"That would be amazing if Shane McCray retired to Cricket Creek," Snake said and shook his shaggy head. "I mean, *wow*—I can't even wrap my brain around that."

"You can't wrap that brain around anything," Colin said and was rewarded with a shove.

"Oh gosh, Pete is announcing us!" Cat did a little happy bounce that Jeff thought was so damned cute. She looked down at her ring and hugged him again, drawing a collective laugh from the band.

"How y'all doin', Cricket Creek, Kentucky?" Pete shouted, and then had to wait for the applause to die down before he could be heard. "As y'all know, we have the honor of having the iconic Shane McCray start his final tour right here in our town! It doesn't get any better than that. . . ." he said and then had to wait again. "Wait. It *does* get better than that. We have our very own Jeff Greenfield and South Street Riot in the house!" The crowd went nuts.

Jeff leaned close to Cat's ear so she could hear him. "Pete is eating this up."

Cat nodded. "This is so awesome. I love it!"

"And as a very special guest, we have the one and only Cat Carson! Wait—she's our own now too!" He waited and waited for the applause to die down and then shouted into the microphone, "Ladies and gentlemen, let's give it up for Jeff Greenfield, Cat Carson, and South Street Riot!"

Jeff grabbed Cat's hand and they all headed onto the stage. He looked out over the crowd and spotted his family. With a grin Jeff grabbed the microphone. "Hey, Cricket Creek, is this exciting or what?" he shouted and raised his hands when the crowd erupted with wild enthusiasm. "Before we begin, I have a little something I want to announce. No . . . I take that back. Make that a *big* something I want to announce," he corrected, and the audience became silent in anticipation. "I just proposed to the beautiful, one and only Cat Carson."

Jeff turned to Cat. She raised her left hand in the air. "And I said yes!"

The crowd erupted with wild applause. "Kiss!" someone shouted, and so he did—not that he needed any encouragement.

"Look over to the left by my family," Jeff said into her ear.

Cat spotted her mother and father and then put her hand over her mouth. She looked back at Jeff and smiled.

"Surprise."

"Oh, Jeff!" Tears immediately slipped out of the corner of her eyes and she waved to her parents, who were clinging to each other. Turning back to Jeff, she said to him, "Just when I think I can't love you any more than I already do . . ." She grabbed him and hugged him while the crowd cheered on and on.

Jeff said to her, "Well, I have one more surprise." Stepping back, he nodded to Snake and then strummed the first four notes to the Beatles song "And I Love Her."

A hush fell over the crowd and Cat put her hands to her cheeks. Looking into her eyes, Jeff sang the lyrics straight from his heart. Simply but eloquently, the words said it all.

Don't miss the next novel in
LuAnn McLane's charming
Cricket Creek series,

WALKING ON SUNSHINE

Available in May 2015 from Signet Eclipse.

"RUSTY, GET BACK HERE RIGHT THIS MINUTE!" MATTIE shouted at her brother's Irish setter, but he bolted from the kitchen with the slab of country ham dangling from his chops. "I mean it!"

Mattie rushed after Rusty, knowing full well that the dog wasn't about to stop. Although the ham could no longer be served to her customers, Mattie felt the need to scold the naughty dog and deprive him of his prize. She also felt the need to scold her brother Mason for leaving Rusty with her again while he went fishing. Apparently, Rusty, who used to be quite the docile dog while riding in Mason's bass boat, now had the odd urge to jump into the water without warning.

"I swear I'm never saving you a bone *ever* again!" Fuming, Mattie dodged tables and chairs while chasing Rusty around the dining room, glad that the restaurant wasn't open for breakfast just yet. For an old dog, Rusty still managed some impressive speed and agility, but this was the second ham heist this week, making Mattie determined to catch him. Country ham and biscuits was a popular item on the breakfast menu! When Rusty headed toward the big booth in the back of the dining room, Mattie threw caution to the wind and did a half dive, half slide across the hardwood floor, hoping to snag him around his haunches and bring him to the justice he so richly deserved. . . .

And she came up with nothing but air.

With a groan, Mattie pounded her fists on the floor. She pictured Rusty doing a wheezy doggy laugh while munching on the salty slab of ham. "I'm gonna tell on you!" Mattie threatened with a bit more fist pounding. After another moment, she started pushing up to her feet, then looked ahead and spotted shoes. Yeah, shoes, not boots. Kinda fancy shoes at that . . .

"Excuse me. Are you . . . are you . . . quite all right?" asked an unusual male voice that made her pause, leaving her in a Pilates plank position.

Two things immediately went through Mattie's head. Number one was that the question held a measure of concern at her plight rather than the amusement that was usually dealt her way; and number two was that his accent was a distinctively clipped British one rather than a slow, Southern drawl. Mattie quickly scooted to her knees, apparently just as he squatted, because suddenly they were eye to—oh . . . very blue eyes. She swallowed, staring. The man was simply gorgeous.

"Um . . ." He tilted his shaggy blond head to the side. "Is something amiss?"

"No, I . . . uh . . ." What did he just ask? Her brain suddenly left the building. "Oh, a . . . ham," she managed, and then realized it sounded is if she were clearing her throat. "H-Ham. I was running after the ham."

"You were chasing after a ham?" He shoved his fingers through his hair, making it stand on end. Mattie had the urge to reach over and smooth it back into its beautiful style. There was something vaguely familiar about him that she couldn't quite place. "So the ham ran away, did it?"

"Yes . . . Well, no. It was a dog."

"A dog named Ham? Now it makes sense."

"What? No . . ." Mattie shook her head hard, making her ponytail swing back and forth.

"Are you quite certain you're all right?"

"Yes. Why do you keep asking that?"

"Well, mainly because you *were* facedown while pounding your fists on the floor when I walked in. Cause for some concern, I'd say."

Mattie looked down at her fists. "Oh, right. I guess I was."

"Early in the day to be so unsettled, don't you think?" he asked gently. "Is there anything I can do? Search for the runaway ham perhaps?"

"I . . ." it was *hard to think* when he looked so cute and sounded so, well, so damned sexy. Mattie suddenly felt silly for having been caught in her fit of frustration on the floor like some kind of crazy person. Should she admit that she was trying to tackle a dog? Would that be better or worse than chasing a ham? "I . . . I was having a . . . moment."

"Ah." He gave her a crooked grin, which made a fluttery thing happen in her stomach. Must be hunger pangs. "Haven't had your coffee yet? I can sympathize. You'd best serve me up a cup, or I'll be joining you in your fist-pounding moment." He stood up and then reached down to help her to her feet.

Mattie took his offered hand, finding his warm, firm grasp to be so pleasant that she felt reluctant to let go. Realizing that she was clinging to his hand, she made a shaking motion that masked her lingering hold with an introduction. "I'm Mattie Mayfield, by the way. Welcome to Breakfast, Books, and Bait . . . or BBB for short." She gave his hand a firm squeeze like her daddy had taught her.

"Well, thank you for the rather odd but warm welcome, Mattie Mayfield. I am duly charmed and also rather fascinated by the wide range of seemingly unrelated items you have to offer here at BBB." He looked over at the bags of fishing bait shelved on the far wall. "Are the worms all dead, then?"

Mattie nodded. "Well, no, I mean, not *dead*. Artificial— you know—plastic, mostly used for bass fishing."

"Ah, and the fish fall for that, do they?" he asked with another boyishly cute grin.

"Oddly, yes."

He chuckled. "It must be quite the letdown to be lured in by a silly piece of plastic instead of a tasty worm. I'd spit it out straightaway."

Mattie had to laugh. "Yes, but there's that tiny complication called the hook."

"Oh . . . true enough." He winced. "Ouch. Adding insult to injury and then ending up in a frying pan."

"No, no . . . *no*." Mattie scrunched up her nose. "You really don't want to consume anything caught in the Ohio River." She waved a hand in the direction of the bait. "This is all mostly for catch and release, for sport and tournaments we host."

"We?"

Mattie jabbed her thumb toward the window that overlooked the dock. "My family owns Mayfield Marina," she answered with a measure of pride. For some reason, she felt it important that he think she was more accomplished than someone who simply slung hash and baked biscuits was, not that there was anything wrong with an honest day's work. "So, what can I get for you?" she asked a bit crisply.

He looked past the bait toward the rear of the shop, where Mattie kept her selection of books. "I think I'll pass on the bait, but breakfast sounds lovely. And perhaps a book later."

"Have a seat, and I'll bring you a menu."

"All right, then."

Mattie thought he'd opt for a booth, but he followed her to the counter lined with old-fashioned round swivel stools in deep red. Mattie had been serving breakfast for several years, and her melt-in-your-mouth biscuits were raved about, but she suddenly found herself feeling a bit nervous. "Coffee?"

"Please."

"So, are you just passing through Cricket Creek and happened to stop down here by the marina?" Mattie asked while pouring strong coffee into a sturdy mug. She was usually a bit on the quiet side, but when hit with a fit of nerves, Mattie tended to chatter.

He reached for a little plastic tub of cream from the dish she'd put in front of him. "No. Actually I just bought the A-frame cabin right next door."

"You did?" From his blue polo shirt to his fancy shoes, he didn't seem the type to settle down in Cricket Creek, but then again, the little town had had quite a few unexpected people move there over the past few years. "Wow." Wait. There really was something familiar about him. Where had she seen him before?

"I'm sorry. I neglected to introduce myself. I'm Garret Ruleman."

"Oh!" Mattie nearly dropped the menu she'd been about to hand to him. She had seen him, all right—on the cover of tabloids at the check-out line at the grocery story. "You are?"

"Last time I looked at my license," he said while pouring cream into his coffee.

Feeling a bit silly because of her question, Mattie decided to add a little sass. "Maybe you should check just to be sure."

"All right, then, I'll have a look." He reached around for his wallet, then flipped it open. "Yes, I'm still Garret Ruleman. Damn the luck," he added with an arch of an eyebrow and a slight grin.

"So you moved to Cricket Creek to live near your father?" Rick Ruleman, famous rock star, owned My Way Records, which was located just a few miles away from the marina. It was well-known that Garret and his father shared a rocky relationship, and Mattie suddenly wished she'd kept her doggone mouth shut.

"No. Actually I'm back in town to rekindle my relationship with Addison Monroe." He calmly took a sip of his coffee and peered at her over the rim of the mug.

Mattie couldn't hold back her gasp. Garret and Addison's broken engagement had been splashed all over the tabloids and was the reason Addison had ended up opening a bridal shop, of all things, in Cricket Creek. Garret looked familiar because she'd seen his face in print so many times—and usually not in a flattering situation. "Addison is, um, married to Reid Greenfield now," Mattie informed him in a hesitant stage whisper.

"You don't say. . . . Well, bollocks, that throws a monkey wrench into my plans." When his mouth twitched, Mattie knew he'd been messing with her. He took a sip of coffee and then added more cream. "This stuff is going to make my hair stand on end."

"It's already standing on end, but maybe that will offset the fact that your nose is going to grow from fibbing," Mattie grumbled.

He reached up and touched his nose. "Oh, wouldn't want that to happen. Actually, Addison and I have mended our fences, and I've met Reid. He's a great chap, and Addison should thank her lucky stars that she dodged a bullet and dumped the likes of me." His grin suggested that he was joking, but there was something in his eyes that made Mattie want to give his shoulder a reassuring squeeze. "So, I had you going, did I?"

"That little deception wasn't one bit funny."

"I didn't really think you'd fall for it. I was just goofing on you."

"Goofing?"

"English slang for *teasing*."

"Well, you'd think that I'd wise up, but I manage to fall for nearly everything." *I could fall for you* zinged through her brain, but she chalked it up to the lack of coffee in her system. "I think I have *tease me* tattooed on my forehead."

Narrowing his eyes, Garret peered at her forehead as if trying to see the tattoo. "Hmm, you do. Get that thing removed straightaway."

"Good advice," Mattie said, and then topped off his coffee.

"Actually, I'm a studio musician and a talent scout for My Way Records." Garret took a sip of the steaming brew. "But yes, it's good to live near my father," he added, but Mattie thought his smile appeared forced, and he started studying the menu as if there would be a pop quiz afterward.

"Do you have any questions about the menu?"

"I do, in fact." Garret looked up at her. "What in the world is redeye gravy?"

"Gravy made with coffee and the drippings from fried county ham." She sighed. "But, unfortunately, I can't offer redeye gravy or country ham on biscuits."

"Ah . . . right, since the ham ran away with the dish and the spoon?"

Mattie nodded. "Something like that."

"Pity. I was curious."

"Well, I do make sausage gravy that will make you sigh with delight."

"As it so happens I adore sighing with delight," Garret informed her with a slow grin that caused the butterflies in Mattie's stomach to take flight once again. "I'm sold." It looked as if he was about to say more when his phone started playing "Hard Day's Night." Standing up, he pulled his cell from his pocket and frowned at the screen. "Excuse me." He smiled, and then answered the call. "Hello, love," he said, making Mattie wonder whether he was speaking to his girlfriend. "Ah, yes, darling, I can be there by noon."

Mattie felt an expected pang of disappointment, which

took her by surprise. Feeling silly, she quickly turned away and started fussing with rolling silverware in napkins. The breakfast crowd would be arriving soon, and she'd best be thinking about getting ready rather than mooning over her sexy new neighbor. *Besides, let's get real,* Mattie thought to herself. Now that she knew who he was, she remembered that Garret Ruleman's bad-boy reputation followed him like his shadow. Along with Addison Monroe, Garret had been linked to various famous actresses and models. If she remembered correctly, his mother was also some kind of celebrity. Garret might have been goofing on her, as he'd said, but Mattie was quite certain that she was as far from being his type as a girl could possibly get. With a sigh, Mattie sternly reminded herself that she was already an expert in the not-his-type field, having been ass over teacups in love with Colby Campbell since, well, ever since she could remember.

Unfortunately, there were several problems with loving Colby, starting with his being Mason's best friend, which made Mattie off-limits because of some sort of hard-and-fast guy-code rule. In addition, the four-year age difference between them had thrown Mattie into the annoying kid-sister category as they grew up. But at twenty-six, she figured that gap surely shouldn't matter! And, let's face it—she was no longer a *kid* but a grown woman, not that Colby seemed to notice. And if Mattie wanted to be honest—and she didn't—that's also where the not-his-type part came into play. Colby always had some sort of prissy, leggy girly thing hanging on his arm, and Mattie was anything but a girly girl. Still, in spite of having the deck stacked against her, every time he walked in the door Mattie's heart beat like a big bass drum.

Unrequited love truly sucked.

Complicating Mattie's love life—or rather the lack thereof—was the fact that her brother Danny, two years her junior, also adhered to the ridiculous don't-date-my-sister rule, leaving Mattie friend-zoned by most of the eligible bachelors close to her age. Perhaps if her brothers would get married, they would get busy raising families and back off on watching her love life like doggone hawks. In fact, their parents had become so frustrated by their lack of grandchildren that they'd up and moved to Florida, vowing not to return to Cricket Creek until they had at least one grandbaby.

Mattie stood on her tiptoes and fumbled around in the cabinet for a coffee filter. Her brothers had been blessed with the tall genes, while she stood barely over five feet two. She was also left-handed and the only blonde in the bunch, but she had the same hazel eyes as her father. Her mother claimed that Mattie's eyes were like mood rings, changing color depending upon her disposition.

Mattie measured the coffee grounds as she tried to listen to Garret's conversation. Eavesdropping was one of her favorite ways to pass the time while serving breakfast. From the old-timers' breakfast club's corny jokes to the really tall fish tales to the gossip from the ladies who came in to browse through the selection of romance novels, Mattie was thoroughly entertained every single morning. While Mattie wasn't one to repeat gossip, she sure did get a kick out of listening to it.

After the coffee started hissing and dripping into the carafe, Mattie decided she needed to refill the saltshakers that were running low. Although she had recently added healthy options such as egg-white omelets and oatmeal to the menu, those selections had remained mostly untouched. She rose on tiptoe once again, but this time her fingers refused to coax the salt container to slide her way.

"Hey, love, do you need some help?" Garret asked in that sweet-ass accent of his.

Love? Wait. Had he just called her *love*? Before Mattie could process the whole love thing, he was standing behind her reaching up for the elusive canister of salt. She could feel the heat from his body standing so close to hers, and *wow*, did he smell heavenly ... something spicy and, well, *delicious*. She had the urge to lean back against him, and when he stepped to the side to hand her the salt, she wanted to grab him by the shirt and bury her nose into his chest just to soak up the smell.

Instead, Mattie had a saucy *I didn't need your help* on the tip of her tongue, but then her fingers brushed against his and she felt a zing all the way to her doggone toes. Still, she lifted her chin, searching her befuddled brain for a retort of some sort, but he tilted his head and said, "You have the most amazing eyes. What color are they?"

"C-Color?"

"Yes. I thought brown at first, but now they look green with a hint of blue. Quite lovely, actually."

Mattie was used to hearing teasing instead of compliments, and she stood there feeling rather perplexed. She licked her bottom lip, something she did when confused, and damn if his gaze didn't seem to drop to her mouth. Mattie swallowed, and although warning bells chimed in her head about bad boy Garret Ruleman, she tipped her head back and leaned closer ... suddenly prepared to risk it for the biscuit.

But just as her eyes started to flutter shut in anticipation of their mouths meeting, Mattie spotted none other than Colby Campbell walk through the front door. Startled, she took a quick step away from Garret and then frowned at him as if he'd done something wrong rather than offer his help. What in the hell had just gotten into her, anyway? Kissing a total stranger wasn't like her at all! She shot Garret a frown so he'd get the message.

"Everything okay, Mattie?" Colby asked in that big-brother tone that never failed to set her teeth on edge.

"Yeah, um, Garret was just helping me reach a canister of salt. Weren't you, Garret?" she asked but kept her focus on Colby. When Garret remained silent, she gave him a little nudge with her elbow and then looked up at him.

"Well, actually . . ."

The mischief in Garret's blue eyes made Mattie's heart start to hammer. She looked at him and held her breath.

Also available from *USA Today* bestselling author

LuAnn McLane

WILDFLOWER WEDDING
A Cricket Creek Novel

Growing up on the wrong side of the tracks, Gabby Goodwin
had more to prove than the rest of Cricket Creek. Even now, as
the successful owner of the flower shop, she hasn't
forgotten her humble beginnings. So when her high school
crush, the former class bad boy, walks back into her life, she
keeps him at arm's length, protecting her heart—and her pride.

Reese Marino gave up most of his wild ways years ago, and is
now part owner of his uncle's pizza parlor. The fact that Gabby
still treats him like a troubled teenager drives him mad. Despite
Gabby's reluctant attitude, Reese is determined to win her over
and show her that love often blooms right where you least
expect it.

"No one does Southern love like LuAnn McLane!"
—The Romance Dish

Available wherever books are sold or at
penguin.com

facebook.com/LoveAlwaysBooks

LOVE
ROMANCE
NOVELS?

For news on all your favorite romance authors,
sneak peeks into the newest releases, book
giveaways, and much more—

"Like" Love Always on Facebook!
 **LoveAlwaysBooks**